Devon, the Demon Duck from HELL

Mark Rude

This is a work of fiction and satire. Names, characters, businesses, places, events and incidents are either the products of the author's imagination or used in a fictitious or satirical manner. Any resemblance to actual persons, living or dead, or actual events is purely coincidental.

Except for the duck. That shit is *real*.

This book is dedicated to author Dawn Cook, who writes under the nom de plume 'Kim Harrison,' for informing me that "Demon duckies are the next big thing. You heard it here first."

Thanks, Dawn.

Libro Hoc Continentur...

Fowl Magic   1

Devon, the Demon Duck from Hell   13

The Infernal Web   22

All Creatures Great and Small   32

Night of the Lepus   46

The Devil You Know   60

Blake the Snake   72

Return of the King   84

Seven Years of Bad Luck   101

Devon Flies South   113

Father Knows Best   131

Annie Puckett and the Broom Closet of Secrets   143

The Story of O   158

Battle of the Basement   174

Deals Are Made to be Broken   187

It Was Not All Better in the Morning   201

How to Escalate a Crisis from
   the Comfort of Your Own Home   214

A Duck By Any Other Name   223

Help Me Rhonda   236

Lost in Translation   247

The Obligatory Chase Scene   259

Truce or Consequences   270

The Good, The Bad, and The Monkey   280

The Cost of Doing Business   292

Chapter 1
Fowl Magic

The demon looked around the room with furious eyes, taking in the faces of those who had summoned him. It had been nearly a century since he had been called to the material plane, and he was in no mood to barter with mortal fools. Besides, the glut of souls in Hell had sent their value spiraling until the market had bottomed out. There was little point in making deals anymore.

"Did we do it?" asked one of the hooded figures, his hushed whisper charged with fear, "Did we really call a demon?" His freckled face was white and drenched with nervous sweat.

"I-I don't know," said another voice from the shadows. The young man stepped forward and peeked from the sides of his deep hood, casting nervous glances about the room with wide bespectacled eyes. The chalk circle in the center of the basement was billowing black smoke, making it difficult to see. The youth held a dagger wet with blood in his shaking hands.

A female voice spoke harshly from the depths of her hooded robe, "Shh! There's something here! What do you think all the smoke is about?" She waved her hands to clear the sulfur-thick air; the glow of a laptop computer added an eerie blue radiance to the smoke-filled room. "Don't step on the chalk, whatever you do." She tossed back her hood and set free a mess of frizzy brown hair as she coughed, moving towards the blackened basement window to get some ventilation.

The demon stepped from the smoke, certain that his fearful countenance would intimidate these obvious amateurs. If he could gain the upper hand early on, things would go more smoothly. He saw the mortals step back uncertainly as he dispersed the black cloud about him.

"What the hell?" exclaimed the freckle-faced lad, tossing back his hood to reveal a mop of ginger hair. "Didn't you kill the sacrifice?" He turned accusingly on his fellow occultist.

Spectacles held up the bloodied dagger and pointed to the altar behind him saying, "What does it look like? It's dead, isn't it?" He looked to the girl for support, but she was turning to her laptop, scrolling up and down the web page with furious concentration.

The demon tested the boundaries of the summoning circle, looking for imperfections. These mortals were inexperienced and may have made a critical mistake. A misplaced rune or a break in the circle could revoke the binding spell… Ah! There it was! One of the runes had been drawn incorrectly! The demon laughed diabolically; ready to unleash his fury before returning to the underworld. *"Fools!"* he roared at the three would-be conjurers, *"I am unbound! Feel my wrath as I devour your souls!"*

"Quack," said the duck in the summoning circle, albeit with an ominous, threatening tone.

Spectacles turned to the ginger, "So how many sacrifices did you bring?"

"Just the one," replied Ginger, scratching his head nervously, "Figured we only needed one."

"We did," said the girl with the frizzy hair, as she looked up from her laptop screen, "Either something went terribly wrong, or this spell isn't all it's... quacked up to be." Frizzy looked at the creature in the circle of chalk and crinkled her nose at it.

"Oh please," moaned Spectacles, "no more puns."

"Quack!" said the duck, beating its wings. The foul smoke spread about the basement and drifted out the open window.

"Well, if this is some kind of joke, it damn well isn't funny," said the ginger. "Mom spent weeks on these robes, and I sank all of my allowance into the candles and that dagger." He stalked about the room flapping the sleeves of his robe. "Plus, it's no easy thing to snatch a duck. They're going to laugh us out of the coven."

"Quack!" repeated the duck, as it stepped from the circle; its webbed feet slapping the concrete floor. It looked back at the summoning circle, then down at its body, flapping about in distress. The duck kept swiveling its head about, examining itself as though for the first time. Finally it cried out with an angry squawk, making the three robed figures jump.

"What are you upset about?" Ginger asked the fowl irritably; "You aren't the one flunking the test!" He scowled at his companions. "We summoned a freaking *duck*." He shook his head as he stamped about.

3

"Maybe we didn't…" Frizzy began carefully, her fingers tapping on the keys as she opened another web page. "The message boards have a few threads about this, about people summoning a copy of their sacrifice." She looked up at the bird with a worried expression and said, "It might not be a normal duck."

The trio stopped and looked at the creature, waiting for it to do something supernatural.

"Quack," was all it said. Before the three fledgling wizards could react, the duck flapped for the open window and squeezed through, leaving nothing but a few white tail feathers behind.

"Well that's just frickin' great!" said Ginger as he threw his hands in the air. "All that work, and we got nothing to show for it." He sniffed his robes, "Except for this smell. You suppose it'll come out?" He gagged at the rotten-egg stench.

Spectacles shrugged and said, "It should. At least we can use them as Halloween costumes, like we told your mom." He looked out the window into the dark street. "Do you think we should go after that bird?" He picked up a feather and turned it in his fingers.

"If you like," said Frizzy, her face aglow with the light of the monitor. She was skimming the Dark Magic message boards and showed no sign of leaving. "I'm going to find out what went wrong; you two can go on a wild goose chase if you want."

"Wild goose chase. Funny." Ginger smirked as he started peeling off his befouled robes. The lad with the round glasses just gazed out the window.

"Well," said Spectacles, "if there's no other screw-ups planned for tonight, I'll need some help cleaning up in here." He looked about for something to wipe off the gaudy ceremonial dagger, just as the clerk at the mall's knife shop recommended.

The demon stalked off into the cool night, waddling down the back alley between the college building and the 24-hour T-Stop. He gnashed his teeth in anguish, or would have had he possessed any, and the clap, clap of his bill echoed into the darkness. *Revenge shall be mine,* he thought to himself as his webbed feet splashed through the puddles of recent rain. *Oh yes, revenge shall be mine...*

Annie Puckett mindlessly scanned in the DVD returns, stacking them alphabetically on the counter. Wednesday nights at Bueller's Big Video consisted of non-stop shelving. The residents of the sleepy mountain town brought back what passed for the weekend's entertainment, spending a few minutes scouting out their next cinematic adventure for the coming Friday. Brainless comedies and CGI-driven action were the regular fare, once the small new release section had been ravaged. Annie was partial to foreign films and always had a good selection to choose from, since no one ever rented them. Occasionally a daring soul would come up with a Bergman or Fellini film and ask, "Is this any good?" to which Annie had learned to answer, "It's subtitled." That usually resulted in the customer putting it back, in the wrong place of course, and picking out something with talking babies or buddy cops instead. Kurosawa samurai films were more commonly rented, but often returned with complaints that there were no high-flying sword fights and gravity-defying stunts. Annie would sigh and scan them back in, reserving comment lest she get fired again.

Devon, The Demon Duck From Hell

Annie was no stranger to being canned, just a side effect of being a natural smart ass. Her student days at Bueller Community College were over, and she had a Bachelor's degree in Fine Arts and a minimum wage job to show for it. To make things worse, she was decidedly a minority in the northern Arizona town, for she was a lonely Goth in a world of neo-hippies, tree-huggers, survival nuts, and rowdy college kids. One of the main reasons she had taken the job at the video store was the uniform; it was a pleasingly black polo shirt with black slacks. Most other jobs required pastel colors, paper hats, suspenders covered with 'flair,' or those hideous multi-colored atrocities they wore at the lemonade stand in the mall. Poor girls. At least Annie had her dignity.

Annie's hair was dyed jet black, of course, and tied back in a ponytail; her eyeliner gave her a hint of Egyptian mystique, while her porcelain skin made for just the right amount of deathly pallor so cherished by her Dark Sisters and Brothers. Her Goth friends in high school had moved on to the bigger university towns, like Flagstaff or Tempe, leaving Annie all alone to fly the freak flag, which she did proudly. She even had some body piercing and tattoos, which were uncommon in Bueller unless you were an ex-marine or one of those classy chicks who sported a tramp-stamp. Luckily, an old biker named Maurice Chekhov had opened a dark, dingy little shop years ago and offered to ink and poke holes in the town's more daring rebels. Annie had just gotten a new tat on the back of her neck recently; the bandage and soreness reminding her where two week's pay had gone.

Annie went out of her way to not get fired. Considering the state of the video rental business in the early

6

twenty-first century, Bueller's Big Video was living on borrowed time. She was lucky to have it so well.

"Ma'am?"

Those red vending machines were taking over like little pieces on a Risk board, claiming territory and putting traditional video stores out of business.

"Excuse me, ma'am?"

It was so cold and impersonal, Annie mused. Those faceless, mindless machines replacing friendly customer service and that personal touch that so many…

"Miss?" came a reedy voice and a rap on the counter.

"Oh my god! What?" Annie exclaimed, jumping at the sudden interruption. "Oh, I'm sorry. I didn't see you," she said to the lone customer in the store. The hippie chick had snuck up on her somehow. "Can I, like, help you with something?" Annie asked, almost apologetically.

"I'm looking for a movie without the black bars. I hate those black bars. Can you tell me which ones have the black bars?" The woman fluttered her hand at the shelves.

Annie's 'Mr. Spock' eyebrow shot up before she could stop it. "You mean letterbox format? Where you see more of the picture?" She'd had this conversation with customers more times than she cared to think about.

"Yeah," said the woman, her enormous hoot-owl glasses turned towards Annie; her long, stringy hair draped over the shoulders of her ochre, teal, and purple knitted vest. "It's like, let me see the top and bottom of the screen, you know? I think it's like, wasting electrons or something, all that black space, don't you think?"

Annie's eyes took on a hooded look she reserved for cretins, but her voice remained perky. She activated her

Idiot Customer Subroutine and let it spew out the oft-repeated words. "It actually lets you see the entire picture, as intended by the director. You can see the sides of the picture that are cut off by the smaller ratio of TV screens." She watched as the information bounced off the woman's head and floated into the atmosphere.

"Oh, my old TV was pretty big, but I still saw the black bars," she said wistfully. "I want to break in my new screen but I want the picture to fill the whole thing."

Annie heard a buzzing in her head as the woman spoke, and she swore she felt her IQ drop ten points. "The entire picture is shown, top to bottom and side to side. Your screen is just squarer than the longer rectangle of the movie screen, so it makes the image smaller in order to fit." She made little goal posts with her fingers and thumbs, trying to illustrate concepts that were obviously beyond the grasp of the big-eyed primate before her. *What were those things called? Tarsiers?*

"Oh, I got a new widescreen TV," said the woman proudly. "I just want a movie that will fill it up." She considered a moment and asked, "I won't see black bars on the sides now, will I?"

Annie looked suddenly to the floor, then back behind her feet. She began looking under the counter and in the drawers.

"Is everything alright?" asked the woman.

"Yeah, I... I think my brain fell out somewhere. Excuse me." Annie wandered off towards the back of the store, leaving the woman to blink and frown behind her enormous eye-wear.

It was almost time to close the store, so Annie went into the office, turned up the music volume to Annoying, and made the final announcement over the intercom. She addressed the single woman as if she was a store full of noisy people. "Good evening Bueller Big Video customers. The time is now midnight and we are closed. Please bring your final selections to the counter and our friendly, helpful staff will assist you. We open again at noon tomorrow. Thank you, and have a wonderful evening."

After helpfully assisting Ms. Widescreen, Annie closed up and counted down the register before locking up for the night. The full moon hung overhead amid a smattering of bright stars; the cold mountain air was crisp and clean, making the breath steam and the skin tingle. Annie locked the doors after checking the parking lot for creeps; it was a small town but it never hurt to be safe. She didn't own a car but it was no big deal. Everything in her life was within walking distance; home, school, the video store, and the coffee shop where she liked to hang out until she made the mistake of working there. *Never work where you like to hang out*, she decided. Everything had gotten better after she got fired, plus now she could gossip with old coworkers about the crappy management.

Annie zipped up her jacket and began to walk home, the traffic light beckoning her towards the T-Stop and a Bladder-Buster of soda to finish off the night. The recent rain had left the streets looking like black glass, reflecting the neon signs and orange streetlights. A few students were returning from an ill-advised mid-week party, stumbling along drunkenly towards the dormitory. *Kids*, she thought. There wasn't another soul on the street except for the little white duck.

Delighted, Annie slowed her pace so the stray duck wouldn't be frightened off. She even bent over in case it wanted to be petted. She made a duck noise to call him over.

"Hey there, ducky duck! Wa-wa-wa-wack!" she said happily. "Whatcha doing out here all alone?"

"Out of my way, mortal." said the duck with a haughty English accent.

"Whoa!" Annie stood bolt upright, looking back and forth to find the hidden camera or college pranksters behind this little stunt. "That was sooo cool!" Her eyes returned to the duck to find the unseen source of the voice.

The duck stopped in its tracks, looking up at her suspiciously. "What?"

"Is this a real duck?" she asked the unseen speaker. "Of course it is. How did you do that?" She wasn't some country bumpkin to be duped by a talking duck. She'd seen hidden camera shows that pulled pranks like this before; she was just really impressed with this one. She bent down to examine the animal.

"Can you... understand me?" asked the duck hesitantly.

His bill even moved as he spoke! How cute! "O-M-G!" she cried. "You guys, that is freakin' awesome! Make him say something else!"

"No one is *making* me speak, mortal fool," said the duck with a sneer, not easy since it had no lips. "*I* am speaking. Obviously you can understand me and so... you shall do my bidding!" It fixed Annie with a penetrating stare over its yellow bill, the white feathers ruffling ominously.

Annie stood transfixed, staring at the duck in awe. Suddenly she squealed, "Oooo I just want to hug you! Can I hug him guys?" She addressed her question to the air. "Will he bite?"

The duck shook its head and waddled off, a string of curses flowing from its bill. Annie just watched it go, sad the prank had ended. She waited for someone to come out of the bushes, collect the duck and have her sign a release to appear on television. No one came.

As she followed the duck with her eyes, the creature turned, heaved a sigh, and waddled back. Seems the joke was not over yet. "You can really understand me?" asked the duck. "You hear my voice?"

"Loud and clear," Annie said. "Hey, where's the antenna?"

The duck pressed her, "But you are not afraid or confounded? Are talking animals not… *unusual* in your experience?"

"Are you kidding? I spent several birthdays at Chuck E. Cheese," she replied. "Pizza and creepy singing rodents. But I still think this is an awesome job. How does the beak sync with the words?"

"It is a bill," the duck responded coldly. "And I assume now that you think this is some trick or illusion. I assure you it is not."

Annie blinked and knelt down to get a closer look. The voice *did* seem to be coming from the vicinity of its beak… er, bill. "Weird…" she said.

"Astute," said the duck. "Once you have come to terms with the reality of your situation, we may continue."

Annie took a moment to put together what her eyes were seeing and her ears were hearing. The duck seemed to be talking, *really* talking. This was no animatronic creation; those things trailed wires, smelled of ozone, and sounded like whirring, clicking servos when you got up close. There was no harness, battery, antenna, or speaker. Its throat moved when it talked. The only thing that looked this real was CGI, but computer generated characters didn't exist in the real world. Then again, neither did talking ducks.

She promptly fell on her butt. "Whoa," she exclaimed, feeling a bit like Keanu Reeves in any of a half-dozen movies.

"Good," said the duck, looking satisfied, "Now we can get to business. I require your help."

"You… you talk!" She pointed at the creature as she scooted away, her sneakers scraping the slick pavement.

"Yes," drawled the duck with exasperation.

"You're, you're a *duck*!" she said.

"Not exactly," said the duck. "I am trapped in this body and require your assistance."

"But, but, but," Annie stammered, searching her brain for an argument, any argument.

"Perhaps if we could adjourn to someplace more private," said the duck as it waddled up to her, "I could answer your questions. It is rather cold and wet out here."

"But," Annie said, as tears welled in her eyes, "but you're a duck!"

The duck sighed, its head drooping. It was going to be a long night.

Chapter 2
Devon, the Demon Duck from Hell

The bus-stop was the closest, best option for a warm, private meeting. The bench was located across from the video store near a vent for the campus steam tunnels, and the bench was covered, with screens on the sides. Anyone approaching would only see a girl and her duck. Even if they caught her talking to the creature, they would likely think it was some weird Goth behavior and ignore it. Just a freak talking to her 'familiar.' Like anyone here would know better.

"So," Annie began awkwardly, "you aren't *really* a duck?"

It answered, "No, I was trapped in a duck's body by an erroneous spell."

"You mean magic? *Magic is real?*" Annie jumped in her seat with excitement.

"Clearly," said the duck. "I am the victim of a mishap,

13

and I am currently powerless to free myself."

"Wow, I thought you were like a science experiment or something, you know, after I decided you weren't a hoax. At least I'm not going all 'Doctor Dolittle.'" She fluttered her fingers about her head.

"Doctor who?" asked the duck.

"Not Doctor Who," she said, "Doctor Dolittle. He talks to animals. You know, in the movies."

"Ah yes," said the duck. "Rex Harrison. He had the Henry VIII contract, I believe."

"Eddie Murphy was Doctor Dolittle," Annie corrected. "You know movies?"

"I know of many actors. They frequently consult my… colleagues. Also, I read the trades." He began preening his feathers, and then stopped himself with disgust.

"So… you're like, what exactly?" she glanced sidelong at the duck, "Some kind of wizard?"

"Something like that," it replied.

"What do I call you?"

"You may call me…" it searched for a name, "Devon."

"Devon," she smiled, "Devon the Duck. Hello Devon, I'm Annie Puckett." She made to shake hands but thought the better of it. "Nice to meet you, Devon."

"Charmed," he said.

"Where are you from?" Annie asked. "You sound like Captain Picard, so I'm guessing you're from England, am I right?"

"I know not of this captain of whom you speak," Devon said, "but yes, I was last eh, living in England."

"Really, where about?" she asked.

"…Devon," said the duck after a pause.

"Like your name," she said. "What are the odds?"

"Hmm," Devon nodded.

"So Devon, are you like a wizard or something? Were you at some magical British school for witchcraft and wizardry when everything went kablooey?" Her eyes were alight with the possibilities.

"Er, no," said the duck.

"Oh," Annie said dejectedly. "Then I guess you're some kind of supernatural entity."

"What makes you say that?" asked Devon.

"Out of my way, mortal!" she said, mimicking his earlier comments. "Mortal fool, you shall do my bidding!" She was butchering the accent but got the swagger essentially right. "No one talks like that unless they're a vampire wannabe, which I am *not*, by the way, or unless they're playing an immortal creature in a movie. Since you aren't in a movie, and you aren't a vampire duck as far as I can tell, you must be something else. What are you, like, a demon?"

Devon eyed her for several moments before answering, "You are shrewd, mortal. Perhaps you will be useful after all."

"No shit! You're a demon?" Annie stood up as if the duck was on fire. "You're a frickin' demon, for real?"

"I am," said Devon, "and I'd rather you didn't make a fuss about it."

"Not make a fuss??" Annie blurted, "I'm talking, *talking* to a demon duck and you tell me not to make a fuss? You just blew my mind, okay? You're a frickin' demon!"

"Yes," he drawled with annoyance, checking to make sure they were alone.

"So," Annie sat down again and turned to face him "does that mean like, God is real then?"

Devon regarded her with mild surprise. "Don't your

religions tell you that humans are the favorite creation, and that God speaks to you?"

"Yeah," she said, "I guess."

Devon replied sourly, "Then you'd be better equipped to answer that question than I, wouldn't you? It's not as if God pops into Hell to chat like he supposedly does here."

She considered this and said, "I thought you were all at war with Heaven and stuff. Weren't you like, cast out?"

"You're talking about upper management," he replied. "They have their own version of events; they say they quit. The rest is just Dante's social critique. But Hell has been the domain of demons since it was created; I've personally only been to earth and back."

"Duck from Hell," Annie said to herself. "So, what brings you here?"

"I was summoned by three neophyte conjurers. Their spell was corrupted, the binding circle incomplete. I was able to leave of my own accord, but I fear I am... diminished. I cannot use my power in this form."

"Bummer," she said. "So what do you want from me? What is your bidding, little dude?"

Devon said, "I require your assistance to exact my revenge and return to Hell."

"Whoa there, duck boy." She waved her hands and said, "I am *not* helping you get revenge on anyone."

"I could make it worth your while," said Devon, silk slipping into his voice. "Is there anything you want, any... agreement we could come to?"

"Ha!" laughed Annie, "Are you asking me to make a deal with a demon? No thanks, I'm not stupid; you aren't getting your hands on my soul, so don't even think about it."

"I didn't ask for your soul, did I?" Devon said. "I am asking if there is a service or reward you require for helping me."

Annie regarded him for a moment and half-jokingly said, "Could you make me a vampire? Not one of those sparkle-vamps though; I hate those guys."

"Only vampires can make other vampires, but maybe I could introduce you."

"Shit, you mean vampires are real too? That's awesome!" She jumped up and down squealing, "I knew it, I knew it!"

"I thought you said you weren't a vampire wannabe?" Devon asked slyly.

"All Goths want to be vampires, ducky. It's just that some of us take it way more seriously than others, with fake fangs and shit, you know?"

"Ah," he said. "What is a sparkle-vamp?"

"Never mind. So like, you can introduce me? Okay wait a minute, what am I saying? I don't even know what this is all about. What is it you want from me?" She folded her arms defensively.

Devon considered for a moment, "I will need your help doing research at first. I must find the summoning spell that brought me here. I will need you to use your machines for me."

"Okies, ducks can't do basic stuff, I get it. No hands. What else?" she asked.

"I will need a translator, obviously; I have spoken to several mortals this night, and it seems that you alone can understand me. I will also need some measure of protection."

"Protection from what?" Annie asked nervously. "Like, other demons and stuff?"

"Dogs and people, mostly," Devon said glumly. "I must stay alive until I am ready to return. Death will limit my options."

"OK, so I keep you alive and do research. Anything else?"

Devon hesitated. "I may require some souls to feed upon if I am to rebuild my strength."

"Oh is that all?" Annie laughed, "Forget it ducky, I'm not feeding you souls, not mine or anyone else's."

"This from the girl who wants to be a vampire," Devon mused.

"Hey now, that's different... isn't it?" she asked uncertainly.

"They kill more often than not," Devon said. "Besides, I wouldn't ask you to help me harvest anyone you care for. Do you have any enemies, perchance?"

"No! I mean, yeah I suppose I do, but I'm not feeding them to a demon! Why would I help you do that to someone?" Annie inched away from the duck.

"Your desire was to become a predator that feeds on humans. Why *wouldn't* you help me?"

"Hey, I take it back, okay? I don't want to be a vampire and I'm not helping you eat people's souls!" She stood up and glared down at the duck. "Why am I even considering this? I should go home and let you fend for yourself."

"So be it," said Devon, "but I *will* get back to Hell and I *will* see you eventually. I shall recall how you abandoned me to my fate and I shall have an eternity to... *discuss* it with you."

"The duck threatens me now," said Annie. "How do you know I'm even going to Hell?"

"Most of you are going to Hell. That's part of the

problem, actually." Devon said gloomily.

"Oh this should be good," Annie smirked. "What is it? Rock music? Video games? Teletubbies? What's sending us all to Hell?"

"Contracts with demons," said Devon calmly.

"I never made a contract with a demon!" Annie protested.

"Have you ever signed something or agreed to terms without reading all the fine print? Do you thoroughly research everything you commit to?" It was Devon's turn to smirk at her.

Annie sat down slowly, afraid to think about how many times she'd clicked the 'Accept' button on the Internet or scrawled her name on a document after skimming the first few lines. "Point taken," she said weakly. Every time she downloaded a software update, or installed a video game, she accepted the terms of usage by reflex. *Crap on a stick. Am I really that screwed?* "Okay, you might have me there. Is there any way I can, you know, fix that?"

Devon ruffled his feathers in a shrug saying, "Not my department. I don't really deal in the direct soul market, so I managed to steer clear of the crash."

Annie looked at him curiously. "The crash? Like a stock market crash?"

"Indeed," said Devon. "Soul trafficking used to be a brisk business; human souls were a valuable commodity for eons. Then came the printing press; the demon responsible for that was quite pleased with himself at the time. One thing led to another and soon the knowledge of the world passed from learned scholars and priests to the common man; radical ideas spread, people gained a little bit of knowledge, which is always dangerous, and eventually lawyers got involved. Ah, lawyers." Devon crooned. "The next thing we knew, lawyers and demons are working together for their clients, one group after money, the other after souls. Hell started filling up faster than anyone anticipated."

Annie was appalled but not surprised; her father was a lawyer. "Wow that sucks." They sat quietly as a pair of young lovebirds walked by, gave them a curious look, and moved on. Annie and the duck waited for them to get out of earshot.

"Yes, it sucks, as you say," agreed Devon. "The market crashed in the late twentieth century and many demons lost their shirts, so to speak. The human souls were piling up and their contracts limited what we could do with them. We had to get creative."

"Couldn't you just, you know, kick them out? Send them to Heaven?" she asked hopefully.

"If there is a Heaven, we don't have any say who gets in. Exclusive club, you know. We deport souls out of Hell all the time, but they keep finding their way back in. One day you cast millions into Purgatory, and the next day they're back looking for work. It's aggravating." Devon huffed.

"Hell has illegal aliens?" she giggled.

"We don't take aliens, just humans." Devon said.

Annie blinked. *Wow, aliens. That was a whole other can of worms.* "So you aren't in the market for souls then?"

"Hardly," the duck replied. "It would take hundreds to begin buying my way back. That's why I need to find out about the summoning spell that trapped me here. If it was brokered by another demon, maybe I can find a way to solve both of our problems."

"So you're saying that a demon is responsible for this mess you're in?"

"Possibly," Devon murmured.

"And I thought *I* had family issues. Okay ducky, I'll help you learn about the spell, and I'll keep you as safe as I can," she pointed at the duck's bill, "but I'm not helping you kill people or get revenge, and I want my soul released from whatever fucked up contract I got myself into."

"Then we have an accord," the demon exclaimed, nodding his head. "The terms are accepted. Now let us begin at once. I assume you have one of those electrical typing machines in your home?"

"A computer? Yeah of course," she said.

"Excellent! One more thing?"

"What?" she asked cautiously.

"Carry me please?"

Chapter 3
The Infernal Web

Annie lived with her mother in a small, two-bedroom house near the outskirts of the campus; close enough to be convenient, but far enough to not be bothered by the sounds of the winter football crowds. Halloween decorations were up; plastic skeletons hung from the trees, and an inflatable, light-up ghost and Frankenstein monster stood in the neighbor's yard, giving the property that used-car-lot vibe. The front door of Annie's house had a cardboard skeleton and witch, both posed dancing a jig, and a jack-o-lantern grinned from its perch on the porch. Devon looked about with interest but said nothing.

Annie's mother was up watching the late night televangelists, mostly for the spectacle of pastel suits, cotton candy hair, and whore make-up.

"Hello Annie honey," mom said.

"Hey mom," Annie said, trying to sneak the duck past the living room.

Mom pointed to the TV saying, "The Fundies are raising money to send the Jews back to Israel so they can kick-start the apocalypse and get Raptured. What was I thinking, using all that money to put you through college?"

"Very funny mom," Annie said, shielding Devon with her body. "You're in the wrong religion if you're waiting to get beamed up. Turns out Tom Cruise was right all along." She didn't mention her college tuition was mostly her dad's money. Mom lived on disability due to being kind of bat-shit crazy.

"Annabelle!" mom exclaimed, freezing Annie in her tracks. "What is that? Is that a duck?"

Caught. "Uh… yeah?" Annie said meekly, feeling like a ten-year-old sneaking cookies.

"What the hell are you doing bringing a duck into my house?"

"He… was lost," she began, the story spilling as she created it, "and I have to look online to see if anyone is missing a duck, but I don't want him to run away so I'm… keeping him in my room."

"I don't want that filthy animal in my house," she said, "We raised ducks and I know how messy they are."

"Quack," said Devon.

"You be nice to my mother!" Annie scolded him. "Look mom, I can keep him in the bathtub or put paper down on the floor. It's only for a night or two. Pleeeeeez?"

Mom relented after ten minutes of wrangling, and Devon sat patiently through it all, offering counter-points for Annie to use. Finally they were alone in her cluttered room.

"Don't you ever do laundry?" asked Devon, as he tried not to get his webbed feet caught in another bra strap.

"Shush duck," Annie said, and she fired up her computer. Her dad had bought her a nice tablet computer last Christmas, but she rarely used it out of spite. Besides, her desktop PC was her baby; she had built it herself. "Can you give me any clues where to start looking?"

"I have no idea how this device works." Devon answered. "That's why I need you."

"Right," she said, "okay, I type in keywords to search for, and the web browser finds the most likely matches."

The duck blinked a few times, digesting this strange information. Finally he said, "I was summoned by two young men and a woman. Try typing 'two men and a woman' and see if we find them."

Annie snickered, "I don't think that will help, unless you're looking for lots of porn. We need to find what they used to summon you. Was it a book, a scroll, what?"

"It was on a device like this," Devon said.

"Awesome! Did you see the screen?"

"It was blue," Devon said.

"Blue. A blue screen. Great. Anything else?" God, he was just like a customer at the video store...

Devon thought hard for a moment and said, "The female mentioned something about a 'board' and a 'thread' and people summoning a copy of their sacrifice," he frowned and asked, "Is this thread on the board part of the 'web' you are browsing?"

"Now you're getting it, ducky." Annie said encouragingly.

"I have no idea what I just said!" Devon replied with frustration. Annie smiled.

"Let's see...people summoning a copy of their sacrifice... did they *sacrifice* a duck to summon you?" Annie asked in horror.

"Yes," Devon replied. "One of the males had a bloodied dagger, and there was a dead duck on a small, makeshift altar."

"Eeew gross. Creepy people. I hope they get what's coming to them."

"Oh, they shall," Devon drawled.

Annie typed several possible combinations of *animal sacrifice*, *demon summoning*, and *copy,* before coming to a series of links to a message board on a site devoted to dark magic and demonology. It was a membership site, so certain areas were off-limits, including the list of popular summoning spells. And it was blue.

"Well, according to the boards, there's been some weird shit happening over the past few months. Looks like a new spell is responsible, something called the "Budget Conjuration.""

Devon shook his head in disgust. "Budget spells. Splendid." He looked down at his webbed feet and sighed.

"I can't check out the spell without joining the site, so let's see…" She began filling out the simple form with her name, e-mail address and age, then clicked 'Continue' and was presented with a screen that said 'Accept Terms of Service' with a big, shiny button next to it. She almost clicked it without thinking.

"Whoa," she said. "I *have* to stop doing that." She looked around the page and found the terms of service as a small, innocuous hotlink under a gaudy banner advertising 'hot singles' looking for 'demon lovers'. Clicking the link, she scanned the small print until her eyes glazed over. "God, I can't believe I'm expected to read the whole thing before accepting."

"Yes," said Devon, "Many people think the same thing about the Bible. Allow me to peruse this..." She set him on her lap and he craned his neck towards the screen; his head weaved back and forth rhythmically as he read, muttering "Next," every ten seconds or so, prompting Annie to scroll down to the next page. Finally, he finished and announced, "One called Memelax declares himself a 'Webmaster,' so I suspect he is one of the Spider Lords. Apparently, he negotiates for other demons and arranges for them to meet with a client base."

"He's a middleman," said Annie.

"Indeed," said the duck. "Memelax gets a percentage of all soul transactions as a finder's fee."

"So it's up to other demons to offer favors for souls then?" Annie nodded as she began to grasp the workings of the Hellish economy. "Like that Henry VIII contract you mentioned; what is that exactly?"

Devon answered. "The Henry VIII contract offers fame and/or power in exchange for broken marriages, the more creative, the better."

"Huh," Annie grimaced, "I wonder if my dad made one."

"Is he a performer?" the duck inquired.

"A lawyer," she said.

"Ah, splendid," Devon crooned, "You must be proud."

"Not really," she said. "So, this Melemax…"

"Memelax," he corrected.

"Right… is that like his real name? It sounds a lot more

'demony' than Devon."

"It is his public name, used for doing business. 'Devon' is just a name I chose to give you," said the duck. "It was the location of the last place I was summoned, in England."

"What were you doing in England? Making Henry VIII contracts?"

"No," Devon said, with a hint of pride, "Have you ever heard of Agatha Christie?"

"Wasn't she that chick from *Murder, She Wrote*?"

Devon's bill dropped open, then clamped shut. He sputtered, "No, she was *not* 'that chick from *Murder, She Wrote*.' Agatha Christie was my crowning achievement, even greater than Ben Jonson." He murmured, "Philistine."

"Who the hell is Ben Jonson?" she asked. "Sounds like a kid I went to school with that used to eat his boogers."

"He was a contemporary of the Bard." The duck retorted.

Annie scrunched up her brow, "You mean Jethro Tull?"

"Shakespeare! William *bleeding* Shakespeare!" Devon barked, truly annoyed now. "Do they teach you nothing in your schools?"

"Hey, I saw *Romeo and Juliet* like three times," Annie said defensively. "Leonardo DiCaprio was-"

"Don't!" Devon snapped. "Just… don't."

"Whatever," she huffed. "So is it safe for me to join this site, or am I selling my soul to Memelax?" Her finger was poised over the mouse button.

Devon swallowed his pride and explained, "Using current demonic legal terms, Memelax is asking for consent to broker an agreement between demons, hereby known as 'consumers' and mortals, hereby known as 'clients'. It states that if you are not under the terms of a pre-existing contract, that Memelax may provide services to facilitate the requests and mutual agreements of clients and consumers, receiving a portion of mortal souls, hereby known as 'revenues'."

"Wow that sounds perfectly harmless. Son of a bitch, you guys are sneaky bastards, you know that Devon?"

"Quite," said the duck. "It is safe to join so long as you do not intend to use or distribute any of the spells. Use constitutes entering an agreement with the consumer that provided the spell."

"Well, I don't and I won't, so I'm gonna click…" she looked at the duck to see if he made any argument. If he was hiding anything, his poker face was too good. She clicked 'Accept'.

The 'Welcome' screen had links to many features and archives, as well as a list of summoning spells members posted to share. They were rated by one to five little animated flames. Annie searched for Budget Conjuration and found it on the list with two flame icons. She read the comments, "Either nothing happens, or you get black smoke and a copy of your dead sacrifice. Hmm, it looks like some people tried killing the copy, but it only made a big mess. Apparently, the spell rates 'two flames' because it actually *does* something. I wonder what a 'five flame' spell does?"

"Let me read the spell," said the duck as he leaned forward again. Annie clicked on the spell link and scrolled down so Devon could examine it. His bill moved as he read; his head weaved back and forth as he squinted against the blue glare of the screen. Finally his bill dropped open and he sat back, his feathers ruffling in distress. "Oh dear," he said.

"What?" Annie asked, tensing up. "Is it bad?"

"The spell was a trap. A demon trap." His head sank in despair, "The instructions to draw the binding circle were intentionally flawed, designed to trap me in this form forever."

"Well, can't you return to Hell by dying?" Annie asked. "I mean just, you know, jump in front of a bus and go to Hell. What's so hard about that?"

"Suicide," Devon said, "sentences me to eternal service in Hell as the property of another demon, in this case, the one who provided the spell in the first place."

"Wow that sounds so... Catholic." Annie said.

"Even the Catholics got some things right," he said. "If I try to take my own life, whether by action or inaction, it qualifies as a suicide and I forfeit my eternal freedom."

"Well then," offered Annie, "what if someone kills you without your permission? Like a surprise? Not that *I* would do that, mind you." *Not yet anyway*, she thought.

"How kind," he remarked. "According to the rules of this summoning spell, if I die in combat or by accident, it's worse."

Annie's eyebrows rose, "What could be worse than eternal servitude in Hell?"

"Being eternal dinner," said Devon.

She shuddered. "That's horrible! Why would one demon do that to another?"

"As I said, the market for human souls crashed; you can't even give them away," the duck sighed, "But demon souls are powerful, versatile, and rather tasty. Since our numbers are finite and we don't breed, the demon market will never be flooded with cheap commodities."

Annie put her hands on her hips and glared at the duck in her lap. "Speaking as one of your cheap commodities, I can't say I feel sorry for you. You guys deserve a taste of your own medicine." She wagged a finger at his bill, "*But* I'm willing to help you if it means helping *me*. I don't intend to go to Hell on some crap legal technicality; there's got to be a loophole somewhere, something we can both exploit."

"Now you are thinking like a lawyer, Annabelle Puckett." Devon said admiringly.

"Screw you, duck. So who's the demon behind this spell? Does it say?" She scrolled up and down the page in annoyance, not really looking for anything.

Devon's voice sneered, compensating for his lack of lips, "Her name is Gothraxess, Mistress of the Infernal Web. She is the greatest of the Spider Lords, and has been very active on Earth over the past few decades. They say her web of influence encompasses the entire world now…"

"The World Wide Web?" Annie asked incredulously. "You're kidding."

"You have heard of it?" he asked. "Is it part of the web-thread you were browsing? I thought as much." He looked down at the wires beneath her desk, half expecting them to be crawling with spiders. "So her web can be accessed by computers now? How interesting."

"You know, that makes a sick kind of sense," she muttered, "Half the Internet is porn and mass stupidity. And LOLcats."

Devon declared, "I know not of LOLcats, but pornography has always been potent bait for human souls. People will make the most foolish decisions in the throes of lust. Consider Herod and Salome."

"Or Bill and Monica," Annie said. "So what does this mean? Is the spider bitch a hard ass or will she deal?"

"How I adore your colloquialisms," said Devon flatly. "Yes, she will deal, but I'm not very hopeful. Normally one can buy their way out of a contract, but the cost in adjusted human souls would be prohibitive... unless you know of a way to start World War III."

"One demon soul is worth that much in human lives?" she gaped. "That doesn't seem right."

"It's simple economics," Devon replied. "How many shiny beads would you trade for a bar of solid gold?"

"Depends on how much gold I have lying around, and how much I like beads."

"Precisely," said the duck.

"That's nice and depressing. So seeing as how the spider queen isn't taking shiny beads in trade, what's a solid gold duck to do?" Annie asked, "I suppose the loophole isn't obvious?"

"No, but I might have a chance," Devon said. "Consuming souls will increase my status, thus eventually voiding the contract. A demon cannot own a higher-ranking demon."

"Good luck with that, duck-face." Annie said. "It's late and I'm going to bed. If you want to surf the Infernal Web, be my guest." She stood, set him on the chair, and made for the shower.

Devon watched her go, then nudged the mouse with his bill experimentally. He found his way back to the web browser and tried using the keyboard, pecking keys one at a time.

B-U-E-L-L-E-R_M-I-S-S-I-N-G_P-E-T-S

Peck, peck, peck.

Chapter 4
All Creatures Great and Small

Devon obliged Annie by spending the night in the bathtub, keeping his duck mess contained. After a long night of navigating the threads of the World Wide Web, he was ready to begin the day; however Annie was less than ready.

"Wake up, mortal." Devon said in her ear. "Annabelle Puckett. Awaken."

She groaned and turned over, peering at him from behind her hair. "Oh god, you're still here. I was hoping you were a dream."

"I am not a dream, Annabelle Puckett. I am ready to continue our mission, but first I must feed."

Annie sat up and glared at him, "You aren't getting any souls, duck. I thought I made that clear last night."

"I was thinking more of wheat toast soaked in milk," he said. "My palette is rather limited for the time being."

"Oh," she said groggily. "I think I can swing some

milky toast. Lemme check my tat first, it itches like mad." She rolled off the bed and made for the bathroom, wearing panties and a black Alien Sex Fiend concert shirt. She peeled off the bandage and examined the neck tattoo in the big mirror, holding up a hand mirror to her face. "Any new ideas on buying out your contract?"

"A few, but we will need to pay a visit to the local constabulary office this morning." Devon replied from her bed, looking at the mess of laundry on the floor like an obstacle course.

"Constab-… oh, the cops? What for?" she asked, as she brushed her hair into pigtails.

"I have a suspicion that there is a cabal of demon enthusiasts in this town," he said.

"In Bueller? You're kidding! Nothing ever happens here, except on Earth Day and the Fourth of July. There are no demon cults here or I would know." Annie said as she poked at her tattoo.

"Why would *you* know?" asked the duck.

"*Look* at me," she replied, gesturing to the tattoo on her arm. "I'm a Goth. They'd have tried to recruit me or something. Most of these mountain yokels think I regularly talk to the devil anyway."

"Do you?" he asked.

"I'd be happy to talk to whoever will answer me at this point. But no, I don't have congress with the Horned One and never have. I dress in black, I write dark, shitty poetry, I like ravens and black cats, but I am *not* evil and I *don't* worship your boss. I'm a good person, duck." She proceeded to apply her Egyptian-style eyeliner and dark lipstick.

"Perhaps that is why no one has approached you," he said.

"Why do you think there's a demon cult in Bueller anyway?" she asked around her lipstick.

"Last night I looked up reports of missing pets in this town. There have been several in the previous months. It stands to reason that they met the same fate as my avian sacrifice."

"Not bad detective work, Sherlock," she said. "Why do we need to talk to the cops?"

'*Sherlock*,' Devon thought with a cringe. *Christie outsold that hack Doyle by a long shot...* "We need names, addresses, information. There must be a pattern. Also, I want to return to the site of my summoning." He flapped over most of the laundry and landed near the bedroom door. As Annie came out of the bathroom, he saw her new tattoo for the first time. "Are you sure you have not had contact with a demon cult?" he asked.

"Yes, Devon. I'm pretty sure," Annie huffed.

"Ah," he said, "It's just that you have a demon symbol tattooed on the back of your neck."

Annie stared at the duck in horror.

Breakfast had been hurried as Annie soaked some toast in milk and fed the demon in the kitchen, much to her mother's disgust. After slapping cream cheese on a bagel, Annie had scooped up the duck and headed out the door, boots clomping on the pavement as she ate and muttered to herself.

"Maurice!" Annie called as she entered the Paradise Lost Tattoo Shop with Devon under her arm. "Are you back there?" The bell over the door rang in distress as she barged in, "Maurice?"

It was late in the morning, but still early for the big biker to get customers. Patterns and sample art cluttered the walls, along with photos of some of the artist's better work. The glass counter held an assortment of inks and body piercing jewelry, and on the counter-top was half a dozen three-ring binders filled with patterns. Towards the back of the shop were a couple of chairs for the artist and his victims. One was the kind used to give back massages, with a hole for the face. Annie had planned to spend some time in that chair after a few more paychecks, but now she wasn't so sure.

"Annie?" called a voice from the back. From the restroom came the hulking shape of Maurice, with his ever-present t-shirt and denim vest emblazoned with patches. His sleeveless arms bore years of tattoos, some faded and obscure, others fresh and vibrant. He had a steel bar through the flesh between his eyebrows and a ring in his nose like a big hairy bull; a mane of brown shag blended into the bushy beard on his face. The toilet flushed in the background as he wrestled with his zipper. His voice was rough from years of cigarettes, and the odor of tobacco smoke hung thickly in the air. There was a citrus air freshener behind the register, and Maurice liked to pretend it compensated for any unpleasant odors, like the one now following him out of the bathroom. "Annie, babe! You up at this time o' day?" he said.

"Not usually, but I got a thing…" she said, fidgeting. "Hey, you know that tat I got the other day?" she motioned to the back of her neck, "Where did you find that again?"

"On the Internet; some tat site had lots of free stuff, you know, like clip-art for the skin." He pointed, "Hey, nice duck."

"Quack," said the duck.

"He says 'hi'," Annie murmured. "Could you show me the site? I want to check something." She went to the counter where he kept his computer. It was a high-performance rig that was sometimes used for keeping records and managing inventory, but mostly for fragging Nazi space-marine zombies or other players. He played first-person shooters when he wasn't inking or piercing, which was most of the time. He went by the gaming handle 'DeadZero-101', which struck more fear into the hearts of his opponents than 'Maurice Chekhov' would have. Maurice flicked the mouse, awakening 'The Monster,' as he lovingly called it, clicked on a couple of icons, and soon had the site on the flat wide-screen monitor. He turned it so she could see.

"You afraid it's a trademark? Think some corporation owns your ass now?" he joked.

"Quack," said the duck. Annie just frowned as she examined the screen.

"So, did you win him or what?" Maurice asked, eying the duck that was oddly interested in the computer screen. It almost seemed to be reading…

"Huh? Oh nah, he's a demon that got summoned and trapped in the body of a duck. I'm trying to help him because the Spider Lord that runs the Internet is gonna drag us all to Hell."

"Okaaay," he said with a coughing laugh. "How's the tat healing?"

"Good. Itches a bit though," she replied.

"Quack," the duck commented, "Quack-wack."

"How would you know?" she asked it.

Maurice just gave them a look and got up to microwave another burrito.

"Hey, has anyone else gotten this tattoo?" she called.

"Not from me. You're the first, babe." He assured her. "But seeing as it's on the net, I can't guarantee…" the microwave beeped at him.

"Do me a favor and let me know if anyone else asks for it? It's kind of important," she pleaded.

"Uh, sure. What's this all about?" Maurice asked.

"Maybe nothing," she said, "But certain tattoos can bring unwanted attention. This might be one of them."

"Quack," said the duck. "Quack, quack."

"Heh, no need to tell me that sweetie," he got his piping hot burrito out of the oven, tossing it from one hand to the other. "Oh hey, I got a special on Russian prison tats! Interested?" She didn't seem interested or amused. Maurice cleared his throat. "What's so bad about this one?" he asked around a mouthful of burrito.

"I have it on good authority that…" she began.

"Quack!" said the duck.

"Shush!" she hissed, "…that it's an occult symbol, and there might be some weirdoes asking after it, or hassling people who have it, so don't tell anyone that I do, okay?"

"Weirdoes?" he asked with a smile. "You mean like LARPers, metal-heads, people who speak Klingon?" He stuck out his tongue and made the 'horned fingers' sign.

"No, I mean like people who sacrifice animals to commune with the forces of darkness," said Annie with a grimace.

"Oh, frat boys!" Maurice said with a knowing wink and a grin.

"I'm serious, Moe! Swear you'll keep it between us." She lifted the duck off the counter and tucked it under her arm.

"Okay, okay I swear on my Harley repair manual." He held up one hand, placing the other below the register on the sacred book, next to the heavy revolver he kept for troublemakers. "Between me and you, sweetie."

"Thanks, Maurice. Take care." She headed out with the duck as the bell over the door jingled merrily.

"So what did we learn?" she asked Devon as they headed for the center of town.

"What is a LARPer?"

"It's uh… a live action role-player," she said. "They dress up and play out fantasies in a game setting, instead of like, just pretending and rolling dice."

"Is it a sexual thing?"

"No… uh… oh god, I hope not." She thought about the people she knew in high school who were into LARPing, and she *never* tried to imagine them naked.

"What is a Klingon?"

"They look like Maurice, but with more bumps on their head," she quipped. "What about the tattoo? Focus, duck."

"It is the sigil of Babel, the Demon of Many Tongues. Those so marked can speak to demons, in whatever form they take. It is fortunate that I found you." Devon said.

"Yeah, great." Annie mused. "Lucky me. How did it get on the Internet?"

"According to the text, the symbol was posted by one called 'Chucknorriss'." Devon stated. "We must locate Chucknorriss immediately and see what he knows."

She replied, "Um, I doubt that's the real name."

"Regardless," he said, "I believe it was placed there by another demon or his minion, as a form of insurance."

"Insurance? What, in case someone used that crap spell and trapped them just like you?" she asked.

"Precisely," he said.

"So they must have some way of reversing it. I bet they

planned ahead, knowing other demons were up to no good. There might be a spell or something to free you, ducky!" Annie exclaimed.

"Possibly," said Devon. "There might be other reasons, but I'd rather not contemplate them."

"Like what?" she asked.

"Did you hear what I just said?" he asked, annoyed. "Not... Contemplating."

"Okay fine, be that way." They walked in silence to the police station, bearing the odd looks of the townspeople.

The Bueller Police Department operated from a temporary location in a strip mall, while the new station was being built up the street. Everyone was looking forward to the new building and the bigger budget, but the current spot did little to raise the esteem of the two dozen or so police officers and staff that had to share the address with a pizza delivery hub and the fabric mart. At least the pizzas came extra hot and fast.

Chief Wagner was a balding man of upper-middle age and lower-middle girth; his leadership and can-do attitude making up for his less-than Olympian shape. A life-long resident of Bueller, he made it his business to get to know as many people as he could during his time on patrol. He was still on a first name basis with most of the business owners and kids who worked in the downtown area. Annie had been one of his favorite baristas. Now she had a duck under her arm.

"Annie," Chief Wagner nodded, sipping his coffee from an enormous insulated mug. He had made his way to the front to get some more sugar packets from the desk sergeant's private stash when the girl and her pet came in.

"Oh, hiya Chief," she said with a smile. "I... I've got a weird request for you."

"Do tell?" he said with mild interest.

"I've been looking into missing pets in town, and was wondering if you could, like, help me out with some of the reports. You know, like copies, addresses." She scratched the back of her neck nervously as the duck looked around the room. "Pictures, if you have any."

Chief Wagner took a long sip from his coffee tank as he looked at her, his police instincts telling him something was decidedly odd. He wouldn't have guessed the reason in a million years, but it didn't stop him from being suspicious. "Those are public reports, so I suppose we could let you have some copies... What's all this about, Annie?"

She hefted the duck and shrugged, "I just thought I could devote some of my time to searching for missing pets. Like Mr. Duck here; he was wandering the streets alone last night and I'm sure someone is missing him."

"Quack," said the duck.

"Mmhm," said the chief.

"And I figured the cops have better things to do than look for lost pets, so I got the idea to help. On my own." She glanced down at the duck.

The desk sergeant had returned to his desk and the chief motioned to him, "Andy, why don't you help out Ms. Puckett here. She needs recent missing pet reports from, what," he asked Annie, "the last few months, maybe?"

"Yeah, that'd be great." Annie smiled, looking relieved.

Andy cracked, "I can get you the cold case files too; someone lost 101 Dalmatian puppies in the middle of last century." Andy was the kind of guy who fancied himself witty and charming. He looked at the duck curiously and the duck looked back with a penetrating stare, as if daring him to comment. Sergeant Andy shrugged and went off to get the files while the chief found several sugar packets in his desk.

"So Annie, you still at the video store?" he asked, as he dumped all the packets into the dark mixture in the mug.

She nodded, "Yeah, still there. Still on the graveyard shift."

"I sure miss you at the café; the new girls don't know how to make my morning boot-to-the-head like you did."

She was genuinely touched. "Aww, is that why you're drinking house blend from that T-Stop bladder-buster? I can leave them the directions next time I'm there."

"Heh, it wouldn't have your magic, Annie." He smiled and took another sip.

"Quack?"

"He's just being figurative," she said to the duck.

Sergeant Andy soon returned with copies of the reports and photos of the missing animals, all tucked into a manila folder. He handed them to the girl with a wink, saying, "Bring 'em back alive, Frank Buck!" He chuckled at his little joke.

Annie gave him a confused frown, but Devon glared at him as they turned to leave.

"Bye now, Annie," the chief called. She thanked him and waved.

After she left, Sergeant Andy said, "Hey chief, I think her duck just gave me the stink-eye."

"Smart duck," the chief said. "You need more sugar packets, by the way."

After the police station, the odd pair swung by the campus grounds to look for the place Devon had been summoned. She followed his directions, retracing his steps from the video store, past the 24 hour T-Stop, onto campus, and into the alley between buildings. They quickly found the basement window Devon claimed to have escaped from.

"This is the math building," Annie said, confused. "What were they doing in the basement of the math building?"

"Summoning demons, obviously." Devon replied with annoyance.

"Yeah, but how did they get in there? It was around midnight, wasn't it? The building would have been locked for hours; I doubt even the janitors would still be working." She walked around to the front of the building, as if the answer might be posted on a sign, like 'Late Night Demon Summoning for Extra Credit.' Nothing.

"I propose we watch the entrance while we examine these reports," said the duck. "Perhaps the culprits will return."

"Yeah, okay. No funny business though." She sat under a tree as students wandered by, lugging backpacks and cappuccinos.

"I could do no 'funny business' if I wished to, Annabelle Puckett. I am sadly powerless in this form." Devon settled by the folder as Annie spread it open on the grass.

"Kinda hard to get revenge then, isn't it?" she asked. "Not like you can peck someone to death."

"No…" Devon said gloomily, "Neither can I speak the

most basic of spells. You have no idea how demeaning this experience has been. Imagine being trapped in the body of a cockroach, and only a rat could understand you."

She glared, "A rat. I'm the rat in this scenario."

"No offense," Devon said.

"None taken, asshole," she snapped. "Now, about these missing critters…"

There were nearly a dozen pets reported lost or stolen in Bueller in the last three months, corresponding with the posting of the Budget Conjuration spell. Some could be considered exotic pets, while most were common enough. Among the first reports was a monkey stolen from the behavioral research lab on campus.

"Makes sense that they'd take something they saw every day before going after people's pets." She did her best Hannibal Lecter voice, but it just came off sounding like Katherine Hepburn. "What does he do, Clarice; this man you seek? He covets." No response from the duck. She flipped some more pages. "These bastards even took some little girl's bunny rabbit. She lives nearby here too." She pointed to the address. "It's not far from campus. Want to check it out?"

The duck was dividing his attention between the math building and the reports. "Perhaps. I would still like to watch for the ones who summoned me," he said with a touch of venom.

Annie nodded, "Well, I work tonight starting at five, so we've got some time to kill." The pair sat in the shade for a few hours before getting bored, and Annie suggested they speak to the girl with the missing rabbit first.

The little girl named Cindy Berger lived just a few blocks from the campus, with a rabbit hutch on the side of the house plainly visible from the street. It would have made an irresistible target to a pet snatcher. There was a little girl, about eight years old, sitting in the front yard; a white and black-spotted rabbit lay in her lap.

Annie approached with Devon tucked under her arm. She smiled and said in her best child-friendly voice, "Hi there, honey. I'm Annie. Is your name Cindy?" She offered the copy of the report showing the picture of the missing pet. "Did you lose a bunny named Bingo?"

Cindy looked from Annie to the duck and back again, nodded, and cuddled her rabbit protectively.

"Can you tell me about him? I want to help you find him."

Cindy gave Annie a curious look and said, "*This* is Bingo. He came back."

Annie and the duck both looked at the photo in the report, then at Bingo. Annie thought maybe the girl's parents had gotten her a new rabbit and told her it was Bingo, but the critter in the girl's lap looked just like the picture.

"Quack," said Devon.

Bingo the bunny twitched his nose and twisted his ears before making a little grunting noise. "Begone, thou fool! The child is mine, and I shall brook no intrusions." The bunny's little pink eyes flashed. Cindy took no notice, but continued to stroke the bunny's head. Annie jumped at the voice, deep and raspy, like one of those demons in the movies. Devon must have been from a more posh part of Hell.

The duck blinked uncertainly and spoke, "I am seeking vengeance on those who summoned us. I invite you to join me in this vendetta, so we might give the mortals pause before entrapping more of our kind thus." It sounded reasonable to Annie, though the idea of a duck and rabbit going on a warpath was kind of disturbing. Silly, but also disturbing.

Bingo didn't see it that way. As Cindy petted him, he spoke again. "I need no assistance from the likes of you, thou fool. Already I am planning my war on the defilers; I have consumed the soul of another to gain strength. Death shall come swiftly to any who interfere, be they demon or mortal. Now, depart, and take thy Egyptian whore with thee!"

"Hey!" Annie barked at the bunny, "The Egyptian whore can understand you and is getting pissed off!"

Cindy flinched and stood up, lifting Bingo in her arms. "I'm going inside now," she said. Bingo's nose twitched again as he made a little growl.

"Same to you, buddy," said Annie, as she realized she had just freaked out a child. *Super. I bet she and her mom come into the store tonight to rent a Disney flick, and little Cindy points out the 'Egyptian whore who yelled at me.' I'm gonna get fired,* she thought. "That went well," she muttered as she turned to leave in a hurry. "Looks like you have competition in the revenge department. Poor kid. I hope she doesn't get hurt. That demon won't hurt her, will he?"

"Doubtful," said Devon. "She is his protection, as you are mine. He will not endanger her."

"Good," she said, "But what did he mean that he'd already consumed a soul? Whose soul?"

"I know not," said Devon, "But I think it bodes ill. The demon rabbit will be more powerful, and now that he knows of my existence…"

Annie asked nervously, "…What?"

"Er… nothing." Devon said.

Chapter 5
Night of the Lepus

The evening at work went smoothly, except for the fact that Devon had to wait outside. Annie wasn't feeling rebellious enough to risk getting caught duck smuggling, or brave the possibility of Mr. Hollis, the manager, coming in for a surprise visit. She told Devon he would have to keep himself busy out front until her shift ended. Devon was not pleased, but there was little he could do. Annie's mother didn't want the animal in her house unsupervised either. She barely tolerated the girl feeding him in the kitchen.

Annie finished shelving a small stack of DVD returns, checked the window to see if Devon was still there, and settled in to do some important-looking paperwork. It was on a clipboard and had lots of little boxes to check off, so she could safely ignore her customers until they asked her a direct question. Besides, the few wandering the floor were regular hour-browsers who could take care of themselves.

Nine o'clock rolled around and Devon had taken to pacing up and down the storefront, making rude noises to any who dared approach him. By the position of the moon, he judged that he had at least three more hours of this drudgery, and resolved to make demands upon his mortal servant for better arrangements during her work hours.

A big, black, overcompensating pickup truck pulled into the parking lot, its headlights swinging towards him until he was almost blinded. The cretin had chosen to park right in front of Devon, even though the lot was mostly empty. The duck squinted in the glare until it died with the engine, and the truck door opened with a heavy squeak.

"Hey there, duck," said a masculine voice from the cab, "You're lucky you're near the window. Maybe I'll see you later, huh?" The young man in the denim jacket and pants made a play of shooting Devon with an invisible shotgun before heading into Bueller's Big Video.

Annie groaned as Tommy Banks entered the store. He was residue from her school days and still acted like he sat behind her on a daily basis, tossing paper wads into her hair. It took all her willpower to manage a phony smile.

"Evening Tommy," she said past her teeth.

"Heya, Puckett pucketpucketpucktpckt… Still rockin' the Wednesday Addams look, huh?" he continued making the stupid 'pucktpuckt' noise as he drifted back towards the action section. At least he didn't treat her like every other female member of the species, and for that, she was grateful. It was better to be tormented than desired by the likes of him. As a card-carrying 'Dude-Brah', he was the type who opened with 'Hey, babe,' followed by whatever lame come-on was currently popular. He took eye-rolling as a sign of interest. As for other guys, they were addressed either as 'dude' or 'brah', often both in the same sentence. *Douche bag*.

Annie went back to her important-looking paperwork, recalling with a little guilt that when Devon asked if she had any enemies he might devour, she had thought of Tommy first.

Tommy came back minutes later with the greatest hits of old-school nineties action and set them on the counter with an obnoxious thump.

"Psyching up for hunting season, Tommy?" she asked with a hint of sarcasm as she scanned his DVDs. *Point Break, Speed, and The Matrix.* "Ooo, someone has a man-crush," she muttered.

He didn't seem to hear, but puffed his chest and replied, "I'm already psyched, Fannie Fuckett." He had thought of that nickname all by himself, back in 7th grade. "You know, you got a duck outside with a death wish." She turned to look and saw Devon watching them from the glass door. Tommy smirked, "If he wasn't next to the glass, he'd be dinner."

"He's a domesticated duck, and I'm watching him for a friend," Annie said harshly. "He's not a target, Tommy." *Asshole*.

"Well, 'tis the season. Maybe you should get him a collar." He snickered and passed her his Bueller Community College student credit card, held between two fingers and presented with a flourish like it was a

48

premium gold card with no limit.

"Ooo, baby's first credit card!" She smirked, "Now you can shop at Walmart like a boss."

"Eat me, Puckett."

"That's not part of the service, *Tommy*." She had a way of saying 'Tommy' and making it sound like 'Asshole.' It was a skill she had honed over many long years.

A collar might not be a bad idea, she thought. *Do they make duck collars? That would be so cute; maybe something with studs...* She had him sign his receipt, and handed him the movies past the anti-theft barricade. "Back by Monday before midnight, *Tommy*." she said. Tommy flipped her off and left the store. Annie watched him taunt Devon with a pantomime shotgun before returning to his truck. Asshole. Maybe Devon *should* eat him.

The duck glared at the denim-clad mortal, but something else had caught the man's eye. Devon came around the front of the truck to see what had distracted him, and to his horror, saw a white and black-spotted bunny sitting in a pool of radiance under the parking lot lamp. His feathers ruffled in dismay and he let out a squawk. The man tossed his movies on the seat and took a pellet rifle from the back seat of his extended cab. Devon flapped and flung himself at the store window, scratching with his claws to get Annie's attention.

Tommy flipped the safety off his pellet gun, chuckling to himself as he sighted the scope on the stray rabbit. "This has got to be my lucky night," he said. "Duck season *and* wabbit season." He squeezed off a shot at the bunny, which leaped straight up in the air, the lead pellet ricocheting harmlessly on the asphalt. The rodent then sat in the light, glowering at the man by the pickup.

Tommy stared in shock at the critter as he chambered another round. "Son of a bitch," he said, taking better aim this time. He held his breath to fire, but the rabbit burst into action, darting back and forth, rushing towards him.

Annie finally heard Devon flapping and scratching at the window and turned just in time to see a spray of blood coat the glass; Tommy's scream choked off as suddenly as it began.

"Shit!" she cried, rushing to the door. She opened it and Devon scrambled inside, specks of blood covering him. The man was on the ground near his truck, with little Bingo the bunny hunched over on his chest; gore dripping from its incisors.

"Flee!" shouted Devon, "Bingo has come for me!" The duck flapped over the display aisle and disappeared into the 'special interest' section.

As Annie watched in disbelief, Bingo trembled upon Tommy's chest, a dim luminance growing around him as his bunny lips parted to suck in the essence of Tommy's soul. His pink eyes flashed with a demonic light and his floppy ears became rigid and pointed at the tips, like horns. He looked up at Annie and roared like a lion, shattering the glass of the storefront as posters collapsed and sparks flew from the marquees.

"He has consumed another soul! He will be more powerful now!" Devon shouted. The other two customers in the store ran for the refuge of the adult section, peeking over the top of the swinging saloon-style doors.

Annie had thrown herself behind the counter to avoid the worst of the flying glass; now she stumbled towards the aisle where Devon was hiding, but his feathery butt was darting around another corner. "Devon?" she cried, hoping he might tell her what the hell was going on. She saw Bingo sniffing around as he hopped over the broken glass and into the store. Annie ducked behind the aisle, watching the bunny in the security mirrors that lined the top of the walls.

"I know you are in here, coward," Bingo said in his booming, raspy voice. "There is no shame in dying thus. You shall return to Hell and be free."

Devon called out, "Lies! I have read the spell! I would be enslaved, or used to stock another's larder. It is not I that shall perish, but you!"

Bingo laughed long and hard, his little mouth stained with blood. "Thou fool! Thou art powerless before me! Behold my wrath!" Annie watched in the mirror as the rabbit burst into flames; his body was engulfed but not consumed, and he began to hop down the aisles, setting little fires in his wake.

"Devon! We got a burning bunny here!" she called out, praying that the duck had a plan.

Bingo turned the corner, setting the shelving ablaze, but he chose not to attack her. "Egyptian whore," he growled, "Thou shalt serve *me* when thy master is slain!" He hopped past her as the sprinklers went off, dousing the fires but not extinguishing the flaming rabbit. The customers in the adult section chose to make a break for the door at that point, rushing through the artificial rain and nearly trampling Devon as he hid nearby. His distressed flapping and quacking drew the attention of the flaming demon rabbit, which rushed to meet him.

"You are mine!" cried Bingo, rounding the corner as the humans screamed and fled.

Devon flapped over several aisles, barely escaping the

bunny's bloody jaws. Annie scooped him up, preparing to run for their lives, but she saw Bingo in the mirror and froze. The rabbit was shaking, almost vibrating beneath the flames. His skin bubbled and bulged; he grew revoltingly wider until his fur split down the middle of his body, exposing red flesh beneath. There was a sickening tearing sound, and suddenly another identical burning bunny was sitting next to Bingo. The two rabbits wriggled their noses at each other, and then split up to search the store. Luckily, they hadn't noticed the mirrors.

"Oh shit," Annie said in a hushed voice. She ran out the store front, crunching glass and nearly slipping in Tommy's blood. "We got two rabbits now," she said to the duck. "Tell me you got a plan!"

"I believe I said 'flee' just a moment ago," Devon exclaimed.

"What about when you said 'it's not I that shall perish, but you?'" Annie squeaked.

"I was bluffing!" shouted the duck.

She cursed and ran into the parking lot, flagging down the two customers who had made it to their car, but they gunned their engine and peeled out of the lot, leaving her behind.

"HEY! I took off your late fees!" she screamed. "Ungrateful bastards!" She flipped off the departing car.

Bingo the bunnies were coming out of the shattered storefront, vibrating and splitting again. Now four flaming rabbits hopped into the lot, trying to surround them.

"Will they attack me?" Annie asked as the rabbits circled menacingly.

"Probably not, unless you provoke them," Devon said,

then immediately regretted it.

Annie tossed Devon away from the rabbits and shouted, "Then FLY duck!" Devon flapped madly into the air as the rabbits leaped after him; he beat his wings, struggling for altitude, but he felt too heavy and quickly became exhausted as the flaming rabbits gained on him. He managed a flap-hop combination that kept him just ahead of the rabbits' snapping incisors.

Annie dashed for Tommy's pickup, squeamishly stepping over his body and searching the cab for anything useful. It wasn't really her fight, but she had a feeling that her ability to understand demon speech was going to make her a popular girl, regardless of which demon survived. *Better the devil I know*, she thought bitterly. Tommy kept a shotgun and rifle in the cab's gun rack, but poor Tommy had been a far better shot than Annie, and look where that got him. No, she needed to run. She jumped in the truck's extended cab, cranked the mighty V8 Hemi engine which rumbled with power, and found to her great dismay that it was a stick shift. She'd only ever driven her mom's automatic subcompact.

"Ah shit," she hissed. "Escape foiled by manual transmission." She stomped the clutch, rattled the gearshift around, stalled the truck and tried again. After probably causing hundreds of dollars' worth of damage to the gearbox, she finally got the truck in reverse and squealed into the parking lot, spinning the big wheel hand over hand as she spotted the flaming rabbits across the street. "Hang on, ducky! I'm coming!" She shifted into first gear, popped the clutch and stalled the engine. "Ah shit," she hissed.

Devon had taken refuge on top of the covered bus stop as the burning bunnies came on, two leaping at him while the other two started chewing the metal framework. Annie had abandoned him and now he was about to have his soul devoured by a more successful demon. He sighed and thought *why couldn't they have summoned me using a dog or... or a Bengal tiger?*

The truck came lurching out of the video store parking lot, its headlights bouncing wildly as it groaned up to speed; Annie was waving out of the window, shouting as she drove past, "Come on, Devon, jump in!" Devon leaped into the air and flapped for the bed of the truck, landing with an inglorious thump against the back of the cab. The truck lurched into second gear and sped up a little, the engine roaring as Annie floored the gas pedal.

Devon breathed a sigh of relief, craning his head over the side to call to Annie, "Well done, my minion! I shall reward you when I am able..."

"Stow it duck!" Annie shouted over her shoulder. "I'm not your minion and we aren't out of the woods yet." Bad choice of words maybe, since the mountain town was surrounded by woods. She saw little bouncing points of light in the rear view mirror. The truck approached the red light at the corner rather too fast, but she didn't want to stop for fear of stalling the engine again; the burning bunnies were gaining... and multiplying. She weaved around the back of a stopped car and ran the light; horns blared, tires squealed, and the duck slid from side to side as he flailed for balance.

Devon looked back over the tailgate and called, "Can this vehicle not move any faster?" The rabbits were crossing the intersection like little comets; an unlucky few getting squished by a passing truck.

Annie yelled back, "I can't drive a stick! We're lucky to be moving at all!"

Devon looked about for the 'stick' she was referring to, but saw only a wheel in her hands. There were two items that resembled broomsticks hanging from the rear window, but he knew them to be gun powder projectile weapons. The sight gave him hope, for though he could never use one in his present form, his minion surely could.

The truck made its way up the road, roaring in low gear. Annie took several deep breaths, reflecting on the fact that she was driving a stolen truck and the owner had died a violent death in front of her store. If the police stopped her and the flaming demon rabbits decided not to make an appearance, she would have a whole lot of explaining to do. Of course, if the rabbits caught her, there would be two murders to solve instead of one. Two murders and one roast duck.

The stoplights seemed to be conspiring against her and she had to brake to avoid rear-ending the minivan ahead. The truck rocked in protest, the engine dying as Annie stamped the clutch a moment too late. Her attempts to start it again were not going well, and Devon was calling from the cargo bed, "We need to move, Annabelle Puckett! Bingo is almost upon us!" Looking back, she saw many flickering points of light coming over the crest of the hill a mere hundred yards away. They were darting to and fro; a deadly tide of flaming fur and floppy ears. *Swell,* Annie thought. *What I wouldn't give for a crate of Holy Hand Grenades.*

She took the keys out of the ignition and unlocked the gun rack as the advancing horde filled the cab's rear window. She didn't know much about firearms, but knew that rifles shot one bullet, while shotguns fired a scattering of lead, and there were a lot of the little suckers to hit. She pulled the shotgun free, pumped it like they did on television, and jumped out of the truck as the fluffy flaming mob advanced. She turned to the duck and said in her best Austrian accent, "Come with me if you want to live." If only she had some dark glasses…

Devon flapped out of the truck and took the lead, waddling for a theater parking lot across the street. There were many cars to choose from, and maybe his minion could find one without a 'stick,' whatever that was. The marquee sign above the theater read:

HALLOWEEN HORROR CLASSICS
SHOWING OCT 29TH
NIGHT OF THE LEPUS

Devon knew his Latin and it was strangely appropriate. *'Night of the Lepus' indeed*. He risked a glance behind him as the burning bunnies reached the abandoned pickup and darted towards the theater. One of them ran under the truck and ignited the gas tank with a squeak and a burst of heat, sending a bright mushroom cloud into the air. The explosion made Annie stumble as a wave of heat and pressurized air hit her in the back.

"Oh shit!" she cried, recalling that 'oh shit' was statistically the most common thing people said before dying a violent death. She wondered how they had gathered those statistics. Bits of Tommy's truck rained down around them, leaving little trails of fire in the night sky.

"The vehicles!" Devon cried, "Lead them to the vehicles!" The bunnies obviously did not want Annie to find another means of escape, but they had to sacrifice one of their number for each car they destroyed. His minion would have to act as bait. Devon flapped madly over the cars, struggling to keep off the ground; as ill-suited as he was for flying, he was even worse on his ridiculous webbed feet.

Annie ran without thinking, trusting the duck to have a plan. The bunnies followed, darting around or under the parked cars, coming on with a whooshing of flame and a hellish scent, like burnt popcorn. It was not long before the first of the cars exploded; the shock wave blew Annie's pigtails forward, the heat warming her skin and pushing her into the hood of a sedan. She gripped the shotgun tighter and chanced a look back. The rabbits were leaving her no escape, igniting every car in the lot one by one as the rest came on. Gouts of fire leaped into the night sky, thunderous noise assaulted her ears, and a panic like she had never known drove her onward as her screams vanished in the chaos. They were running out of cars, but Devon crossed to the next row, waiting for Annie to follow. Her heart was racing as she fled the onslaught of fire and flying metal, dashing towards the duck with a dozen burning bunnies in pursuit.

"Run, Annabelle Puckett!" Devon cried, flapping his wings. "Run to me!" The rabbits came on, spreading out to dart under the next row of cars, each emitting a cute little squeak before erupting into an inferno. Metal, rubber, and plastic rose into the air and came crashing down, nearly crushing the fleeing pair.

Annie was thrown to the ground, the shotgun flying from her grip as her hands and face met the pavement. Groaning, she lifted her head to see Devon surrounded by the last three rabbits from Hell. Their flames were a pale blue aura about their furry bodies, and their little pink eyes glowed in the light of the burning wreckage. Devon was backing away, hissing and ruffling his feathers in a last effort to seem dangerous. The bunnies were not impressed.

The rabbits spoke in unison, saying, "Now, thou shalt perish and thy soul be tormented in Hell for all eternity!" The raspy demon voices sounded so odd coming from such cute little bunny mouths, "But before we consume thy soul and send it hence, know that it is Haggarath, Demon of Itchy Sores that has conquered thee!"

"Oh no," said Devon miserably, "a common dermal demon. This is *so* embarrassing…"

"Silence!" cried Haggarath, "Itchy sores are not to be mocked, as you shall learn to your great-"

A loud *BANG* sounded, and one of the flaming rabbits burst into bloody chunks. *Ca-Chick* went the shotgun as Annie chambered another shell.

Both remaining bunnies turned on Annie and leaped at her, their flames burning brightly. "Die Egyptian whore!" they cried. One was struck with a blast of hot lead, but the last bunny knocked her to the ground, incisors gnashing as it lunged for her throat.

"Haggarath, I bind thee!" cried Devon. The bunny froze in place, giving Annie a chance to toss him aside as she regained her feet.

Ca-Chick!

Haggarath began to move just as Annie pulled the trigger and splattered him across the asphalt. Devon leaped on the remains and a steady quacking arose from his bill, like an evil laugh. His duck body shook as a terrible dark radiance began to leech out of the rabbit's bloody form; the tangible miasma of evil surrounded Devon, twisting about him defiantly. The demon duck absorbed it with his wings spread out, as his quacking became almost maniacal, chilling Annie's blood. The lights of the marquee exploded and sparks showered

58

down upon the scene, as the duck consumed the soul of Haggarath, Demon of Itchy Sores, formerly Bingo the bunny.

Wow, thought Annie, *Totally 'Highlander.' There can be only one.*

Moviegoers began to pour out into the devastation with unbelieving eyes, soon to discover whether or not their auto insurance was any good.

Chapter 6
The Devil You Know

"Okay, Ms. Puckett. Let's go over this again…" the chief had been called in to deal with the catastrophe, interrupting fried chicken night at the Wagner house. He was in a poor mood but insisted on handling the interviews personally, since a death was involved. A fresh pizza and two large sodas sat on the table between them at the station, a tape recorder monitoring the scene.

Annie was frazzled and exhausted; her Egyptian eyeliner had run and smeared in a way that looked both creepy and cool, at least to her mind. She took her time chewing the pizza, for not only was it much needed food, but also it gave her time to think about her cover story.

"I told you I could only tell you what happened, but I can't explain it." She sipped her soda and looked into the man's weary eyes.

"Annie," the chief began, "Tommy Banks is dead. You

60

stole his truck and blew up half the cars in Bueller. I'm gonna need you to help me understand."

"I didn't blow them up!" she squeaked. "It was the rabbits. Some psychos must have tied explosives to them and let them loose." It was far-fetched, but not as much as the truth. Besides, they were dynamiting bunnies in Australia.

"And Tommy?" the chief asked. "You want to go over what happened to him again?"

Annie took a breath and sighed, "He came in, rented a bunch of movies and left. A minute later there was blood on the window, and I looked outside... I didn't see what got him but there was this roar, like a mountain lion or something... then the shop window exploded... I ran into the store and there was a fire, the sprinklers went off. That's when I ran out and jumped in his truck."

"And you didn't see who or what killed Tommy?" Chief Wagner had asked her this same question about six times tonight. "Or why he had a pellet rifle in his hand?"

"No, I just grabbed his keys and drove off; I don't know why he had the rifle." She really hadn't seen him use it, but knowing Tommy, he probably took a shot at Bingo and got himself eaten for it.

The chief said, "If he'd been trying to protect himself against a bear or big cat, he had two better weapons to choose from. Kind of odd, don't you think?"

Annie smirked, "Plenty of odd to go around. I didn't *want* to take his truck, but those two customers left me there to die, can you believe that? Even after I'd taken care of their late fees! They had some bogus story about mixing up movie boxes and tearing apart the house to find them..." *Divert, divert, divert...*

"Do you remember who they were?" he asked. "If they

were witnesses, we'll need to talk to them too."

"I'm sure it's in the computer at work," she said. "I can't think now."

"Well, Mr. Hollis is there now, working with my men. I'll give him a call. He's also gonna pull the security tape…" he waited to see if this news would make Annie nervous.

Annie chewed another bite. Mr. Hollis was the store manager and would no doubt be even more interested than the police to find out what happened. She made sure her story was factual, but omitted the absurd reality of demon bunnies. If they saw something bizarre on the tape, like a rabbit tearing out Tommy's throat before setting the place on fire, then maybe they could all share a cell in the loony bin with her. She wasn't going to volunteer *that* kind of info.

Chief Wagner made some more notes on his pad. "You didn't see anyone else who might have been responsible for these rabbits rigged with explosives?"

"No one, chief. At first I thought it might be some horrible college stunt, you know?" She considered pointing his investigation towards the college, but without enough specific information, there was little hope he'd make the connection to a demon cult and possessed pets. "Who could do a thing like that?"

"Well, it's a major animal cruelty offense," said the chief, "but that's nothing compared to what will happen if the same people are responsible for Tommy Banks getting killed." He stood and motioned across the room where Annie's mother was waiting nervously. "I think we've got all we need, Rosemarie. You can take her home."

Rosemarie Puckett clutched her purse and weaved

between the desks to embrace her daughter. "Let's go Annie," she said in a shaking voice. "Got all your things?"

Annie was really sorry for all the stress she put her mom through in the last few hours. Mom was on medication for anxiety disorder and did not need the added drama of her daughter surrounded by exploding rabbits and exploding cars.

"Where's Devon?" Annie asked, looking around nervously.

"Who?"

"The duck. His name is Devon." Annie said. "I left him with you."

"Oh, that damned duck!" said mom, "The animal control people were here earlier, and I had them take it away."

Annie stopped dead in her tracks, "You did WHAT? He's in prison now?" She stomped about furiously as the police officers all turned their heads. "You sent my duck to the Big House?"

"Annabelle Puckett, calm down!" mom said, getting more frazzled herself, "You can't keep that duck in the house any longer! Whoever lost him will claim him. Now let's get you home, it's almost 3 am."

Annie let herself be led out to the car, livid with her mother for taking matters into her own hands. If it were a normal duck, Annie would have been upset enough, but Devon had just devoured a demon soul tonight, and was more powerful for it. If his abilities were anything like Bingo the burning bunny, he could cause untold damage. The first place he'd go would be Annie's house, possibly to share some choice words with mom, using Annie as an interpreter, of course. Talk about awkward.

Early the next morning, Annie got a call from Mr. Hollis, who wanted her version of events, and kept asking if she was okay or injured. Annie figured he had nothing on her and was trying to avoid a possible lawsuit, so she was purposefully vague. It never hurt to make the boss squirm. Nevertheless, her morning was officially ruined. Since she was already up and unlikely to get back to sleep, she joined mom for breakfast.

Mom was even more concerned now than she had been at the police station, since she had the whole night to absorb what had happened. She watched Annie over her coffee and between bites of waffles, looking for signs of post-traumatic stress.

"Mom, you're starting to creep me out," Annie said without looking up from her tablet. The Bueller Bugle had the biggest headline she had ever seen on the town's little excuse for a news site, and she wondered with dread when the wannabe investigative reporters would come asking the biting, hard-hitting questions. *What was your relationship with the deceased? Is it true you hated his guts since grade school?*

"Sorry to stare honey, but I'm worried about you," mom said. "It's not every day someone dies right outside your door."

Let's hope that doesn't become a trend, Annie thought. "I'm alright mom, it was a crazy night, but I'm okay." In truth she had been badly shaken up, but the recent shift in her reality had made the death of Tommy Banks seem more surreal than unnerving. She was deeper in the shit of the universe than anyone in this town, except maybe the demon cult that started this mess in the first place. People thought Tommy was simply killed, but his soul had actually been *eaten* by a demon, and *that* demon's soul had been eaten by Devon. By the twisted rules of some spiritual food chain, Tommy's eternal soul was percolating in the guts of a duck locked up at the pound. Try sharing *that* over waffles.

"Mr. Hollis called," said Annie, "I guess the store will be closed while the fire and water damage people work on it, so I've got some time off."

"That's good," mom said, "Tommy's funeral will be this Monday if the police finish with him…" she trailed off, not wanting to think about the details. Her thoughts went out to the boy's parents, waiting for answers and demanding justice be done. If what Annie said was true, one or more cruel pranksters were responsible. What kind of maniacs would let a cougar loose in town, and set dozens of rabbits on fire?

"I'm going to the pound to get my duck," Annie said resolutely.

Mom started to protest, but thought the better of it. Maybe caring for the duck would be therapeutic for her daughter. She grumbled and muttered a bit, to give the impression of having the last word, but she didn't say no.

Annie put on a black skirt, sleeveless concert tee, lace and denim vest, and thick-soled boots painted with cute little skulls. If the press was going to be in her face, she might as well look nice as she wandered the streets trying to solve the mystery of the demon cult. She borrowed mom's car and drove across town to the animal control building, practicing apologies to the angry demon that would keep her mom out of hot water. She hoped that devouring a soul hadn't gone to the duck's head.

Bueller Animal Control and Shelter was an unremarkable building near the edge of town, with a small vet's office and space for many guests, mostly dogs, cats, and the occasional raccoon. The front office was abuzz with sports talk as the uniformed employees finished their morning coffee and donuts, but they all fell silent as Annie walked in, her outfit generating raised eyebrows and smirks. The group broke up to look busy, leaving the guy at the reception desk to handle the newcomer and try to keep a straight face.

"Let me guess," he said to her, "black cat?" His coworkers giggled in the background.

"White duck," Annie said with a glare. "Brought in last night."

"Oh yeah," he said, still pleased with himself. "We got him in the back. Quite a temper." He buzzed for assistance and a young woman came from the back to take Annie to the holding area. It was a long hall with a concrete floor that held rows of cages, and the smell of disinfectant and animal scent filled the room. A distant quacking could be heard amid the barks of stray dogs and the mewing of kittens. She wished she could adopt them all, but unfortunately she was here for a damned demon.

"Annabelle Puckett!" came a familiar voice from a cage near the back. "I knew you would come. You shall be rewarded for your loyalty, my minion. Now release me."

Annie wasn't about to start a conversation with Devon in front of the pound employee, but she allowed herself some pet talk. "There you are!" she said to him, "Momma was worried about you, yes she was! I'll get you out of here in no time, ducky-wucky." She turned to the woman, asking, "Has my baby behaved himself?"

The woman mouthed some inaudible words and tapped

her throat, indicating the loss of her voice, but she also held up a bandaged finger. She opened the cage, stepping back to allow Annie to retrieve Devon.

Annie heard a hissing chuckle coming from a nearby cage. A sibilant voice called out from the depths of the enclosure, "Oh yessss, she is a special one, ducky-wucky. Truly a rare and valuable mortal, yessss."

Devon replied to the unseen speaker, "You doubt me? She bears the mark of Babel and does my bidding," then, under his breath, he said to Annie, "Try to show some reverence, if you please."

Annie lifted him from the cage and turned to the woman, "Could I look for a few minutes?" The woman smiled, nodded and walked off, giving Devon a departing glare. Annie peered into the cage for the source of the creepy voice. Coiled in the low light was the thick, muscular body of a boa constrictor; the angular head was poised to examine her as its forked tongue flickered, scenting the air. "Now *that's* more like it," Annie said in awe, as she bent to admire the snake. "*Much* more demony."

"Annabelle Puckett, I require you to release the snake, for we have an accord." Devon said haughtily. A little *too* haughtily.

"Okay duck, I don't know what kind of jail-house gossip you two have been swapping, but I am NOT your minion and I DON'T do your bidding, so cut the master-servant crap." Annie shook Devon gently as she spoke, wagging a finger at him. The snake hissed with glee.

"I… have given her the illusion of free will," said Devon quickly. "But she is bound to me, I promise you."

"Oh, yesssss…" hissed the snake. "That I can

67

sssseeee."

"Annabelle Puckett, a word please." Devon said. He motioned with his bill toward the far end of the room. Annie huffed and carried him out of the snake's earshot, her anger making her forget to apologize for mom. Devon looked back towards the cage and said quietly, "I need you to play at being my minion in the presence of the snake."

"Oh you do, do you?" she snarled, "What is this, some kind of demon pissing contest? I'm not your slave, duck-face, so don't treat me like it! And what's the idea, telling him about my stupid Babel thingy? I don't need every trapped demon on earth knowing I can understand them."

Devon said, "The snake has information that I require. He was kept by the demon cult for weeks before escaping, and he knows where they may be found!" Then he whispered, "Besides, playing the part of my minion will grant you certain protections. There are rules…"

"Yeah, I think it's time you let me in on some of those rules," she scoffed. "I'm not gonna end up like Tommy Banks." A thought struck her and she asked, "Is Tommy… you know, in there?" She pointed to his general stomach area.

"His soul has given me power, yes," Devon said. "It shall pass on soon, and will likely return to the place of his death. Such is the way of souls stripped of energy and purpose."

"Pass on?" she asked.

"I am trying to be polite," said Devon. "Pass out. Pass through. Pass."

She closed her eyes, shaking her head, "Are you telling

me you're gonna, what, shit him out? And this ghostly Tommy-shit is gonna haunt the fucking video store parking lot?"

"Ever the lady," Devon drawled. "It's more of a ghostly Tommy-fart, but essentially… yes."

"Oh, *hell no*," she hissed. "That is NOT happening to me. Tell me about these damn rules of yours, duck. Like right now!"

"Very well," he began, "First, it is forbidden to harm a demon's minion except in self-defense. That is why the rabbit avoided you last night."

"He blew up cars all around me!" she said.

"He was trying to destroy the cars, not you. Not until you attacked him."

"Well, that sounds like splitting hairs to me," she said. *Heh. Splitting hares. Ba DUM bum.* "What if I'm not your minion? Can they kill me at will?"

"Yes, if they wish," he said, "But they can only devour the soul of one who attacks them. This keeps demons from going on wasteful killing sprees."

"Oh yay," she said. "So I'm slightly less killable than anyone else. What other wonderful perks do I get?"

"As my minion, you cannot be cajoled or ensnared by another demon. As a matter of courtesy, they will leave you alone."

"Swell," she said.

"Also as my minion, I am able to deal on your behalf." Devon said.

"Deal?" she asked, suddenly alert. "What kind of deals?"

"The kind that can get your soul released from a demon contract, once we find out who has the legal rights to it," Devon explained. "It is the essence of our agreement

Annabelle Puckett. You serve me and I help you."

"I thought we were *helping each other*, Devon. I don't recall agreeing to *serve* you."

"Splitting hairs," Devon said mildly. "Besides, this way you are protected. I need only give you my summoning name to seal the bargain."

"Okay..." she said hesitantly. "What is it?" Devon whispered in her ear. "Wow, that's a mouthful," she laughed. "OW! What the hell?" she nearly dropped him and grabbed her ear. "You bit me, you little creep!"

"Sealed in blood," Devon said. "Now it is binding. The name I gave is for you only. If you share it with another, it is within my rights to punish you."

"What??" She did drop him this time, resisting the urge to kick him; she was in an animal shelter after all, and punting the animals was frowned upon.

"My summoning name grants a degree of power over me; that is why it is not shared." Devon explained, trying to keep his dignity as he righted himself on the cement floor. "Haggarath made the mistake of giving his name last night, and I was able to briefly hinder him. It was not his summoning name, but still..."

"You think you're going to *punish* me?" she shouted, "What the fuck! How dare you!"

"I am not powerful enough to make it anything severe," Devon reassured her. "But I figured you should know."

"Fuck a duck!" she stomped around, upsetting the nearby kittens and waking a sleeping mutt. "You little bastard! I should leave you here to rot, you and your little snake buddy. Hell, I should *feed* you to him."

"He has not consumed a soul, demon or otherwise," Devon said patiently. "I would have the upper hand, and

70

besides, I require his information. We made an agreement to assist one another."

"Screw you, duck. You're on your own." She turned to leave when a sudden splitting headache stopped her in her tracks. Dizziness took her and she grabbed a cage to steady herself.

"I cannot allow that, Annabelle Puckett. Please, I need your help and you need mine. Let us not end our relationship on such a sour note." Devon looked up at her calmly as the animals went silent.

For the first time since meeting the demon duck, Annie felt genuinely afraid for herself. Last night had been freaky, panicky and exhilarating, but not personally terrifying in such an… invasive way. Things had taken a new direction, and she had the feeling that direction was sliding downward. She turned to face Devon and the headache subsided, vanishing in seconds.

The pound employee came into the silent room, looking about with concern. Her voice seemed to have returned a little as she rasped, "Is everything okay in here?"

Annie spun around at the voice and said, "Fine," quickly covering her look of panic. "Um, I don't suppose I could take the snake too?" she asked meekly.

"Quack," said the duck, sounding pleased.

Chapter 7
Blake the Snake

Smuggling an eight-foot boa constrictor past mom was a feat worthy of *Mission: Impossible*, but somehow Annie managed. Once in the bedroom, the snake had no problem hiding amid the mess of laundry, or under the bed. Feeding him would be another matter, but Annie hoped the duck and snake would conclude their business quickly before that became necessary.

"Annie, honey," called mom through the door, "I'm gonna go pick up some Halloween candy and frozen dinners. Need anything at the store?"

A dozen mice, she thought to herself, but looking at the snake, she reconsidered. *He could probably eat a small dog, or rabbit. Or duck.*

"Um, some ice cream would be good." Annie called back; mom agonized over ice cream flavors, so her shopping would take longer, and Annie needed time.

"What flavor?" mom asked.

"Surprise me," Annie said. She heard mom grumble through the door and knew she had tacked on at least another fifteen minutes to the shopping trip.

The duck and snake waited for the sound of the front door closing before they began to talk in earnest. Annie sat on the bed, wondering what she'd gotten herself into this time.

"The occultists are sssstudents at the school," said the snake, "there are a dozen members, sssome of which live on campussss. The three you described are initiates." He coiled under Annie's black work jeans as he spoke.

"What were they doing in the math building?" Annie asked.

"They use the sssteam tunnels under the school to move about. They perform their rituals in the basementsss."

"So they do not disturb the other students," Devon said from the corner of the bed, "or raise questions. Clever."

The snake said, "Yessss, I used one such tunnel to escape after I had learned all I could."

Annie asked, "But why did they keep you around? Don't get me wrong, snakes are awesome, but I figured they'd, you know, try and get rid of the evidence of their snake-napping."

"They disposed of the snake they sacrificed, yessss, but I convinced them to allow me to stay." He flicked his tongue at her, "I can nod for 'yessss' and shake my head for 'no'. They ssssoon realized I was no ordinary sssnake."

Devon said, "Annabelle Puckett, I require a map of the school, if you please." His voice held a commanding tone that grated Annie's nerves, but she knew better than to argue.

"Yes, *master*," she said snidely. She got on her computer, printed a map of Bueller Community College, returned to the bed, and waited sullenly for the duck to examine it. *Little shit*, she thought to herself.

The snake crept up the side of the mattress, "They reside in thisss dormitory," he said, flicking his tongue at the map, "the leader lives on the top floor."

"And the ones who summoned me?" Devon asked, "The initiates?"

"One lives in the same building, and two others are local students," said the snake. "It would be possible to lure them all to one room."

"Yes," Devon said with anticipation. "Revenge shall be sweeter if they are all together."

Annie spoke up, "If you remember the terms of our agreement, Devon, I'm not helping you get revenge or hurt anyone." She was firm but mildly respectful, "If you want to go after them, you do it alone."

Devon nodded, "I have not forgotten, Annabelle Puckett. However, I am now powerful enough to deal with them myself. They are mine by right anyway."

The snake piped up, turning to Annie, "That is well, Msssss. Puckett, for I will require your assisssstance to meet with he who leads the coven, if your master will permit."

"I'm not helping you kill anyone either," she said sharply.

"Oh no, I do not wish to kill," said the snake, "I need you to translate for me. This treacherous ssspell must never again be used, and I hope to prevent it. I must convince him that it is wise to lissssten."

Annie looked at Devon, hating the fact that she needed

his permission and hoping he'd give it. A talking snake was damned cool, and she'd rather spend time with him spooking a college kid than helping the stupid duck get his stupid revenge.

"Very well," Devon said, "But I warn you, she is mine and I will brook no intrusions." Annie flinched, for it was almost exactly what Bingo the bunny had said about little Cindy.

"Fine," Annie said, relieved. She turned to the snake, "What do I call you anyway? I can't just call you 'snake' all the time."

"What do you wish to call me, Msssss. Puckett?"

She cocked her head at him and asked, "How do you like Blake? I suppose I could get all *Harry Potter* and call you 'Salazar' or 'Nagini,' but it doesn't rhyme like Devon the Duck."

"Devon the Duck is alliteration, not rhyme," Devon remarked.

Blake the snake nodded and hissed, "Ssssso be it, Mssss. Puckett. Blake the Snake."

"Call me Annie," she said with a smile. *He is so cool.*

The plan was simple; Annie and Blake would contact the leader of the demon cult, and Devon would scout out the dormitory on his own, plotting his revenge. That suited Annie just fine; the little feathered shit-loaf had stepped over the line. Besides, she had always wanted a snake. Snakes were so very Goth, much more so than ducks.

Leaving the house with a duck under her arm and a boa constrictor about her shoulders was a lot easier with mom gone, but Annie missed having the car. Blake was kinda heavy and the campus was several blocks away.

She clomped on in her tall black boots, feeling like a circus sideshow, and drawing odd looks from passing cars and people. *Laugh all you want, sheeple*, Annie thought. *You have no idea how fucked up this really is.*

The trio arrived on campus in the middle of the school day, but there was already a buzz in the air; it was Friday, there would be a football game tonight, and tomorrow was Halloween. Kids of all ages went out trick-or-treating in the sleepy mountain town, and being old enough to drive, vote, or drink was no reason to stop. The dormitories were all into the spirit, decking the halls with rubber bats and spiders, orange and black streamers, paper skeletons, and bloody rubber body parts hanging from doorknobs. A myriad of smells came from each room; dirty socks, hints of weed, incense, and pizza were the most common.

Devon knew one of the initiates lived on the first floor, but Blake did not know which room. The duck began to feel discouraged as he gazed down the long hall full of closed doors, and he swore to never take thumbs for granted if ever he possessed them again. Annie and Blake headed upstairs, leaving Devon to ponder his predicament.

Annie had to stop a couple of times on the stairwell as students admired her snake, answering their questions from her own extensive studies. Mom would never let her have a snake of any size, but that didn't mean Annie couldn't plan for the future. Someday she would move out, and a snake was what she planned to buy first, even before a TV.

Once they reached the third floor, the pair passed under hanging decorations and blinking orange and purple lights until they reached the door in the middle of the long hall. It boasted a big cardboard devil, posed doing a jig, with the words 'Abandon all hope, ye who enter here' written above in calligraphy.

"Subtle," Annie remarked. "I wonder if this only comes out on Halloween?"

"The hall was been decorated for weeksssss," said Blake. "I could not say."

She knocked on the door, listening to the muffled song on the other side. *Sounds like 'To Lose My Life' by White Lies,* she thought. *At least he has good taste in bands.* The door opened and the smell of incense wafted over her, and the glorious music hit her in the chest.

The college cult leader framed in the doorway was like a Goth god, his mop of unkempt hair was dark, spiky, and full; his pale, waxy complexion caught the glow of the orange and purple lights in the hall; his thin, willowy frame was draped in black; he wore a concert tee of 'The Smiths' over his narrow chest; his torn, black jeans hung precariously about his tiny waist. Eyeliner accented piercing blue eyes under thick, dark brows. In a word, he was gorgeous, with the kind of looks and manner that made tween girls squeal and pee themselves. Annie had to remind herself that she was old enough to be his... slightly older sister? Old enough to have driven him to high school his freshman year. *Just a kid, just a kid...*

"Hi!" she said, a little too loudly, "I'm Annie, and this is..."

"Nagini!" he said, his eyes popping. "You found the snake!" He ushered her in, looking up and down the hall before closing the door.

The room was classic dorm decor, with bad lighting, mismatched furniture, unmade beds, and Suicide Girls pin-up art mixed with movie and music posters. Annie had always laughed at the ads for back-to-school sales that showed parents moving college kids into bright, cheerful, perfectly decorated rooms. Yeah right. If they ever looked like that, it lasted until mommy and daddy left. She took a seat on The Couch That Came from the Eighties, letting Blake the snake unwind next to her.

Before the kid could ask any questions, Annie held up her hands and said, "Okay look, I know that you're the leader of a demon cult; I know you kidnap and sacrifice animals to summon demons, which I think is totally gross and stupid by the way; and I know that this snake was the result of one of your messed up rituals."

She watched him stumble and try to make excuses, but finally his shoulders slumped, and he sat down on a footlocker that served as a coffee table. "How did you know?" he asked quietly, looking at the snake. "Did Nagini tell you that somehow?"

"Pretty much," she said. *No need to tell him about Devon.*

The kid sighed, "We knew he was special; the way he understood us, answered our yes-and-no questions, it was eerie. He's something from the Other Side." Tearing his eyes from the serpent, he told Annie, "I'm Blake, by the way."

"No way!" she exclaimed, "I named the snake Blake!" She turned to Blake the snake, "Why didn't you say *his* name was Blake too?"

Blake the snake hissed and flicked his tongue.

"Okay look, non-snake Blake, this is gonna sound really freaky, but I need you to listen and stick with me." She leaned forward and looked into his pretty blue eyes. "Blake the snake, or Nagini, or whatever you want to call him, is not just from the Other Side; he's… a demon.

78

The spell you used *did* summon a demon, but trapped him in a copy of the sacrifice, in this case, a snake."

"A demon?" he asked quietly, "A real demon? I had a demon living with me for weeks?" His voice was shaking.

"Yep," she said, almost feeling sorry for him. "Sorry Blake, but when you play with fire…"

"That's incredible!" he blurted, far more thrilled than Annie would have been. "We made contact! The summoning spells worked! I have to tell the others, we thought we've been doing something wrong…" He got on his computer and pulled up his e-mail service.

"Blake, listen to me!" Annie yelled, "You didn't do it right, the spells are flawed. Demons aren't supposed to be trapped like that."

Blake said, "Are you kidding? Demons that can be kept as pets? That's beyond cool! Think of the possibilities, the arcane knowledge…"

"The soul eating," Annie said. "They're dangerous, Blake!"

Blake the snake hissed and said, "Annie, down here, please." She glanced at him and he locked her in his reptilian gaze. "There is no need to worry him. Perhaps if you told him how you undersssstand me?"

Annie felt the words twisting in her head. *Yeah, that sounded like a fine idea.* She turned to the kid and said, "A few days ago I got this tattoo," she showed him the back of her neck, "it turns out it's the symbol of Babel, and it lets me understand demons. I can hear Blake the snake talking just as clearly as I hear you."

Blake the college student was awestruck. "He speaks to you? In words? What does he say?" She had his full attention now.

Blake the snake hissed and Annie translated, "He says it's very important that you stop using the Budget Conjuration spell. He says it does more harm than good. He says... what?" She looked down at the serpent for clarification.

Blake the snake locked her in his gaze. "Tell him where you got the tattoo, Annie. Tell him how to get one like yourssss."

Annie blinked. *Yeah, that sounded like a fine idea.* She turned to the kid and said, "I got the tat at Paradise Lost Tattoo, a few blocks south. If you get one like mine, you could understand the snake too. Tell Maurice that Annie sent you."

Blake the coven leader thought it over for a few seconds and then went to look for his wallet. "This is awesome, so freaking awesome! Wait till the coven hears about this. Hell, wait till the forums hear about it! I'll have the whole occult web ring on fire!"

"One lasssst thing," said Blake the snake. "Annie, look at me please." She did, and his eyes seemed to bore into her head, "You should tell Devon all issss well. Tell him I will ssssstay with the leader. But forget about the tattoo discussion, if you please. Forget, Annie."

Yeah, that sounded like a fine idea. The snake sure had lots of fine ideas. "Sure thing, snake-Blake. I'll be going; I'll catch up with you later." She rose and let herself out. "Bye non-snake-Blake!" *He was cute*, she thought as she headed down the hall.

Passing students, some wondering aloud if they should call animal control, had harassed Devon as he tried to find the right door. The last thing he wanted was to have the men in green show up with their nets and nooses again, so he decided to wait for Annie and Blake outside under a tree. It was not long before she came out of the building alone, her mood lighter than it had been all day.

"There you are, ducky! I've been looking for you." She came over and sat down under the tree, crossing her big black boots.

"Where is Blake?" he asked suspiciously.

"Oh, he's gonna stay with the cult leader." She perked up, "He's kinda cute, by the way. The kid, not the snake. He's named Blake too, how weird is that?"

Devon thought for a moment and said, "I suppose that will be well. I did not trust the snake."

Annie turned to the duck, "I thought you were like, buddies or something, making plans together."

"No, it was an arrangement of convenience," said Devon, "He feared me, sensing my power, and I needed his information about the cult. I gave him freedom in exchange for furthering my revenge. I also agreed not to devour his soul."

"Nice of you," she said. "Speaking of your precious revenge, how did it go?"

Devon sighed, "I think it will be harder than I imagined. Doorknobs are a bit beyond the scope of my power." He examined his wingtips sadly. "Besides, it is obvious I don't belong there."

"Well, sucks for you," she smiled. "It'll be easier tomorrow night, I'm sure."

"How so?" he asked, eying her suspiciously.

"Party time," she said. "It's Halloween and a weekend all in one. That means a hall party, open doors, drunken students stumbling around."

"Interesting," Devon said. It seemed his minion was in a helpful mood after all.

"But you're still on your own. I have plans that don't involve demon revenge." She got up to leave, lifting him and tucking him under her arm.

"Annabelle Puckett," Devon said hesitantly, "I hope you understand my actions during our time around Blake, as you call him." Sensing her stiffen, he continued, "I was acting in your best interests as well as my own. I do not wish harm to come to you."

"I guess that doesn't include brain-splitting headaches," she said sharply. "Or biting."

"Weak as I am, I had to draw blood to invoke my power over you," he said, "I am sorry, but the binding spell will protect you by the laws of Hell."

"Super-duper," she said, "What more could a girl ask for?" Annie was in no mood to chat about Devon's asshole-ish behavior, or the threat he held over her, rules or no. She wasn't even sure why she told him about the dorm Halloween parties; for some reason, she just felt like divulging the information. Her mind wandered back to Blake the snake and his freaky eyes...

They walked in silence for a time, then got lunch at a fast food joint. Annie had a cheeseburger and Devon ate her fries, though neither spoke much, apart from "thank you" and "ketchup please." On the way home, the pair came upon a lady walking her toy poodle down the street. The little dog had an almost embarrassed expression, for it was wearing a tiny 1950s-style 'poodle skirt' and sweater, with pink bows on its ears.

"Oh, how cute!" Annie squealed, bending down to see. Devon drew the dog's attention, earning a few sniffs as he quacked a warning.

"Nice duck," the woman said, beaming as Annie fawned over her poodle. "Are you dressing him up for

Halloween?" She asked as if it was the most natural thing to do, although in fact, it was considered by most self-respecting animals to be a crime against nature.

"Heh, maybe," she said, as the poodle did a pirouette. Annie looked at Devon tucked under her arm, "What do you think, ducky-wucky? Want to dress up this year?" She gave him a little shake, as if she needed to get his attention.

Devon was about to say something extremely rude when he reconsidered. Annie and the woman with the leash kept making inane baby-talk at the creature, treating his appearance as a novelty. The dog was, so to speak, in the holiday spirit. An idea formed in Devon's brain.

After Annie got the temporary insanity out of her system and moved on up the street, Devon said, "I think a costume would be a good idea, Annabelle Puckett."

She stopped dead and said, "OMG really? No way, that'll be so adorable! There's a pet store down the next street, we can pop in and find you something." She giggled at the prospect. "Maybe you can go trick-or-treating with me after all?"

"What is OMG?" he asked, "You said that once before, the night we met."

She explained, "It stands for Oh My God. We shorten it to save space when texting."

"Hmm," Devon said. "I'm sure I don't know what 'texting' is, but I'll wager the Mistress of the Infernal Web is to blame."

"You're probably right," said Annie, chuckling. "LOL."

Devon peered up at her. "Whatever," he said with annoyance.

Chapter 8
Return of the King

Halloween was Annie's favorite night of the year, and the nice thing about having it on a weekend was that the party started well before dark. If Bingo the burning bunny hadn't wrecked the video store, Annie would have had to work until midnight, but now she could attend one of the many parties in town without calling in sick. It was the only positive she could get out of the whole affair.

The place to be was the Ferris Wheel Bar and Grill, where Oktoberfest was already in full swing, and Halloween was just another reason to throw a party. People were encouraged to come in costume, so long as the masks could be removed to check ID. A few local bands kept things lively, while the owner, old Howard Ferris, played the role of Master of Ceremonies in between tending bar and spinning stories about his new ex-girlfriend, who got younger and prettier with each telling.

Annie hadn't worked on a costume, but the nice thing about being a full-time fashion rebel was that you always had something to throw on. She got dolled up in her Gothic Slut getup, looking like a spooky, Burton-esqe harlot. Her hair was bound up in big pigtails, with black and white bows; her black leather corset left her arms and shoulders exposed, better to show off her tattoos; around her waist she wore a frilled, spider-web lace draping that served as a half-dress, complete with little plastic spiders; her black and white striped stockings were held up by visible garters; and the whole ensemble was completed with her big, black, platform boots. Her typical black lipstick was accented with glitter gloss, and her Egyptian-style eyeliner was done up more ornately than usual. Under her arm was her escort for the evening; the one and only King of Rock and Roll himself.

Devon had found few costumes at the pet store that would fit, but the Elvis disguise was simple enough without hindering him. Annie could not get over how adorable he looked; but Devon was more concerned with not being molested or arrested during his mission, a fact he did not share this with his minion. The duck wore a little felt duck-tail hairdo complete with sideburns, held in place by an elastic thread. Over his back was draped a white cape with a stand-up collar, and patterned rhinestones that glittered in the bar's neon light. It was simple, elegant, and effective; already he was being cooed over and cheered by costumed party-goers.

"I feel like the beginning of a bad joke," Annie called to him over the music, "A girl and a duck walk into a bar…"

"I do not know this joke, Annabelle Puckett." Devon said, "How does it go?"

She said, "The punch line is usually something like, 'put it on his bill'."

"Ah. Amusing," he said without conviction.

She moved up to the bar, careful not to get Devon squished, and ordered a beer. A banner advertised Fantasy Football Night every Wednesday, and Halloween drink specials were listed on blackboards; the drinks all had 'spooky' themed names like Blood Brew, Deathly Pale Ale, and Lycanthrope Lager. You could even purchase the drinks in a souvenir Franken-Stein. She had to give Howard props for that. Clever.

Devon had been to many a pub and tavern in his day, finding them a great place to meet mortals willing to make a deal, but he had not been to one for a very long time. "What is this Fantasy Football?" he asked over the noise.

Annie replied sourly, "Some kind of statistics game for football fans. I thought it involved like, unicorns and elves, but I was wrong. Real disappointment." She still remembered that day in high school when she asked if she could play a unicorn quarterback; Tommy Banks had heard about it, and gave her a ration of shit for a year. *Well, you're dead now Tommy. Suck on **that**.*

Devon blinked. So the elves had been relegated to creatures of fantasy, had they? Interesting. As for unicorns, well, the very idea was preposterous.

Annie got away drinking with a duck under her arm for nearly two hours, until one of Howard's sharp-eyed bartenders noticed that Devon was not a toy or prop. Fearing a health code violation, they asked her to take the duck outside.

Devon, The Demon Duck From Hell

"What's the world coming to when a girl and her duck can't get a beer?" she cried, teetering a bit as people filed past her. "Elvis has left the frickin' building."

"Annabelle Puckett, do not despair," Devon said. "If you wish to return to your party, you may leave me on my own."

"I couldn't do that," she slurred, "you can't walk down the street alone. What if someone duck-naps you?"

"I shall be safe tonight, I think. I am in disguise, after all." He tried to smile but lacked the proper facial muscles.

Annie set him down on the sidewalk, careful to maintain her balance. "You're a good guy, you know that? Deep down you are. Sorry I called you a little feathered shit-loaf."

Devon peered up at her, "I don't remember you *ever* calling me that."

"Oh," she said, "Well, not out loud I didn't. But it's okay, 'cause you're a good duck." She saluted him, turned on her heel, and called as she reentered the bar; "I got my cell phone, so call me if you need to."

Devon shook his head as his drunken minion went back inside to rejoin the party. *It will be better this way*, he thought, *for there are some things a king must do alone*. He waddled off down the street towards the college campus, his cape glittering in the moonlight.

Annie capered back into the midst of the festivities, first showing the bartenders she was duck-free before ordering another beer. The band was doing loads of cover songs with a Halloween theme, currently playing *Werewolves of London;* she joined in the chorus of howls with the rest of the bar, making herself light-headed near the end of the song. "*Awoooooo, werewolves of London! Awooooooo!"*

Nearly an hour went by before she felt her back teeth floating, and she headed for the ladies room. Bueller's Ferris Wheel Bar was known for two things: amazing cheese fries, and enormous restrooms. Finding an open stall with ease, she swept the facilities with her gaze before getting comfortable. *Scanning for puke... All clear. Proceed with HazMat disposal.*

Sighing in relief, her lace skirt gathered around her waist, Annie's peaceful moment was disturbed by the sound of the girl in the next stall dialing her cell phone. She peeked under the partition and saw her neighbor had her jeans around her ankles. *Who calls people on the toilet?* Annie wondered, slurring her thoughts. The girl was talking to a prospective boyfriend by the sound of it, trying to come off as playful and sexy, so Annie decided to give her some ambient sound effects to enhance the mood. She turned up the pressure on her bladder release valve, but it didn't have the desired effect; the girl just giggled and babbled to cover the noise. *Gimme a break,* Annie thought. *Some people have no manners. Time to go nuclear on this bitch.* She shouted "Incoming!" and let loose a wet rumble in the thunder-bucket that echoed in the vast restroom, making Ms. Chatty jump; the toilet seat stuck to the girl's ass and slammed back down, striking like a judge's gavel. *Guilty!*

"Ohmygodwhatdafuck!" the girl shouted, "No, no, baby, it was the bitch next to me... No, I'm not on the shitter, god, what kind of girl... hello? Hello??"

Mission accomplished, Annie thought, smiling with satisfaction. *Enemy communications disrupted. Return to base.*

Hiking up her jeans, Ms. Chatty thumped her fist on

Annie's stall and shouted, "Thanks, you frickin' sow!" before stomping out of the restroom.

Annie cackled maniacally. *Serves you right, princess.* While thinking of cell phones, she suddenly remembered telling a duck to call her if he needed to. *How the hell was Devon supposed to call?* She fumbled in her little purse for her cell phone and found it wasn't even on. "Shit," she muttered, waiting for the signal bars to show up. She had a voice message from Maurice from earlier in the day.

"Yeah, hey babe, its Maurice... ah look, you know when you said to call if someone came in for that tat? Well, someone did; college kid with a big fuckin' snake, said you sent him, so I figure it's okay, but I said I'd call, so... this is me calling. Later."

It took a few moments for the words to register. *Blake the cult leader is getting a Babel tat? He says I sent him? When did I mention any of that?* It didn't make any sense, but then again she was very drunk. She got up, flushed, and called Maurice back. It was after 6:00 pm, so Paradise Lost was closed, but DeadZero-101 was probably on the Internet, raiding a dungeon with his all-female elf guild.

The phone rang and rang, until the message picked up with the store hours. She knew to call again immediately, because gamers almost never answered the first time. After the second set of rings went unanswered, she began to worry. She called one more time, just to be sure, before leaving the bar in a hurry.

The walk down to Paradise Lost was only a few blocks, and the cool air helped clear her head. Why did she not remember telling Blake about the Babel tattoo? It must have come up in the course of their chat; she had to explain how she understood the snake. Come to think of it, she didn't remember much about the meeting at all, other than it went well, and the kid was seriously hot. God, she wasn't *that* drunk, was she? Costumed kids and adults passed her on the street as she wandered towards the shop, a bad feeling growing in the pit of her stomach that had nothing to do with drinking too much.

Paradise Lost Tattoo was closed, as expected; the lights dim and the door locked. A weird smell lingered in the air, like something burning, but no smoke or fire could be seen. It was different than the fragrant fireplace scent that permeated the winter skies over Bueller; this was more like… burnt chicken? There was no movement in the store, and even the wide-screen monitor of the Monster was dark behind the counter. Being more curious than cautious, Annie walked down the side alley toward the rear parking lot, asphalt crunching under her thick-heeled boots. The smell was much stronger back there, acrid and vile. Her eyes began to sting. As she turned the corner, she found herself staring into the barrel of a big revolver held by a fuzzy giant.

"Annie!" Maurice cried, lowering the weapon, "Don't sneak around on me, babe! I nearly fragged you."

"Jeez Maurice, what gives?" Annie squeaked, her heart thumping madly. "You scared the shit outta me. I thought I was about to get shot by Dirty Hagrid." She took in the scene behind the tattoo shop, noticing a thick, dark, curving line scorched into the asphalt near the dumpster. The horrid burnt chicken smell emanated from it, she was certain.

Maurice holstered his sidearm, picked up his broom and resumed sweeping the charred remains of the fire. "Shit Annie, frickin' Halloween night, ya know? Brings out all the weird ones. Did you get my message?"

"Yeah, just a while ago back at the bar," she said.

Maurice shook his head, "That kid with the snake, he came in earlier and asked for the tat I gave you. I figured since you sent him, it was alright, but man… freaky shit."

"What happened?" she asked with a growing sense of dread.

"After I finish, he gets all weird and distracted with his snake. He didn't even want to check out the tat, he just paid and left, like forty minutes ago. Then I smell smoke back here. I come out and the kid runs off… he burned his snake, Annie. Burned it to a crisp right behind my store. What kind of freak does that?"

Annie stared at the curved line of char on the ground. *Poor Blake the snake*, she thought. "Maurice, I gotta tell you, I just met the kid yesterday and I don't remember telling him about you or my tat, although I must have, I guess."

"Well, you see the little shit again, you tell him to stay the hell away from my store. I better not catch him in a dark alley." The big man almost seemed scared as he fingered the handle of his revolver.

"Sorry Maurice," Annie said meekly as she wandered away. It wasn't her fault, was it? Maybe Blake the snake said something that freaked out Blake the non-snake; maybe the kid got smart and sent the demon back to Hell. *Yeah with what, a Zippo lighter? How do you torch an eight-foot long snake?*

Then it struck her. *Magic*. Blake the kid could summon demons, but Blake the snake *was* a demon, and he could now talk to the coven leader directly. This didn't sound good at all. *I need to find Devon*, she thought, *I need to find him now*. She began to recite his summoning name over and over in her head, wondering if he might appear before her like 'Beetlejuice' or something.

"I have no idea how this works," she said to herself, "but it's all I got."

Malgamadalard, Malgamadalard, Malgamadalard...

When Devon-Elvis entered the dormitory, the party really got started. Costumed college kids cheered and pointed, everyone asking, "Who brought the wicked duck?" but no one tried to remove him or call animal control. He came and went freely, stopping only to endure the drunken attempts to pet him by nubile female students dressed as slutty nurses, slutty witches, slutty librarians, slutty police officers, slutty nuns and slutty cartoon princesses. One girl in a black robe and slutty school outfit made him look twice, but alas, it was not the girl he was hunting tonight. Nevertheless, his feet got tangled in her red and gold scarf, and she had to straighten out his rhinestone-studded cape, giggling an apology.

Some doors were closed to him, but he only needed to knock with his bill and be admitted, or wait for someone else to come and go. Some people offered him beer from their cupped hands, but he could not afford to have his wits addled tonight. Revenge was neigh. He examined all their faces, waiting for the ones in masks to take a drink and reveal themselves. Not finding his quarry, he moved on as students hooted and cheered him. *If they only knew*, he thought. He stopped briefly to peck cheese puffs off the floor; he needed to build his strength.

He had been searching the dorm for nearly an hour before he came to the right room. Had he started at the other end, he would have found it much sooner, but no matter. The door was open to let the party atmosphere filter in; the windows cranked open to make the room less stuffy. Within were three robed figures, a young man with dark hair and glasses, a girl with frizzy brown locks, and a ginger lad with freckles. They were all drinking beer and talking amongst themselves, and they were otherwise alone. *Perfect.*

Suddenly, he sensed his minion calling him with his summoning name, her frantic state of mind distracting him from his mission. She would know his whereabouts and soon, so he must act quickly. Not *too* quickly though; he wanted to enjoy this…

"Here's to a job well done," said Ginger, toasting with his beer bottle. "And to the three newest members of the Mystic Star and Circle."

Mystic Star and Circle, Devon thought. *How original.*

"Here's to not screwing up as bad as we thought we did," said the bespectacled boy.

"Isn't the Grand Master supposed to meet us tonight?" Frizzy asked.

"Blake's e-mail was kind of vague," said Spectacles, "but he'll be here."

Devon savored the moment as he waddled into the room, his high-collared cape casting a diabolical shadow across the floor. The three students looked at the new arrival with curious faces before, one at a time, a strange realization dawned on them. The duck had a swagger that seemed menacing, a stare that penetrated their very souls. He ruffled his feathers and addressed the three robed students as they slowly got to their feet.

"Ne invoces expellere non possis…" he intoned ominously, "Do not call up that which you cannot put down."

The students, of course, heard only "Quack wack, wack quack, wack…" but the sound sent a collective chill through their bones. Then the door slammed shut, seemingly of its own accord.

That's when the screaming began.

Annie had repeated the duck's summoning name in her head about a dozen times before she got the sudden sense he was at the BCC campus. She let out a curse and ran as fast as her big boots would allow. *I need to get in shape*, she thought. *I need to not jog after drinking*, she also thought. She was out of breath well before making it to the dormitory, and she really felt like puking, not that anyone would have noticed here tonight. The stitch in her side was a grim reminder that her quarter century on Earth had not been spent as well as it might have been; if there was going to be much more running around, she would have to make some changes, definitely. New Years was coming up in a few months; she made a mental note to make a resolution to stay fit. Again.

Everyone in the multi-room party had seen the duck dressed as Elvis, but no one had seen him lately. Devon had wandered from room to room apparently, because everyone she asked on the first floor thought he was the coolest thing they had ever seen. Annie had to admit the sideburns were adorable and the cape was darling, but she didn't come here to take credit. If he was here looking for revenge, it was her fault for mentioning the party and buying him a costume. *Stupid chick*, she thought, *not putting two and two together because you wanted to play dress-up with a demon duck*. She began skipping the open doors and tried the closed ones; if

Devon were up to no good, he would be discrete about it.

Annie knocked, called out, and then listened at the doors if no one answered. When someone did answer, she had to contend with a few clumsy propositions. It was pathetic, but still flattering in a sick way; hopefully they weren't all looking at her through beer goggles. Dorm parties could be so much fun, but not if you were the sober one.

Some doors were not locked, but should have been. There were just some things you couldn't un-see, like a guy bending over to change soiled underwear; a passed-out kid getting posed for homo-erotic pictures by his 'friends'; and some chick playing at being a stripper before barfing in her boyfriend's lap. She also figured she would see herself in an amateur porn video called 'Goth Chick Interrupts Dorm Sex.' *Freaks,* she thought. *Higher education, my ass.*

One door was locked and silent within, but looking down, Annie noticed a pool of what looked like blood seeping under the door. A sick feeling overtook her and she backed away, afraid she might puke then and there. She headed for the exit and ran around the side of the dorm, counting windows to find the right room. Devon was on the grass up ahead, his costume discarded.

Annie approached carefully, noticing the window was open and the screen had been torn. She glared at the duck, who only watched her passively. He should have been white, but he was splattered in red. Her breathing came in gasps and her heart started thumping madly; all of her instincts told her to flee the scene, but she had to know what had happened, she had to find out what her carelessness had led to. She peered through the window into the dimly lit room. The scene of bloody carnage sent her doubling over in the bushes, puking out nearly $50 worth of good beer.

"It is done, Annabelle Puckett," said Devon with some satisfaction. "I have taken the souls that were rightfully mine."

"Oh god…" she said as she coughed and spit, "What did you… *how* did you…?" There was no explanation for what she saw in that room; a mountain lion could do that, but a duck? "You told me you couldn't…"

"It wasn't easy to slay three at a time, but they were in my power, such as it is. When you summon a demon, you had better bind him properly, or he can claim your soul. With the power I had already gained from Bingo, er, Haggarath, I was able to wreak a considerable amount of havoc." His smug attitude dwindled as he saw Annie's look of horror and betrayal. "I didn't *lie* to you earlier; that was before I consumed the demon bunny."

"How could you murder three kids? Oh God, what are their parent's going to do?" The guilt and self-loathing took her, but she forced herself to think of the others who would be hurt most. "They had families, Devon… futures."

"Their families didn't teach them very well, did they?" Devon asked. "As for their futures, I think we both know where they would have ended up. At least now they will serve as an example to others of their coven…"

"You could have just scared them, damn you! You didn't have to… oh God…" She felt like her world was spinning, and it wasn't just because of the alcohol. "Do you realize how much shit you just brought down? This isn't the 1930's! We have DNA, FBI, CSI; shit like that!"

"L-O-L?" Devon ventured.

"F-U!" Annie shouted. "This place is gonna be swarming with cops soon, and we're both at the scene! That's *my puke* over there! *Evidence puke!*"

"Can they dust for puke?" Devon asked, interested. "Miss Marple never dusted for puke…"

"Miss Marple didn't have a modern crime lab, duck! God, what are we going to do? Those poor kids!" She still couldn't believe what she had seen. This was a nightmare. She was living in a nightmare. *Devon is going to crap college students in my bathtub later. Son of a bitch.*

"I think we should focus now upon this coven leader," Devon said. "We might learn if there are others that need-"

"Oh shit, Blake!" Annie cried. "Blake the coven leader got the tattoo, and Blake the snake was burned to a crisp behind Maurice's shop! That's why I came to find you."

Devon's bill dropped open, "The coven leader received the Sigil of Babel? How did he learn? Did you tell him how to get it?"

"No! I think… I'm not sure. I don't remember telling him anything about it." Annie cried.

"Annabelle Puckett," Devon said gravely, "If the coven leader was the one who summoned the demon into the snake, that demon would be able to lay claim to his soul. Using the Sigil of Babel, the demon could trick the boy into giving up his body, allowing the demon to possess him." He waddled into the light of a street lamp, "Since the snake body was tied to the demon, it would be consumed by fire if he willingly left it behind. I think we have a terrible problem."

Annie stumbled away from the dorm window, and from Devon, repulsed by the blood that stained his feathers. He had what looked like a piece of flesh dangling from his bill.

"Fuck, is that a piece of flesh dangling from your bill?" Annie gasped, "I'm gonna be sick again…" Devon shook his head, sending bits of gore flying everywhere. "Gah! Don't flick it all over me, you goddamned monster!"

Devon said calmly, "Pull yourself together, Annabelle Puckett. Blake is now possessed, increasing the demon's power tenfold."

"Huh?" she said weakly, "Why?" Her stomach roiled again.

"He inhabits a body that can speak and cast spells," Devon explained. "Hissing or quacking won't get you very far."

"Then how come you didn't try to possess one of those kids?" she asked.

A voice came from the side of the dorm, young and masculine. "Because he wasn't clever enough to do what I did," said Blake the demon. "He thought only of revenge; he never thought to trick one of them into getting the tattoo, then have them repeat the words to a spell that would offer him a new body." Blake chuckled, "Now his chance is gone."

"Fake Blake!" Annie said in horror. "Is the real Blake dead?"

"His spirit is mine, so he's as good as," said Fake Blake. "I'm going to consume him more slowly, another pleasure Devon has denied himself. Silly duck, believing I was powerless, letting me spend some quality time with dear Annie…"

"You got her to tell the lad where to get the mark, and then made her forget," Devon said. "This meddling is forbidden, for she is my minion."

"Yes, well it's not a hard and fast law, but more of a matter of courtesy," said Fake Blake. "You can take it up with a High Underlord when you return to Hell, but of course, that depends on the manner of your return. Snacks have no legal rights."

Annie dared not move, unsure of what terrors the next moments would bring. She knew not to attack Fake Blake, but couldn't he kill her anyway? Would he kill Devon and consume his soul, then turn on her for fun? She knew that whatever he chose to do, the bastard would look totally gorgeous doing it. *Shut up Annie,* she chided herself.

"Annie, repeat after me," Devon said quietly. "a posse ad esse…"

"A posse ad esse…" Annie repeated, uncertainty on her face.

"What are you doing now?" Fake Blake smirked, raising his hand to strike.

"Absolutum dominium." Devon said.

Annie repeated the words and doubled over in enormous pain; the world was drowned out in a wash of fire that raced over her nerves, turning her blood to lava and her bones to molten metal. She collapsed to the ground; her fingernails chipping as she reflexively scratched the asphalt. Then the pain was gone as quickly as it had come. When she lifted her head, she found they were alone in the parking lot. Fake Blake was nowhere to be seen. "What happened?" she rasped, getting shakily to her feet.

"I used you as a conduit for a protection spell," Devon said. "For all his posturing, he is still a lesser demon, never having consumed another. I, on the other hand, have fed rather well the last few days. Through you, I was able to protect us both. He fled rather than wait around for the protection to fade."

"How long will it last?" Annie asked weakly.

"How did it feel?"

"Like getting hit by a freight train made of flaming hot razor weasels," she croaked.

"Then it will likely last for some time. How I love your colorful descriptions," he crooned. "You make Shakespeare seem the bungling amateur."

"Screw you, duck." Annie groaned as she shuffled off to call the police.

Devon watched her go, uttering with all the affection he could muster, "Screw you too, Annabelle Puckett. Screw you too."

He waddled after her, quacking in contentment.

Devon, The Demon Duck From Hell

Chapter 9
Seven Years of Bad Luck

The sleepy northern Arizona town of Bueller had not endured a media circus since the early nineties, when someone thought they spotted a notorious escaped convict in their backyard. The fugitive had been evading law enforcement in the northern part of the state for weeks, and worse, doing it with style. Bueller had suffered the presence of news vans and reporters for days after the sighting, all hoping to be there when the outlaw was caught. Local motels and restaurants still referred to it as the Golden Age. Of course back then, no one had been murdered in town.

Annie Puckett found herself in the middle of a media circus now, one that was likely to put Bueller back on the map for all the wrong reasons. They were calling it the 'Bueller Halloween Massacre' in the national press, though the regional papers tried to be less sensational, out of respect for the families. Still, the 'Wilson Hall Slayings' were all anyone could talk about. Three students murdered on campus, hundreds of residents partying in the building, and no witnesses; it had all the makings of a horror film. The killer was still at large, and the public was terrified. Annie knew the truth of course; the murderer was sitting on her lap at the moment.

Devon complained, "How long is this going to take?"

Annie knew better than to answer his question directly. She was in a police station, with the chief himself sitting across from her. If she was going to get out of this mess, she had to avoid looking bat-shit crazy, so she used pet-talk that wouldn't raise suspicions. "Shush Devon, shush. We'll go home soon."

Chief Wagner shifted his considerable girth in the plastic chair and motioned for more coffee. "So you want to tell me what you were doing on campus last night?" His voice was weary, and he looked disheveled and grumpy, but his eyes were sharp and alert, noticing her every facial tic.

"I was looking for my duck," she said innocently. "I thought he might head that way, and sure enough, he was making the rounds." The adorable Elvis costume she had dressed him in was now covered in blood in an evidence bag on the table.

"What made you think your duck would be there?" asked the chief.

"Well," Annie began, "It all goes back to my theory about the missing pets." She'd had a few hours to concoct her story, and now was the moment of truth, so to speak. In other words, it was time to see if the lie could pass muster with the cops. "I figured Devon here had been duck-napped, and was being held on campus before I found him, so he might go back to a familiar place, a place where he'd been fed before. Maybe he'd even go right for the culprit!"

The chief leaned forward, "Why did you come to believe the missing animals had been kept on campus? Seems like a leap to me."

Annie got excited; she loved this part of her story because it made her feel rather brilliant, even if it was kind of a retroactive theory. "Okay, what I did was, I looked at the missing pet reports like they were all related, you know? I learned the first animal to go missing was a monkey from the campus research lab three months back." She paused for a reaction, but the chief was unmoved. "How do we begin to covet?" she slipped into a Hannibal Lector voice, "Do we seek out things to covet? No, we begin by coveting what we see every day."

The chief said wearily, "I don't think *Silence of the Lambs* is relevant to the pet abductions, Annie. Maybe the murders, now…"

Shit, girl; this is the wrong time to be doing serial killer impressions. No matter, Annie had made up a good story, and she was gonna stick to it. "It's relevant if you look for a pattern in the animal thefts," she said. "The first was on campus, the next was up the street, then the little Jack Russell Terrorist two blocks south, and so on, until the snake was stolen from a reptile farm on the edge of town. It all began on campus and moved out, like the territory of a serial killer or something." Hey, she watched TV crime dramas, so she knew her theory was sound.

"Then I started asking around campus and learned that certain people had been keeping animals in their dorm rooms. One even had a boa constrictor! Case solved!" That was all crap; the few students she spoke to hardly gave her anything useful, and she learned almost everything relevant from a pair of demons trapped in animal bodies. Whoever said 'The truth shall set you free' had never had the kind of bullshit week Annie had just experienced.

"What's more," she said, heaping more bullshit on the pile, "the same day I start asking questions on campus, someone pulls that burning bunny stunt, and Tommy Banks gets killed!" She thumped the table for emphasis, but only succeeded in startling Devon out of his bored stupor.

"Waaah," he complained.

"Why didn't you tell us about your investigative breakthrough the night of Tommy's death?" asked the chief, making notes on his old-fashioned paper flip-pad.

"I didn't make the connection at the time, and I was really shaken up. It was kinda traumatic, you know?" Annie played the Freaked-Out Girl card yet again. *Hey, it's a good card.* She stared intently at the top of the duck's head, playing up her post-traumatic stress.

"So you figured the duck would go back to the people who stole him." Chief Wagner made some more notes on his pad as he spoke, "Now, what's all this other crap about the snake again?"

It's not crap, she thought defensively. *It's a solid half-truth.* "Well, when I sprung Devon from the pound, I saw the snake; I thought it might be the missing one, and I heard a certain student kept one in his dorm room for a while." Annie tapped her fingers on the table nervously, "I guess I was stupid to try confronting that Blake kid. It might have been *me* getting murdered..." Her eyes returned to the top of Devon's head, boring into his feathered skull. *Damned little monster.*

Chief Wagner flipped through his notes, "Is this the

same kid who allegedly torched the snake behind Paradise Lost Tattoos? The one Mr. Chekhov called about?"

Annie sniffed and nodded. Fake Blake was on the loose and up to no good, and she couldn't tell anyone how dangerous he really was. Maybe it was wrong to point the police in his direction for the slayings, but the kid wasn't exactly innocent. He had been the leader of the coven that sacrificed animals to summon demons. This mess was all his fault anyway. *Too bad; he was really cute.*

The chief called to one of his subordinates and gave him a slip of paper. "I want to have Blake Kingsley brought in as a person of interest. We may also have to call the feds in on this, God help us."

The officer sighed and looked out the window at the caravan of news vans camped in the parking lot. "Yes chief," he said, as he headed for the door.

Mom was there to take Annie home, but a swarm of reporters at the police station door were standing between them and their car. Chief Wagner had a couple of officers escort them out, but it was still an overwhelming experience for the small town girl.

"Annie! Are you a suspect?"

"Mrs. Puckett! Does your daughter belong to a satanic cult?"

"Annie over here! How well did you know the murdered students?"

"Is it true that you hated the late Tommy Banks since grade school?"

"Annie! What's with the duck? Is he a witness?"

"Are you trying to get attention from your estranged

father?"

"How do you explain the death and property damage that follows you wherever you go?"

"No freakin' comment!" she yelled frantically, fumbling for the car door. Devon nipped at reporters as they jostled Annie, even managing to rip the foam cover off a microphone that got too close to him. Finally, they were in the car and driving for home, with some of the news vans following in the distance.

"Are you okay, baby?" mom asked nervously. No doubt she had some of the same questions as the reporters, but didn't want to ask.

"I'll be alright mom, I'm just shaken up. Those kids…" Seeing Devon's handiwork was not something she could have been prepared for. She held the feathered killing machine uneasily on her lap, remembering the blood and flesh hanging from his bill the night before. She'd woofed her cookies upon seeing the mangled victims, leaving material evidence behind. If she had fled the scene like she wanted to, they surely would have traced her puke back to her, DNA and all that. She watched enough TV to know the puke would be sent to a crime lab in Phoenix, and a short investigative montage later, they would match it to her. She wondered, *Do they have my DNA on file?* The last time she threw up was in high school biology class, when Tommy Banks made her fetal pig sing and dance before being dissected. But they didn't need previous puke for a DNA match; they could get that from a cheek swab. Better to come clean and make up a good lie.

As for Devon, he had been bloody enough to place him in the room when the killings occurred, but of course, no one suspected that he was the murderer. Luckily, she had refused to touch him before the police arrived, so there was no blood on her hands or clothes, except for a few specks that he flicked on her accidentally.

"Your father called this morning," mom said hesitantly. "He wanted to know what was going on, and I had to tell him you were in the police station for questioning."

"You told him that?" Annie cried, "Mom, can't you lie for once?"

"Lying is *his* specialty, not mine," mom said. "Besides, he... wants to help. Not that you need a lawyer or anything..."

"Quack waak waak," said Devon, suddenly interested.

"...But it might be nice to get out of town for a while until this whole thing blows over," mom said. "At least your father lives in a gated community with security guards. If the press, or some wacko tries to come after you, you'll have a safe place to be."

Annie sighed, "Dad has security because he has enemies of his own."

"Yes," said mom, "But most of them are decent people who have good reason to hate him. It's not like he's being stalked by psychotic killers..." She shook her head, unable to accept that her daughter was mixed up in something so horrible. *I should never have bought her those Anne Rice books in grade school*, she thought, charting her daughter's descent into darkness in a fit of motherly guilt.

"Mom, I'm not moving in with dad and the hyphens," Anne huffed.

"Quack," said Devon, "Waakwaak quack!"

"NO!" said Annie harshly. Mom pretended not to notice; her daughter had good reason to crack up a bit, and she wasn't going to judge her if she wanted to argue with her duck.

Once they got home and Annie took Devon up to her room, they had their first private discussion since she reported the murders the night before. She had a lot bottled up, but didn't want to scare mom by screaming at the top of her lungs.

"You tricked me, Devon. You tricked me into helping you get revenge!" She glared at the duck on her bed, hissing her accusation.

"I did no such thing. I left you to listen to your loud music in that pub with the other drunken mortals," he said defensively. "You seemed to be having a good time."

"You asked me to dress you up as Elvis so you could walk into a dorm party and kill people!"

"How was I to know the King would still be so popular with the young people today?" Devon shuffled his webbed feet. He missed his sequined cape, blood stains and all; pity that it was evidence now.

"You were cute! You were adorable! It didn't matter if you were Elvis, or Yoda, or frickin' Kim Jong-il! You *knew* a costume would help you get close to your victims, and that's why you asked me to dress you up!"

"So I tricked you," Devon admitted, "So sue me. If you will not willingly do my bidding, then I must be creative. Your precious morals were not compromised."

"People are dead!" she hissed. "Don't tell me about my morals. I had no idea you were capable of… what you did." She covered her eyes and took a deep breath.

"I cannot use the usual magic in this form, not without your aid," Devon explained. "I had to resort to a more… direct approach."

"You tore them apart!" she screeched, hopping up and down.

Devon shook his head, "Their souls were already mine when they summoned me unbound. I was just collecting on a debt. I could not repeat the deed again if I wished to."

Annie looked sideways at him, mistrustfully. "No? Why not?"

"Ducks are not very efficient killers," he explained in a lecturing tone, "Usually, a soul must be devoured after the victim's death, but as I said, their souls were mine by right. I used their living essences to fuel my revenge, combined with the power of the demon soul from the rabbit. It wasn't easy, let me tell you. But it was worth it."

"I don't suppose you considered what kind of shit you'd bring down on my life, did you?" Annie accused. "Fake Blake was right; you were so stuck on revenge, you didn't even *think* of alternatives."

"Fake Blake, as you call him, is being sought by the authorities for my actions, thanks to you. I do not see how he was so very clever in the end."

"He can talk now instead of just quack," Annie pointed out.

"Hmm, yes, point taken." Devon conceded. They sat in silence for a time until he declared, "Annabelle Puckett, I would like you to reconsider staying with your father."

"What the hell for?" she asked, getting even more annoyed. "You're suddenly concerned for my safety?"

"He is a lawyer, is he not?" asked the duck. "That will present certain benefits."

Annie smirked, "I can't think of a single one."

Devon explained, "Every law school has secret

societies, many of which are devoted to extra-planar relations. It is likely that he, or a paralegal in his employ, has access to the *Arcana Curiae*."

"The huh?" Annie stared blankly.

"The *Arcana Curiae*; it is a collection of contracts between mortals and demons, updated regularly, and used by the High Underlords to settle legal disputes." Devon sat on the bed and ruffled his feathers to get comfortable. "Any active contracts are kept on file for review, but one must know how to find them."

"So all lawyers know about demon contracts?" she asked, not entirely shocked.

Devon replied, "Not specifically, although I'm sure many of the more influential ones do. Demons don't present themselves as such in legal matters; we are clients like any other, offering goods and services in exchange for payment, all couched in benign legal terminology. Contracts used to be much more simplistic and binding, but alas, those were simpler times."

"And now?" Annie asked.

"Proper Law Doctrine has made things trickier, but lawyers have stepped up to the challenge," Devon crooned. "Some will take the most absurd cases if they think it will go to court. They just want to make a name for themselves, regardless of the precedent being set. It's wonderful, really. Did you know that in some states in this country, a soul now qualifies as intellectual property?"

"Hm. Interesting," she lied. "So you think my dad will get us access to this demon library of soul contracts? How am I supposed to approach him with that?"

"Leave that to me, Annabelle Puckett," he said, "I will guide you through the labyrinth of diabolical dealings and find out who, if anyone, might have the legal rights to your soul."

"And then we fix it and we're finished, duck." Annie said firmly. "I helped you find the spell that summoned you, I kept you from harm, you even used me as a surrogate to cast a protection spell, which hurt like a bitch, by the way. I think it's time you upheld your end of the deal. I want out."

"Yes, yes, if it turns out you are entangled in a demon contract, I shall certainly help you to get out of it." Devon looked about the room, avoiding her gaze.

Annie felt something was amiss. "If I'm not, if I'm free and clear, then we're still done." She stared hard at him, daring him to argue.

Devon shifted uneasily, "Well, if it turns out that you have no demon contract, then our other arrangement takes priority…"

"What arrangement?" she growled, her eyes narrowing.

"Well… you *are* my minion after all. It was sealed in blood and has a term of seven years…" He quickly flapped off the bed as she swung a fist at him; she had tried to knock his bill around his head, like in a Daffy Duck cartoon.

"Fuck you! Seven years, seven *fucking* years? I never signed up for that!" She began throwing laundry at him as he ducked and dodged, looking for good cover.

"You should be grateful, Annabelle Puckett. Getting out of a demon contract could take years, and the cost might be prohibitive. If you are not so obligated…" he ducked under a flying pair of jeans, "…then seven years of minion-hood is hardly worth complaining about. It is a win-win situation, really."

"Win-win? You got some nerve, you little shit nugget!" she picked up one of her big, knee-high, black leather Demonia boots with elevated heels; a lethal weapon if thrown with enough force.

"Annabelle Puckett, I am on your side either way. You will find I am a fair and generous master…"

"ASSHOLE!" she threw the boot, but it missed and hit the wall, causing mom to call from downstairs.

"Annie? Are you alright?"

"I'm fine mom, just venting!" Annie pointed at Devon, "No more deals, duck! You're not my goddamn master!" She stomped around her room, pulling her pigtails as her mind reeled, "Seven years! Shit, I'm never gonna get to Heaven like this!"

"I never promised you Heaven, Annabelle Puckett; only to help keep you out of Hell by your own folly. Few mortals of this age get a chance like that."

Annie wanted to cry, but she wasn't going to break down in front of Devon. "How is being a demon minion going to look?" she whimpered. "That can't be a gold star on my report card."

"It's not as if you're doing it for selfish gain," Devon said, sympathetically. "You are helping someone in desperate need…"

"Don't gimme that Good Samaritan shit, you little monster. If the road to Hell is paved with good intentions, I'm on the freaking Autobahn to Hell on rocket skates because of you. I need… I need to hook up with an angel or something…" she buried her face in her hands.

Devon regarded her with mild amusement and said, "Well, if I see one, I'll let you know."

Chapter 10
Devon Flies South

Mom drove Annie and Devon to Pulliam Airport outside of Flagstaff, where Mr. Puckett had arranged for a plane to pick her up. The last time she had been on a flight to the valley, she and mom had chartered an ancient looking twin turboprop. It reminded Annie of the poultry cargo plane that Indiana Jones jumped out of, after the pilots dumped the fuel and bailed. The fact that she had been eight at the time hadn't helped ease her fears; she'd still believed *Gremlins* was real too, silly child. Now, for all she knew, *Gremlins* might have been a documentary. *Shit*.

Mom walked her to the tarmac where a gleaming white private jet was waiting. Begrudgingly impressed, Annie set Devon's pet carrier down and gave mom a hug, letting the steward load her baggage in the cargo compartment.

"You'll be home before Thanksgiving, so remember to

try and play nice honey," mom was saying, "I know you can get a little testy around your father…"

"I'll avoid being a testy if he avoids being a dick." Annie quipped. Mom gave her a disapproving look but said nothing; her ex had earned his reputation with his daughter.

"Call me when you land," she said, waving goodbye. "And make sure the pilot doesn't fly through any chemtrails! You never know what they're releasing up there!"

Annie saluted, picked up the pet carrier and climbed aboard. *Chemtrails. God, mom.*

"Chemtrails?" asked the duck.

"High altitude bullshit," Annie explained. She picked a seat farther from the cockpit so they could talk without being overheard.

"This is quite stylish," Devon said, as Annie strapped the seatbelt over his plastic carrier. "I've never been in a flying machine before. The seats are so plush, and there is no trash on the floor like in your mother's car."

"Yeah, yeah, she's a pig, I know," Annie mumbled.

"I see where you get it from," he remarked. "Are we alone on this flight? May I come out soon? I think I would like one of those peanut butter cookies now. Do we have milk?"

Annie peeked at the duck in the carrier. "Are you nervous, Devon?" she asked with a smile. "You sound nervous."

"I have never flown before, as I said," Devon remarked irritably. "It is strange enough using my own useless wings, but I have seen how high these machines go… I still do not understand how they keep from dropping out of the sky."

A wicked grin spread across Annie's face. "Hey, did I ever tell you about that Indiana Jones movie where he takes a ride on a plane full of live poultry?"

Devon blinked at her, not sure he wanted to hear what happened to the poultry.

The pilot made his announcement, advising his passenger to buckle up until the seatbelt light was turned off. The engines whined, the plane began taxiing, and Devon groaned a little. As they accelerated down the runway, Annie heard the duck's little claws scratching on the floor of the carrier as the g-forces pushed him back into the box. "Ugh, Annabull Puh... is this normal?"

"You gonna hurl, duck? Maybe you shouldn't have eaten all those people last night; they probably gave you a tummy ache." She was going to enjoy this while it lasted.

Devon was quiet for the next few minutes as Annie took in the view of the departing treetops, which soon gave way to scrub-covered plains, hills, and valleys. Clouds created a dance of moving shadows across the purple terrain. Arizona was really beautiful, especially in the high country. Unfortunately, she was on her way to the valley and its dystopian urban sprawl. The Phoenix metropolitan area was growing like a weed, spreading out and soaking up precious water; its asphalt arteries trapped the heat in summer, keeping the temperature above 90 degrees Fahrenheit well past midnight. Luckily, it was early November, and the fall months were the nicest you could ask for. *There's always a trade-off,* she thought. *At least we don't get earthquakes. Or hurricanes. Or volcanoes, mudslides, tornadoes, tsunami, sinkholes, massive blizzards, alligators, or*

Godzilla.

The seatbelt light went off and Devon peeked through the cage door. "Is it safe to come out now, Annabelle Puckett?"

"Yeah, come on out and enjoy the scenery while it lasts." She opened the cage and lifted him to the circular window. "I've never been in a private jet before. This is nice."

"Most people do not fly this way?" he asked.

"Nah, most take crowded passenger jets. It's cramped, noisy; people bump you when they move; and when they put their seats back to sleep, you get to stare at their head in your lap. It's like a big flying bus, only with recycled air and more radiation," she explained as she got him a cookie.

"Flying bus," said Devon. "How novel." He ate the Nutter Butter she broke up for him, and they both got comfortable.

"So Devon, you must have some clue about this," she began, making sure the pilot wasn't able to hear, "I know you don't have anything to do with Heaven, but you must know how people avoid going to Hell. I mean, you said the soul market was good for a long, long time, right? What did they all do to stay out of trouble?"

"People said their prayers, ate their vegetables... you know, the usual." He said airily.

"Don't be flip! I'm serious. I don't think people have changed all that much, so what kept Hell empty for so long?"

"Oh, it has never been empty, but there have been droughts," he said. "After the Jesus Incident, for example."

Annie stared in shock. "Huh?"

"You've heard of him," Devon said. "A carpenter from Nazareth made a wager with Hell's Upper Management, betting that if he could get people to believe he was the Son of God, the believers would stay out of Hell. They took the bet, and have been kicking themselves for two thousand years. I personally suspect it was rigged..."

"So wait, are you saying Christianity is based on a bet, and that he's *not* the Son of God?" Annie was staggered to get a revelation like this from a duck on a plane.

"I have no idea if he is or not; we don't get their newsletter," Devon said, chagrined. "But that isn't the point of the wager, is it? He got people to believe in him and they were saved, at least until they did something really stupid."

"But a freakin' *bet?*" Annie was exasperated. *Did God really work that way?*

"Have you not heard the story of Job?" Devon asked. "I'm sure it made it into the Bible, though perhaps it ought not to have; it's such bad PR. Also, there are things like free will, genetic mutation, and papal infallibility. If *that* doesn't prove that God has a gambling problem, I don't know what will."

Annie was deflated at first, but she saw a ray of hope and asked, "So, if I were to like... believe again and stuff, I'd like, be saved from Hell?"

Devon thought for a moment, "I'm not sure it works that way, now that you know about the wager."

"But you just told me about it! That's not fair!" She folded her arms and sat back. "Stupid duck, ruining my eternal salvation."

"I take it you're not a person of faith," Devon asked.

Annie looked out the window, "I used to be, but shit happens..."

Devon nodded, "And your faith wasn't strong enough."

"Oh, my faith was plenty strong," she sighed, "God just didn't measure up to it."

"Hmm yes, that is a common theme," he said smugly. "What happened, you didn't get the pony you prayed for on your birthday?"

She said, "I was twelve. My parents divorced, my mom had her first nervous breakdown, my cat got sick and died, and we moved away from all of my friends. Nothing much in the big scheme of things, but when you grow up hearing that faith can move mountains… well, it's kind of crappy when it doesn't even save a sick cat."

"Mmm," Devon agreed.

"It's like, they tell you all this super, magic stuff about God when you're a kid. Then, once you get older, you find out that things don't work that way anymore; like God has retired from the miracle gig and we all missed the show. You start to lower your expectations, you know? Instead of miracles, the preacher tells you to pray for things like serenity and clarity. Hell, you can get that from a bag of weed!" She shook her head, "Soon you realize that prayer is just a coping mechanism, like drugs and alcohol, psychiatric therapy, or screaming into your pillow. No one's really listening."

The demon duck nodded his head, familiar with this part of the human condition. Faith was one of God's biggest gambles, and occasionally, He lost. "So, what now?" Devon asked, "Do you believe again?"

"What, believe in God? Or that he loves us, and there's a plan or something?" she shook her head, "I believe that if there is a god, he's got a damned sick sense of humor."

Devon looked down at his webbed feet and drawled in

agreement, "Yes…."

Before they knew it, they were coming in for an approach to Scottsdale Airpark. Annie put Devon back in his carrier, more out of concern for the upholstery than his safety, and they prepared for landing. The pilot announced that the temperature was a lovely 90 degrees in the valley, and that they would touch down in seven minutes. It was the most nerve-wracking seven minutes of the entire flight, and Devon asked about every change in the engine's pitch, every hydraulic whine, every bump and bank.

"Is that normal?" he would mutter from his box.

Annie considered reassuring him, but then decided to have some fun instead. She would reply in a worried tone, "I don't know, Devon. I don't think so."

The plane touched down with a screech of rubber on the tarmac, and the rapid deceleration made the duck slide around in his carrier again. Annie let the g-forces have their way with her just for kicks, leaning forward a little more than was necessary. The plane taxied off the runway and came to a stop near a black SUV parked near a hangar. She thanked the pilot for a lovely flight, though Devon vocally disagreed, and stepped down the ramp into the Valley of the Sun. The warm, dry air hit her as if she had flung open the door to a kiln. The skin on her forehead tingled and tightened.

"90 degrees in November," she huffed. "I bet you feel right at home, being a demon and all." She wandered towards the black SUV, as a rather handsome man strode forward to meet her.

Devon's voice was muffled, "Oh yes, I *love* being confined to a tiny box while I slip about in my own filth.

All I need is a spot of tea and a muffin, and it'll be *just like home*."

"Do I detect a note of sarcasm, duck?" she quipped.
"Hey, at least it's not someone else's filth."

The man spoke, his deep voice obscuring Devon's sharp reply. "Ms. Puckett? I'm here to drive you to your father's house."

The guy looked like a catalog model. He was in his mid-thirties with a smooth, angular face, blond hair, and ice-blue eyes. He was dressed in business casual, with a teal Polo shirt, neatly pressed khaki slacks, a Rolex worth three times as much as her mom's car, nice Italian shoes made of some poor reptile, and Aviator sunglasses. *Standard desert camouflage in this part of town,* she thought. His cologne, no doubt expensive, was sadly mingled with the scent of jet exhaust and asphalt.

"That's me," she said, as he gallantly took her bags. She couldn't help but ogle him a bit as he turned, and the SUV's power lift gate rose as if by magic. He was way out of her league, but hey, a free show is a free show.

For her part, Annie looked like she was going to play a rock concert in a dive bar. She wore one of her many black concert tees, ratty jeans with holes in the knees, her skull boots, and she accessorized with a studded wristband and collar. Her black hair was up in pigtails again, hanging to the sides of her head like a bunny's lop-ears.

"So, dad couldn't make time to pick me up himself?" Her tone was sharp; she had nothing against the driver, but she was the disgruntled daughter, after all. The man would just have to deal.

He said, "No ma'am, I'm sorry. He's tied up in a case today. Mrs. Winslow-Puckett sent me to collect you."

"Hmph," she said, "So I have her to thank for remembering my existence. How is Mrs. Hyphen Puckett?"

"Doing well, ma'am. She and her daughter are at the salon today; they'll be home later." The man had not responded to her attitude, and hadn't used 'stepmother' or 'stepsister' at all so far. *You dance well, my friend*, Annie thought. *Now I just have to make you stop calling me ma'am.*

"So what do you do for my dad, besides chauffeur his offspring?" She was being a bit of an asshole, it was true, but her father brought it out in her.

"I actually don't work for him," the driver said. "This is just a favor for Amanda."

Eeeeenteresting, Annie thought. *On a first-name basis with my step-harpy? This guy is cougar meat, you can bet on it.*

North Scottsdale was about as upscale as urban sprawl could get. To say it was the Beverly Hills of the Desert was not far off the mark; if you were rich, famous, and trying to get away from the L.A. scene, or New York's glass and steel canyons, North Scottsdale was the place to spend a luxury vacation. Five star resorts, golf courses, country clubs, and a big overpriced mall were the main attractions. The strip malls were built with genuine architecture, and had more sushi bars, specialty boutiques, and nail, tanning, and hair salons per square mile than Annie thought possible. It was a snob's paradise; at least for snobs who had never been around real wealth. They had money, sure, but most of the residents were either *nouveau riche* who liked to show it off, or upper-working-class shlubs who ran up their credit cards trying to fit in. The northern residents thought of Old Town Scottsdale as quaint and touristy, and they thought of South Scottsdale like a Third World country. The rest of the valley called the city 'Snottsdale,' though it really only applied to half of it.

Almost every third car on the road was a either a luxury touring sedan, a single occupant SUV, or a shiny Midlife Crisis Mobile. These were driven by either older men with a self-satisfied look, or bleach blond women with enormous sunglasses perched over amplified lips and tits. The rest of the traffic was made up of subcompacts, delivery vans, and other lesser vehicles, driven by those who had to commute to this part of town. After all, someone had to make all those triple-shot, half-foam, double-whip, non-fat lattes.

Annie's SUV drove farther north, past the Loop 101 freeway, and into the resort communities at the foot of the mountains, or 'buttes' as the locals called them. As far as Annie could tell, buttes were just mountains with higher property values.

"How was your flight, Ms. Puckett?" asked the driver.

"Short, but comfortable," she replied. *I should probably ask his name; it's only polite.* Devon again offered his opinion of the trip, but all the man heard was a string of quacks. Just as well.

"Good, good. Is this your first trip to the valley?" he asked.

"Nope. I used to live here… Phoenix, that is. Dad had a practice downtown until he made a name for himself, suing a homeowner on behalf of his client." They had lived on Central Avenue, just blocks from a part of town where the billboards advertised criminal defense attorneys and bail bonds. She crossed her arms, and disgust crept into her voice, "He was representing a burglar who hurt himself trying to break into some guy's house. Helped the bastard steal more from the homeowner than he could have ever gotten from a burglary."

"Ouch," said the driver.

"How delicious," said the duck.

"So what's your name, dude?" Annie asked. This guy seemed nice enough.

"Frank Wilcox," he said. "But you can call me 'Dude' if you like." He flashed a charming smile. Perfect teeth. They would have glinted and made a chime sound if this were a toothpaste commercial.

Sunhawk was an exclusive neighborhood behind a tall, masonry wall, which was designed to look all Mesoamerican and ancient; it bore pictographs of half-naked people making offerings, and jungle creatures sticking out their tongues, looking fierce. Annie imagined the injection-molded symbols meant, in Aztec, "If you have to ask, you can't afford it." Or maybe it just said "Please don't feed the cougars."

Beyond the wall was a variety of imposing estates in shades of earth tones, many of which had columns, arches and plastered walls to invoke Roman or Tuscan architecture. Curved brick tiles capped the starter castles with rows of terracotta ridges, and almost every house sported wide, manicured lawns; tall, neatly-trimmed shrubbery; and broad, curving driveways. Multi-car garages held the classics of automotive high fashion, and often next year's model of luxury sedan.

Her father's house was on Tail Feather Lane, which gave Annie a creepy sense of foreboding. *Isn't there a Bible passage about not bringing evil into your father's house? Or was it ducks? Don't bring evil ducks.* Most of the scripture she knew came from movies anyway, so her knowledge was suspect. She'd have to look it up online later.

The home of William Byron Puckett, Attorney at Law, was at the end of a broad cul-de-sac and stood like a palace overlooking the street; its columns and mix of flat and slanted roofing were in a pseudo-Pueblo-Palladian style, the walls crawled with creeping ivy, and large windows rose along the vaulted ceilings. Annie had never been to her father's house, but she had seen it from orbit, spying with a map program. The satellite photos didn't do it justice.

The driver helped Annie into the house with her bags. "Thanks for the lift, Frank," she said.

"Beau chance, Ms. Puckett. Have a good one." He smiled and waved as he drove off. *Nice guy*, she thought, *He must know the family well, wishing me luck.*

She rang the doorbell, which tolled like a freaking cathedral tower. Soon, the nine-foot-tall door swung open to reveal a little Hispanic housekeeper, whose eyes widened at the sight of the unkempt Goth girl with the duck.

"Are joo Annie?" she asked with a thick accent.

"That's me," Annie said, hefting the pet carrier and duffel bag.

"Aaaah, come een, come een." She smiled and ushered her inside, "I yam Estela. Jour room es ready downstairs, Ms. Annie. De lady will be home in a few hours."

The foyer was vast and impressive, with one of those spiral staircases you always see rich people have on TV. Daylight flooded in through the high windows, shining on lush potted plants and sparkling floors. She saw a cavernous living room beyond, and a vast patio with a swimming pool. The low patio walls allowed for a stunning view of the mountains and city below. *Holy shit, this is nice.*

Estela began to lead her down the plush stairs, when a scampering and yipping stopped them. A white Chihuahua came up the steps, barring their way, his little belled collar tinkling as he postured menacingly. Devon glared from his cage.

"Ay, Taco, callate la boca, cabron." Estela scolded the little rat dog.

*Taco? They named it **Taco**?*

"He es a rascal," Estela said as she shooed him away, "Like a leetle baby. Yust ignore heem." She led Annie to the basement, with the dog in tow, and opened the automatic window shades.

Annie had to gasp; the basement was really an entertainment complex, complete with a large plasma flat-screen TV, leather theater-style seats, lush plants along the walls, and a wet bar towards the back. The guest room was down a short hall to the side, adjacent to a combined workout and laundry room. Her room had a queen-sized bed, a roll-top desk with a laptop computer, a small entertainment center with a TV, Blue Ray, and stereo system, and even a little playpen for Devon. The bathroom was bigger than her bedroom back home, and had a Jacuzzi. *Holy. Shit.*

Estela asked if she needed anything before leaving her to settle in. Annie could only shake her head mutely. *What more could I need, other than my own fully stocked fridge? I'd never have to leave.*

"I approve, I *very much* approve," said Devon, after she let him out of his carrier. "Were it not for the barking rat, this would be a perfect place to live." He waddled into the bathroom and checked out the tub. "Splendid, it is deep and wide enough to make a wading pool. I desire a swim, Annabelle Puckett."

She snorted a laugh, wondering if swimming was something the demon did often, or if the duck's body was asserting itself.

"Don't get too comfortable, Devon. We aren't making a long stay of it; it's only three weeks."

"But why?" asked the duck, waddling about the vast space. "This is so very much nicer than *your* shabby dwelling. Your own bedroom looks like it could be a closet in this bedroom, albeit a messy closet. They even have a servant to pick up after you."

"Yeah, it's *nice*," she said with a sharp tone, not appreciating his opinions. "But we'd have to put up with my dad and the steps, and that's not going to be a picnic for me, so just shut your bill about it."

"What exactly is your issue with your father?" Devon asked. Not that he cared for his minion's family troubles, but it would be so very nice to live here instead.

"Oh, I don't know," she began with exasperation, throwing up her hands, "Maybe it's that he never gave a shit about me, or he always had a lame excuse for missing birthdays and school plays, or he drove my mom to have a nervous breakdown with all the shit he put her through. Maybe it's that."

"What did he put her through?" the duck inquired.

Annie sighed and looked down at him. *Can't fault him for being curious,* she figured. "He cheated on her a couple of times. He lied about business trips and meetings; he lied to cover trips to Vegas with his buddies and parties with call girls. Mom found a business card for an escort service in one of his suit coats. I was eleven years old, but I still remember that fight like it was yesterday."

Devon nodded, "Infidelity. Yes, it is one of the most common sins we see. It's rather amusing that you people make such strict rules for yourselves; rules that you are biologically programmed to break."

"Yeah, hilarious." Annie murmured. She began to fill the tub, angrily adding some scented bath balls at Devon's request.

While he was happily paddling around, Annie decided to check out the laptop computer on the desk. It had good specs, comparable to the desktop 'Monster' that Maurice kept at the tattoo parlor. She wondered if her dad bought it so she'd have something to occupy herself; it was a typical enough gesture for him to make. The user profile was labeled 'Guest' instead of 'Annie,' so she didn't flatter herself to think he'd given it more than a cursory thought. *'Here, pumpkin. Have a shiny.'* Jerk.

"Hey Devon," she called, "Something has been bothering me for a while." She got up to check on the duck, who was enjoying his swim. "Your summoning name is like, a secret, because it's used to summon you, right?" Her voice echoed in the cavernous bathroom.

"Very clever, Annabelle Puckett," he intoned. "That is correct. It can also be used to bind me, much more powerfully than my business name." Strangely, his voice did *not* echo.

She filed that info away. "Well, if it's such a big secret, how did those kids get it?"

Devon stopped swimming and considered, "I had wondered the same thing, but my thirst for revenge clouded my judgment on the matter…" Again, he regretted his decision to devour all of his summoners at once. "Usually one makes inquiries with a prominent demonologist, lawyer, or political party. One has to know the demon's business name to learn the correct summoning name. These are found in ancient Kabbalistic tomes that have made their way onto various college campuses, though the secret societies that keep them are normally found at much more… prestigious schools. Such information is not easy to come by."

Annie went back to her computer and typed 'Malgamadalard' into the search field. "Oh, here it is," she said. "It's on Wikipedia."

"Wiki-what?" Devon squawked, clearly dismayed.

"It's an encyclopedia on the Internet that anyone can edit… there's a big list of freaky names here." She read his entry. "Your business name is *Farquatz*? Sounds dorky; no wonder you prefer Devon. Hey, it says you're a literary demon! What's that?"

There was a splashing as Devon fluttered out of the tub and waddled to the computer desk. "It has my summoning name *and* professional information on that machine? Curse Gothraxess and her meddling ways!"

Annie scrolled up and down the page. "You think Gothraxess did this?"

"It would make sense. The Budget Conjuration spell that trapped me was hers, and it is useless without summoning names." Devon glared at the screen.

"So… what's a literary demon?" she asked again.

Devon sighed, "We find a market for works of literature, helping the author gain fame and renown."

"So, you're like a muse?"

"No, more like a publicist or agent; we don't provide inspiration or ideas." He explained, "We generate interest in their work; we manipulate people into wanting to read a book, attend a play, what have you. As for the quality of the writing, well…" he shuffled a bit, "The harder the sell, the steeper the rates."

Annie frowned, "So if I wanted to publish my shitty poetry, you could make it popular?"

"Oh yes," Devon said. "A colleague of mine worked with Jewel."

"But the cost would be insane, I suppose," she made a face. "Not worth it."

Devon tilted his head at her, "There is little difference in the fate of the soul; the rates of a literary demon are based on commission. The worship and acclaim given to an author after death is consumed by the demon and…"

"Wait a minute," she interrupted, "Back home, you mentioned Ben-something; that guy that was big in Shakespeare's day."

"Yes…" he replied.

"Did you have something to do with Shakespeare too? Were you like, the agent of the Bard Man himself?"

Devon hung his head. "No, that wasn't me," he muttered. "I thought Shakespeare was a bit too wordy, too steeped in the romantic style; I was looking for a glib realist with mass market appeal…"

"O-M-G, you *passed* on Shakespeare?" She broke into a huge grin and laughed as she spoke, "He's like, the best known writer in the history of English… history! He's even been translated into Klingon! What were you *thinking?*" Her mirth ended when a piercing headache struck her between the eyes; the pain was brief but effective. "Ow! Jeez, don't be so touchy, duck!"

"Touchy?" he scoffed, "Do you know how much Shakespeare's demon gets in commission? He was able to move into a mansion in the Karrkan Pits within the *first fifty years* after the man died! The soul of King Edward I does his *laundry!*" Devon flapped about in circles, "*My* greatest achievement was the best-selling novelist of all time, but she died in 1976, just before the big market crash! Thirty-three years, and all I have to show for it is a split-level flat in the hills. I have half a mind to file a lawsuit against *Murder, She Wrote* for a piece of their residuals..."

"A place in the hills sounds nice," she offered, rubbing her temples.

"It's Hell. The deeper it is, the more exclusive." He sank down and ruffled his feathers. "Blasted economy."

Annie had never seen him so upset. "So what did your guy do?" she asked meekly.

Devon sighed, "Ben Jonson? He was quite a character, and very popular in his day. He wrote a number of plays and masques for the royal court of James I." He asked hopefully, "Perhaps you are familiar with one of his comedies? *The Devil is an Ass?*"

"Never heard of it," she replied.

"Yes, well *you're* hardly a bloody English scholar, are you?" He stalked back to his bath, muttering. Annie smiled to herself, glad that she'd found one of his buttons. *Push with care and stand back.*

"Annabelle Puckett! My bathwater is tepid!" he called with displeasure, "And I require bubbles! Step lively!"

"Right away, *Farquatz*," she muttered under her breath.

Estela heard the ominous, echo-less quacking in the basement and crossed herself, trembling. "El pato es no bueno," she whispered.

Chapter 11
Father Knows Best

Amanda Winslow-Puckett and her daughter Tiffany Winslow-Dyer-Puckett arrived almost an hour later in a flurry of chatter and the rustling of designer shopping bags. Taco raced to the door to greet them, his yapping adding to the racket, as the ladies made their way into the cavernous living room to disgorge their treasures on one of the plush couches.

"Estela? Has Annie arrived yet?" Amanda called towards the kitchen as the housekeeper came in behind her.

"Sí, Mrs. Weenslow-Pockett. She es downstairs..." Estela began.

"Oh!" Amanda jumped a little, "There you are. Good, I'll go and check on her, I suppose. Was everything alright for her um, pet?"

"I theenk so, ma'am... about de duck, there es something not right about him..." she stopped speaking

131

as Annie came up the stairs.

"Hi," Annie said awkwardly, giving a little wave. "I was just on the phone with mom." The steps were not her favorite people, but mom had just reminded her that she was a guest, and it wouldn't do to come out of the gate all bitchy.

"Annie," Amanda said musically, opening her arms. Instead of hugging Annie, she held her at arm's length and made little kissy noises toward either side of her face; it was like some exotic greeting for germaphobes. "How was your flight?"

Standard perfunctory question, Annie thought. "It was good. Devon wasn't happy. He doesn't like to fly."

"Devon?" Amanda asked, "Oh, your duck. He doesn't like to fly, how funny! Isn't that funny, Tiffy?" she turned to her daughter, who gave a kind of congenial smirk.

Amanda Winslow-Puckett was a tall, leggy trophy wife in her early forties, freshly coiffed and ex-foliated from a day at the spa. Amanda's hair had been platinum blond the last time Annie saw it; the color more closely resembled something natural now, if highlights like that were natural. Her breed of cougar was common in this part of town, with a body half her age, and a face that was smooth from regular tune-ups, but she had managed to avoid habits like smoking and excessive tanning. Such habits contributed to the sphincter-lipped, leather-faced, turkey-necked horrors that prowled the bars and nightclubs, seeking dark places to hunt.

Tiffany Winslow-Dyer-Puckett bore her biological father's name between her mother's and stepfather's, making her 'Tiffany Hyphen-Hyphen Puckett' in Annie's book. Tiffany had just turned eighteen, and her perky, perfect breasts had just turned two. The three of them were going to college sometime next year, just as soon as she decided where all the hot guys were going and what courses they were taking. Annie foresaw a great future for her stepsister, that is, if 'Girls Gone Wild' ever led to greatness. Maybe she'd land a rich bastard lawyer, like Amanda had?

Tiffany made eye contact for the first and last time, saying, "Hello Annie," in a pleasant voice. She then ignored her and took her shopping upstairs, leaving Annie to envy the tight butt that wiggled up the steps in those Capri pants. Tiffany had a way of sucking all the self-esteem out of the room, damn her.

"So dad is busy at work, huh?" Annie asked, "Expecting him sometime this year?"

"Oh, he'll be back tonight. Busy busy busy, you know your father." Amanda said.

"Mhmm, Darth Puckett." Annie made a face, "Know him, I do." She looked around the room and asked, "So, what's within walking distance around here?"

Amanda laughed a bit too loud, "Oh my, Annie! Walking distance? I have no idea. If you like, I can call you a cab if you want to go into town." She amended quickly, "On your father's tab, of course."

"Thanks, maybe later." Annie replied. She had made herself known, and could now disappear downstairs until dinner.

Devon was sitting at the computer desk, pecking at the flat, compact keyboard in frustration. "What nonsense is this? How do you type on such a thing?" He kept shifting in the chair and hitting 'delete' to undo his mistakes.

She replied, "It's designed for fingers, not peckers. Whatcha looking for?"

"I am seeking clues to finding Gothraxess in her corporeal form," he said. "I assume she must have obtained a human body to become so influential; it is the only explanation for her success."

"Gothraxess possessed someone like Fake Blake did?" Annie was troubled. "How common is this possession thing anyway?"

"It has become more common of late," he said, "One of the exciting things about this age is the desire for new experiences. Mortals like to feel powerful and in control, and demons like to have actual living bodies to inhabit." He looked at his feathers and added, "Human bodies, that is. Some demons even pay a monthly fee for the privilege, trading wealth for the chance to share a human life on earth."

"World of Warlock-craft, huh?" Annie smiled. "People do that on computers, you know. They pay a monthly fee to play an avatar in a virtual world; stuff like wizards, warriors, and monsters. You do quests and fight each other. Kind of addictive though."

"Do you play such games, Annabelle Puckett?"

She said, "I used to, but there were too many creepy stalkers and griefers."

"What is a griefer?"

"Someone who enjoys messing up your game, getting you killed, stealing your experience points or whatever," she said, "Oh, but there was this one grief prank I heard of that was epic; these guys playing orcs and trolls bent the rules and pulled a demon lord out of a high-level zone, right into the main human city! It started killing newbs and everything else in sight. No one could defeat it, so the admins had to reset the game world..." She looked at Devon, suddenly remembering what she was talking too.

"Interesting," he drawled. "Sounds like fun." He was almost smiling.

"Yeah…" she said, turning back to the computer, "So, what are we looking for exactly?"

Devon gave up the chair to his minion saying, "Gothraxess thrives on manipulating thought and opinion, luring mortals to her will. She takes the work of mortals and other demons, making it part of her web, tying it all together so she may feel the distant vibrations of new trends and paradigms. She does not make typical contracts with mortals for fame and fortune, but instead creates great enthusiasm and then feeds on it."

"Demons can feed on enthusiasm?" Annie asked surprised.

"Yes, as well as other mass emotions; fear, hatred, guilt, disappointment," he said. "Election years are big for us. So is war. And the World Cup."

"Hmm, maybe that's why those Joss Whedon shows keep getting canceled," she remarked. "Some demon is feeding on the disappointment and outrage."

Devon replied, "I do not know of these *Ja Sweden* shows you speak of."

"Oh come on," she said, "He did *Buffy* and *Angel*. You know, the vampire shows?"

"Oh, *him*." Devon said. "I read about him in the trades; he's the mortal who tried to expose the relationship between lawyers and demons. Everyone thought he was being funny."

"Yeah, that's the guy." Annie said. "So what do you want to search for? Obviously she won't go by 'Gothraxess' in real life."

"No," he agreed, "She will use a business name here on

earth, so whoever speaks it will be known to her, like an insect twitching on her web."

"Something better than Farquatz, I hope."

"Every joke you have, I have heard," he snapped.

"Heh, I bet. So, what do you plan to do when you find her?" Annie asked. "If she's such a big shot, she probably has all kinds of security and people trying to get her attention."

"I'm not sure," he said, "I think combat is out of the question, and I have almost nothing to bargain with, however the knowledge might prove useful."

They spent the next hour looking on line for wealthy, reclusive women with 'spidery' tendencies. Devon explained, "She will be unmarried, for a spider queen would be driven to devour her mate, which would be socially awkward among humans. She may have a large adopted brood however, for her maternal instincts are strong."

"Well, celebrity adoptions are really common," Annie said, "Assuming she's a celebrity. She might be working behind the scenes, like an executive or something."

"Ms. Annie!" called Estela from upstairs, "deener is served."

Annie sighed. If dad was home, he hadn't bothered to come downstairs. If he wasn't, then she might enjoy dinner a little more. "Okay duck, I'm off to battle. Wish me luck." She headed upstairs, leaving Devon at the computer.

The smell of food was enthralling, though Annie had little appetite. Dad and the steps were already at the table when she arrived; her father noticed her with mild surprise, "Annabelle! Have a seat. Welcome to your new sanctuary." He motioned to the empty chair opposite

Tiffany. "How was the flight? Comfortable, I hope." Estela began setting food on the table as Annie took her place.

"Hi dad. The flight was good. Frank was nice too."

Mr. Puckett looked up, "Frank?" he asked.

"The guy who picked me up from the airport?" she explained. "Because you were *busy*?"

Amanda piped up, "Victoria's Frank, dear. From the club. I had him swing by and pick up Annie." She pierced her salad a bit forcefully; Tiffany glanced from her mother to her stepfather as he sipped his wine, a hesitant expression on his face. Annie looked around the table as the silence lingered. *Awkward moment*, she thought.

"Ah," Mr. Puckett said finally. He served himself a helping of roast beef before passing it around to his bio-daughter.

William Byron Puckett was a balding man in his fifties with a band of dark hair around the back of his head, a sharp nose and a bit of middle-age paunch. His eyes, once his best feature, had been considered sincere and puppy dog-like, but now had a world-weariness that made him appear more like a Bassett hound. Mom told Annie she started dating him because his eyes made her feel sorry for him. Pity was a great way to start a relationship.

"I uh, understand things have been pretty crazy up there in the mountains," Mr. Puckett began.

"Up there in the mountains, dad?" Annie remarked, "You make it sound like *Deliverance* or something. It's just your average psychopathic-murder-on-the-loose scenario; it could happen anywhere."

Tiffany was not about to be upstaged. "We had a

shooting at one of the nightclubs just last month! Of course that was in *south* Scottsdale, near the university. It was totally gangsta."

Annie feigned interest, "Oh wow, did you see it happen?" *In front of you, with blood?*

"No," Tiffany scoffed, "It was *south* Scottsdale. It was on the news though, and my friend Jennifer from school had a friend whose brother was like, totally shot."

"Is that the kid who took a bullet in the ass?" Mr. Puckett asked.

"Yeah," said Tiffany. "Left cheek."

Annie said, "I saw a guy I knew get killed right in front of the video store," she took on a haunted expression. "His blood splattered on the window, just like in a horror movie... then there were the burning bunnies..." She stared at the mashed potatoes like the scene was replaying itself on the creamy, whipped surface.

"Oh my god," said Amanda, "That was for real? Someone set rabbits on fire with explosives? How cruel! I hope they catch the bastards who did that."

"Did I mention a guy was killed?" Annie said. "They think it was a wild animal attack, like a mountain lion or something." *Or a possessed rabbit. Whatever.*

"I thought it was a psycho," said Tiffany, "The news said three kids were killed."

"They were," Annie said, playing for effect. "Murdered in a dorm full of partying students. I found the bodies and... oh man, what he did to them... I just had to puke..." She braced herself against the table and heaved a breath like she was getting sick; everyone tensed up, preparing for a possible spew all over their dinner. *Perfect.* She held them in suspense for a moment longer, and then asked cheerily, "Pass the horseradish?"

A collective sigh of relief passed around the table.

The food went around and everyone ate in silence for a while, until Annie spoke up again, "Do you believe in demons, dad?"

Mr. Puckett looked up with a curious expression, "Demons? You mean like, 'The devil made me do it,' or like personal demons that you overcome?"

Annie shook her head, "No, like demons that make contracts for human souls. Demons you can summon. *El Diablo*." She made her fingers into pointy horns at her temples and flicked her tongue. Estela made a muffled noise from the kitchen.

"That's an odd question Annie," he said, looking at his wife and stepdaughter with a touch of embarrassment. "Why do you ask?"

"I think the victims, and maybe the killers, were part of a demon cult in Bueller. I think they were dealing with forces beyond their control." She watched him to see if he got nervous in a guilty way. Instead, he used the same tone she remembered at the age of six, when he told her there was no Santa Claus.

"Annie honey," he said, "Demons aren't real in any real sense. They're mythology, like unicorns and elves. People who summon demons are just sad, delusional individuals who are looking for power and control that they can't get in their daily lives."

"So, you don't believe that there's a place called Hell, or demons that want our souls?" She knew he was an excellent liar, but he was also insufferably smug when he thought he was right. Like now.

"No Annie," he said while cutting his food, "There's no divine judgment for the wicked, it's up to society to make its own justice. That's why I do what I do. If evil people went to Hell and good people went to Heaven, there'd be no need for lawyers or the courts."

"But you don't send criminals to jail," Annie replied, "You help idiots sue pizza parlors when they burn their mouth on the cheese."

Mr. Puckett looked mildly annoyed, "I help people find justice while on earth, so they don't have to die to get what's coming to them, and I make a good living doing it, by the way." He sipped his wine. "I managed to get your mother the best medical care, didn't I?"

"Only after you drove her insane," she retorted, quietly.

"Pass the mashed potatoes, will you dear?" Amanda said to her daughter. Tiffany did so with a bit of a smirk. Distract and Ignore was her mom's favorite tactic.

Mr. Puckett cleared his throat, "Annie, your mother and I had our problems, it's true. Mistakes were made on both sides, and unfortunately you were caught in the middle." It was a statement of fact, and the closest he ever came to making an apology. Not that a real one would have helped much.

"What about you, Annie?" asked Tiffany. "Do you think demons are real?" She might as well have been holding a straight jacket and a big butterfly net, judging by her tone.

Annie noticed Estela peeking around the corner, but the maid quickly disappeared back into the kitchen. Annie said, "I don't know for sure, but in the last week, I've seen some pretty twisted shit. You think you know about the world and then something happens that turns everything upside-down. I've seen things; things that would make you question your sanity."

"What kind of things?" Tiffany asked anxiously.

Devon, The Demon Duck From Hell

Annie looked her dead in the eye, and said dramatically, "Things from Hell."

Taco started barking downstairs as Estela dropped a spoon in the kitchen; it clattered noisily as she scrambled to pick it up, muttering in Spanish.

"I'm sure you've been through a lot, Annabelle," said Mr. Puckett, "and I respect that it's had a profound effect on you, but I don't think that indulging in silly superstitions is going to help. There is evil in the world, but it is Man…" he raised his finger, *actually raised his finger*, like he was giving a lecture in a bad movie, "Man that is the source of all evil, not some mythical being that sits on your shoulder and makes you do things you wouldn't have done otherwise. Passing it off on the devil is just a way of denying responsibility."

"So I guess you won't know about the *Arcana Curiae* then, huh?" She watched him closely.

"What is that, some *Harry Potter* thing?" he asked, obviously confused. "I told your mother not to let you get lost in those books. Serious literature, young lady. *That's* what you need to fill your head with." Tiffany smiled and Amanda sighed.

"You're such a muggle, dad." Annie said. So it seems he was really in the dark about the whole 'demons and lawyers' thing. Just as well, she didn't need another reason to loathe the man.

"Muggle?" he asked, "What, does that mean I'm un-cool or something? Ask your stepsister; I'm totally down with it. I'm hip." He swiveled his head and bobbed his shoulders in an absurd chair-dance.

Tiffany smiled, "Oh, he's in da hizzay, fo sho," she said, in her best rich-white-girl-ghetto.

"See?" dad remarked. "What she said."

141

Annie smiled despite herself. Dad always had a way of disarming people at his own expense. It was a good tactic at the dinner table, or in front of a jury.

Annie didn't like the next part of her plan, but it was the most critical. "So, do you think I can visit at the office later? You know, like a 'Bring Your Daughter To Work Day' or something?" The last thing she wanted was to seem all needy and clingy.

Amanda piped up, "That sounds like a wonderful idea, Bill. Doesn't that sound nice, Tiffy?" Tiffany rolled her eyes.

"I… don't know, Annie," said Mr. Puckett. "There isn't much to see, and I'll be very busy. Maybe we can do lunch sometime instead… I'd have to check my schedule of course…" He poked his vegetables as if his calendar was buried underneath.

"Oh, I don't need to be constantly entertained," said Annie, cringing inside as her bio-dad tried to dodge her. "I'd keep out of the way. Totally incognito, like a shadow in the night."

"That'd be something to see," muttered Tiffany under her breath. Her mother shot her a look.

Annie persisted, "I could get a cab to the mall and walk to the office. I'll have my people call your people and we'll do lunch… or I could just like, hang with the paralegals…"

Mr. Puckett still seemed unsure, but the look his wife was giving him meant that the subject would be picked up after dinner if he didn't agree.

"…Fine," he said to his daughter, looking very uncomfortable. "Lunch."

"Awesome!" exclaimed Annie, though a dentist appointment sounded more fun.

Chapter 12
Annie Puckett and the Broom Closet of Secrets

It was nine in the morning before Annie woke up. Not that she was usually an early riser, especially on a Monday, but she rarely got the kind of amazing sleep she had just experienced. The bed was damned comfortable, and the room was secluded enough to dampen the household noises. There were no train whistles like back home, no traffic noise, no high school band practice echoing through the trees. Dad was likely out of the house by six o'clock, but Amanda and Tiffany had little reason to be up before the sun. Only Estela could be heard puttering around in the kitchen, whistling some wavering tune. *When did she leave or come in? Did she live here?* Annie had no idea.

She took her time getting ready, letting Devon sleep in until after she was dressed. He seemed to like his playpen for the security it offered; he had Annie drape the sides with a sheet to conceal him from the prying eyes of Taco, who would look in on them every hour or so. Annie dressed in a black and white striped top with long sleeves, a black vinyl skirt that went down to mid-thigh, and cute leather ankle boots. She tied her hair back to conceal the demon tattoo, and donned a pair of sunglasses that made her look like that chick from *The Matrix*. She woke Devon by bumping his playpen, and he looked up at her, surprised and bleary-eyed.

"You awoke before me, Annabelle Puckett. I am shocked," he said.

"Yeah, yeah. Come on, breakfast time." She had not considered feeding Devon in his playpen, and if anyone had a problem with a duck in the kitchen, they would just have to say so.

She picked up Devon and his food bowl and climbed the stairs. Taco came from behind the couch and followed cautiously, still unsure of the new animal. He made silly little huffs as he hopped up each stair, just behind Annie's ankles. They followed their noses to the kitchen, enticed by the smell of delicious eggs, potatoes, and ham.

Amanda and Tiffany, who were already primped and dressed for the day, sat in the breakfast nook overlooking the patio, chatting like teenagers. Amanda wore a purple spandex leotard with matching sweatbands, leg-warmers, and designer sneakers. Her hair was styled and perfect. Tiffany was dressed in a pink velvet hoodie, and tight, white warm-up pants that looked painted on. *Probably has a black thong underneath,* Annie thought. *Tramp.* They both seemed ready to work out, but not ready to sweat.

"Going to the gym?" asked Annie.

"Shopping," said Tiffany, "at the health food store and the organic market."

"And... then the gym?" Annie asked.

Amanda laughed, "No silly. We can't leave food in the car while we work out. Besides, we have an appointment at the masseur later, so we have to come home and change."

"So that's your duck?" asked Tiffany. "Isn't that like, a farm animal?" She crinkled her nose at Devon as Annie set him on the floor with his plastic cereal bowl.

"Oh no, ducks are considered exotic pets," she lied, "especially his breed."

"What breed is that?" Tiffany asked, seeing nothing special about the white duck.

Annie glanced at Devon uncertainly, and he quacked at her.

"Pekin. He's a Pekin duck," she said.

"Sounds like Chinese takeout," Tiffany remarked with a slight smile.

"Yeah, sometimes I could just eat him up," Annie said, as she poured him some corn flakes. "I'm going to get him a proper collar and leash today."

"*What*," Devon said flatly. Everyone else heard "*WACK!*"

"So he doesn't get picked up by the pound again," Annie said, "mustn't flaunt the leash laws after all."

"Hrmm," Devon muttered.

"It's almost like he understands you," giggled Amanda.

"I know, weird isn't it?" Annie said. Just then she noticed Estela; the woman was watching the duck with a curious, fearful expression.

"Oh, Estela," said Amanda, "We'll be going out, so no

need to bother with lunch."

"Okay, Mrs. Weenslow-Pockett," she said. "What about de duck? Es he going tambien?"

"Yeah," said Annie, as she poured some milk over his corn flakes. "I need to get him some stuff."

Amanda produced a little purse from somewhere and said, "That reminds me Annie, take your father's credit card for the cab ride and shopping. Just don't go crazy with it; no diamond duck collars!" She laughed as she handed Annie the plastic. Annie wondered if Amanda had been made to return a diamond-studded collar for her rat dog. *Probably*.

"Thanks," she said, taking the card. She didn't want her dad's money, but saving her soul was a good cause to spend it on. In this day and age, it helped to have a little moral flexibility.

The steps left shortly thereafter, driving to the health food store in their pristine workout clothes, looking like Barbie and Skipper; that is, if Skipper had a boob job, and Barbie had begun to show signs of age. Annie checked the infernal web for a map of the downtown area, charted out her course, and ordered up a cab. She figured she'd hit a pet store in the mall first, and then make for dad's law office, which was southeast across the canal.

The cab took her into town, dropping her off at the Scottsdale Fashion Square. The complex was both impressive and inviting - three levels of retail heaven, with wide, airy spaces and a big circular fountain for a centerpiece. There was a good mix of classy and casual, so Annie didn't feel *too* much out of place, but then, no one else had a duck under their arm. She could have been more discrete and lug him around in the pet carrier, but Devon forbade it. *What I need is a big, over-sized purse; one that I can wash.* She peeked in a few stores that sold purses, but never got past the entrance. Something about the looks she got from the saleswomen told her she would not find what she was seeking here. *'Try Ghettrocenter Mall on the west side, honey.'*

Annie found a pet store that had a nice selection of tags and collars for every taste. She even found pet costumes on clearance, and winced as she recognized the Elvis cape Devon had worn.

"I miss my cape," Devon said wistfully.

"Tough shit, Hell Beast." Annie replied quietly. "You got blood all over it."

She bought Devon a little red collar, and had a tag made with his name on one side, and her cell phone number on the other.

The inscription read:

Devon
DDFH

The clerk asked, "Would you like your address on the back too? There's room."

"Noooo," Annie said aversely. Then, noticing the clerk's expression said, "Um, no thank you."

She also picked out a pink retracting leash, but Devon forbade her to try it out. He muttered, "It's bad enough that I have to wear a collar, but you expect me to endure a leash as well? My patience has its limits, Annabelle Puckett."

Annie explained in a hushed voice, "There are leash laws, duck. If you need to wear one to avoid trouble, then that's the way it'll be. I can't do this research stuff without you, since I'm not a lawyer or a demon."

"Very well," he conceded, "But you will not use it to tug me around like a beast. I expect you to remember my dignity."

"Remind me to have you watch the original *Planet of the Apes* sometime," she muttered, "You aren't exactly Charlton Heston, you know."

"*Planet of the Apes*," he smirked, "how appropriate."

"Yeah, and it's Ape Law, so deal with it." Annie said, and she clipped the thin leash to his collar. She really had no idea if there were leash laws that covered ducks in this town, or any town for that matter. Annie just wanted to put the little sucker in his place. *Master, my ass.*

A short time later they were walking down the street towards her dad's law practice, located kitty-corner from the tall buildings that rose above the canal. 'Tall' was a relative term, as a ten-story building was considered tall in Scottsdale and these looked to be eleven or twelve stories. They were luxury apartments, according to the signs, which read 'Scottsdale Waterfront Residences.'

Annie chuckled, *"Waterfront*, huh? I wonder how much it costs to live by a landscaped strip of dirt next to a smelly canal. Oh well. People cross oceans to visit Venice, Italy. Who am I to judge?"

Devon felt the urge to swim in the smelly canal, but kept this to himself.

The sun was warm, but the breeze was cool and refreshing as they walked along, Annie slowing her pace to match Devon's waddle. He took to complaining about the heat of the sidewalk, which for some reason, Annie found hilarious.

"I thought you were from Hell," she said. "Isn't it kinda hot there?"

"I am a demon in Hell, Annabelle Puckett, not a duck," he said. "This body is not as resilient as my true form, and these ridiculous webbed feet are not made for pavement."

"So… what do you look like in your true form anyway? Bat wings and cloven hooves?"

"A colleague of mine once said that I resembled the villain in *Die Hard*, whatever that is." Devon said. "I assume it is one of your 'epic' motion pictures."

"Wow, I'm impressed. Not bad, Devon. Yippie ka yay, muthaducker."

"Yippie…? Dare I ask?" the duck gazed up at her quizzically. "No, no never mind."

THUM *THOOM* THUM THUM *THOOOM* was the next thing she heard, the thumping baseline of a rap song creeping up and goosing her; its lyrics and sentiments extremely out of place in *this* hood. Before she could turn around, she was showered with a spray of cold water and ice cubes, making her shriek and jump. Devon squawked in alarm as the ice clattered around him, unsure if it was a magical attack from another demon. Annie saw the hand of the driver retracting into the car's sunroof, soda cup in hand. The silver sports car, license plate 'LGLEGL', took off up the street, accelerating as if it mattered.

"Asshole!" she shouted, "Frickin' Scottsdouche!" She flipped him the bird, but it was all she could do.

"Who in the world was that?" asked Devon, as the water slid off his back.

"That," she said, "was a douche bag. Scottsdale has more of them than a porn convention."

"Why did he throw ice at us?"

"Probably because I'm wearing the wrong clothes, or

not driving a nice car; maybe because I'm walking and can't chase him. Maybe he has something against ducks. Who the hell knows?"

Devon glared at the retreating car as it squealed into a right turn a block away. "Philistine."

They arrived at the office complex about five minutes later, and Devon hopped gratefully onto the scant grass as they walked up to the shaded entryway. They looked for the suite number and soon found the Law Offices of William Byron Puckett, spelled out in plain, unassuming, white letters. Annie watched herself in the reflection of the glass doors, admiring her sunglasses and boots and checking for water stains. Her eyes came across a little sign near the door that read 'No Pets Allowed' and she stopped in her tracks. "Devon, we have a problem."

"What?" he asked.

"No pets allowed. You can't go in."

"Is this not your father's building?"

"He leases an office, he doesn't own the whole thing," she explained. She looked around, assessing her options, when she noticed a familiar silver sports car with a 'LGLEGL' custom license plate. Her eyes narrowed. "Mr. Ice Cube works here. Interesting." *Revenge will come before the water has dried*, she thought.

Devon looked towards the covered parking and saw the offending car. "I did not see it there. I must be going blind."

A little spark went off in Annie's brain and she cried, "Devon, you're a genius! We are *so* lucky I bought this leash! But first things first; Mr. Ice Cube left his sun roof open…"

"And I am done with my morning cornflakes," Devon

said evilly.

The guard at the security desk looked up at the sound of a tap on the glass doors. They were opened by an oddly dressed girl with a duck on a leash. The guard stood to get her attention, but she didn't seem to notice. "Excuse me, ma'am. No pets allowed in the building."

Annie swung her dark glasses in his direction saying, "Oh! Hello, I'm here to visit William Puckett, attorney at law. This is my seeing-eye duck. Where is the elevator please?"

The guard blinked a few times at the duck on the leash before pointing towards the elevator; he then checked himself and said, "About twenty feet ahead of you, ma'am. Do you have an appointment?"

"I'm his biological daughter, actually. From his first marriage. If you want, you can call up and say his Little Orphan Annie is waiting in the lobby. That's his pet name for me; Little Orphan Annie. Are there any chairs? My feet are kinda sore." She could see there weren't.

The guard hesitated, "Uh, why don't you go on up, ma'am."

"Thanks! Forward, Devon," she said, letting the duck lead the way. Devon waddled to the elevator and pecked on the door, and Annie lifted him up. "Going up, Devon," she said. He pecked the proper button. "Second floor, Devon," she said, and he pecked again. She enjoyed the look on the guard's face as the doors closed.

"That was strangely empowering," said Devon. "Perhaps I can push the buttons on the way down?" he asked.

"Sure thing, ducky."

The doors opened on an elegant hallway leading to her

dad's law firm. The offices took up two suites, with windows overlooking the east valley and the mountains; the wood paneling, brass fixtures, and carpet looked like the backdrop of every lawyer commercial she had ever seen. It smelled of old leather, paperwork and fresh coffee. There was even a big bookcase with legal tomes, which were probably there for show. The receptionist looked up in surprise, her eyes going from Annie, to Devon, and back again as she put on her best, professional 'what-the-hell' face.

"May I… help you?"

Annie, sans sunglasses, still had Devon tucked under her arm; the blind act wouldn't be needed here. "Annabelle Puckett to see William Puckett. I'm his bio-daughter, from his disastrous first marriage."

The woman blinked away her attitude and smiled awkwardly, "Yes of course, we arranged for your flight. Your father is in a meeting with clients and it may be awhile. Would you like to wait?" She motioned to some lovely leather couches by the door. The magazine selection ranged from gossip/fashion to fashion/gossip, plus *Time*, in case anyone cared.

"Actually, I need some legal assistance, it's part of the reason I'm in town." She looked around the office at the low cubicles with their hanging plants and busy people. "Dad mentioned that I might be able to talk to someone about research…" She really hadn't thought this through, but bullshitting was a talent of hers. "I just need to ask around, it'll only take a minute. I mean, we can bother him if you think that would be best, but it's kind of private, like family stuff, you know? I'd just rather not involve the whole firm. Could I wander a bit? I'll be quiet, I swear."

The woman looked from Annie to the duck again, trying to make sense out of the request, but the girl was already heading towards the office floor. The woman made as if to stop her, but thought the better of it; Annie *was* the boss's daughter, and blood was thicker than coffee after all.

Annie poked her nose in a few cubicles, finding the usual array of family photos, knickknacks and inspirational posters. A few female paralegals looked up at her as she walked past, but a male voice could be heard yammering on the phone. *Target acquired*, she thought, switching into Terminator mode. Annie peeked over the cubical wall and saw a head full of gelled hair and a shiny earphone. The man was youngish and well-dressed. His business clothes were neat and pressed, but his expensive shoes were up on the desk as he leaned back in his pneumatic chair. The desk was a shrine to Tiger Woods, with a room-full of golf paraphernalia packed into the limited space.

"Yeah bro... yeah. Ah, bro it was awesome. Totally showered, like a hailstorm... yeah, Goth chick or something, black and white stripes and a mini, looked like a prison dominatrix... Ship that shit back to high school, bish. Wez tryin' to class up the Square! Man, bro, she had a duck on a leash! No shit dude, a duck! I know, right? Like who walks around with a fuckin' duck..."

"Annabelle, this fool can help us. How very lucky... for us." Devon said softly.

Annie chose that moment to move into his field of view. The douche that showered her with ice was about her age, clean cut and well-dressed, but with an arrogant smirk etched on his face. That smirk vanished as he saw her, and he sat up quickly and ended his call. "Gotta go bro."

"Hey… bro," Annie said, savoring the moment. "Ain't this a bitch? It's like you can't abuse some random person anymore without them tracking you down."

"Look lady, I don't know what you think I did, but my dad is a junior partner here, so if you're harassing me in my workplace, then you're gonna have some serious legal problems." His threat gave him a bit of courage as he composed himself.

"Oh, your daddy works here too? How special. Did he buy you that silver pasta rocket with the 'Legal Eagle' license plate, or did you save up your allowance?"

The kid was smart, because his brain picked out the pertinent information. "Your dad works here?" he asked nervously.

"William Puckett," she said with little joy. It was rare that her father came in useful, but the name served to terrify the douche, and that's what was really important. "I'm his bio-daughter. Flesh… and *blood*." She leaned over the desk as Devon hissed menacingly.

"Oh," he said weakly. "Uh, look, it was a total misunderstanding, okay? I thought you were someone else, and…"

"Don't!" she slammed her hand on the desk, but kept her voice low. "Don't try to worm your way out of this. If you want to get back into my good graces, you can answer a question or two." She looked down at the duck before saying; "I want you to tell me about the *Arcana Curiae*."

The douche looked pale and began to sweat. He looked around the office as some of his coworkers began to take notice of his strange visitor and their quiet but intense conversation. "Look, I don't know anything about that," he stammered.

"Quack! Waakwaakwaak," Devon said, motioning with his bill.

"That ring on your finger means you were a member of the Silver Serpent club in law school, which helps train paralegals for extra-planar relations," she said. "As in demons. You deal with demon contracts."

The douche made a nervous laugh, attempting to brush her off. Annie set Devon on the desk and the duck gave him a baleful glare, his eyes glowing red. Suddenly, a blue flame surrounded him, and his webbed feet began scorching the paperwork. The douche jumped back and held up his hands in surrender. Devon's flame died down as quickly as it began.

"The *Arcana Curiae*," Annie said again. "I need to see it."

"Okay, okay," said the douche, breathlessly, not taking his eyes from Devon. "I can take you to it, just... don't tell my dad. Or yours." He got up, opened a drawer in the desk, and removed a key. "We uh, need to go to the basement." They walked past the receptionist, who looked up curiously. "I'm just taking Ms. Puckett down to the commissary to get a snack," he said. The three of them got into the elevator and the douche pushed the button, much to Devon's chagrin.

"So uh, what's with the duck?" he asked as Devon hissed at him. "Is he like a super-charged demon minion?"

"Quack!"

"Oh, he's not the minion, I'm kinda the minion. Devon here is a demon trapped in a duck's body." She hefted him as he glared at the man.

"Whoa," said the douche to the duck. "Bummer bro. So you've got to figure a way out of it, huh?"

"Quack," Devon said.

"Can you understand him?" he asked.

"Of course," she said, giving no further explanation.

The elevator reached the basement and the three of them stepped off into the dim hallway. Bare spiral light bulbs illuminated the space, casting pools of cold light on cold concrete. The place smelled like industrial solvent; the fresh scent of chemical pine trees lingered above the mildew. The douche lead the way past large electrical breakers, maintenance equipment and locked doors. He stopped before a door marked 'Private' and inserted the key.

Annie waited to be impressed; she held her breath, preparing for gloomy tunnels, flickering torches, ghoulish statues and arcane symbols. She braced herself for a cold breeze, a blast furnace of heat, the stench of tortured souls. She steeled her nerve to meet deadly traps, and ghastly creatures asking riddles in the dark. What she got was a small closet, a steel table and chair, and a single light bulb hanging over a ten-year old computer.

"This is it?" she asked. "This is the *Arcana Curiae?* This is the big secret place?"

The douche explained, "*Arcana Curiae* means Secrets of the Court. It's all on computers now; all you need is a connection to the secured network. Let me log you on..." he fired up the relic, which took a minute and a half to allow input, and he typed in his password. "Just shut it down when you're done. The door will lock behind you." He scratched his head nervously, "So... are we cool?"

"You have served... *for now*," said Annie, waving her hand dismissively. "Leave us." She was going to play this up. *Fear me, for I am the Keeper of the Duck.*

The paralegal gave Devon a last look before departing, closing them in the closet. The cooling fan whirred loudly in the dusty old computer tower, stirring the stale air.

"I wanted to frighten him more," said Devon moodily. "Also, he got to push the button."

Annie shrugged, "You can push it on the way up. That flame trick was pretty cool, by the way. I was impressed." She clicked the icon labeled 'AC' on the computer screen, opening the program with turtle-like slowness. *What was this processor speed, less than 800 MHz? 533?* She was prompted to enter a password, which Devon did with his bill. *Peck, peck, peck.* What came up was a simple application with a standard gray background and a few typing fields. Total turn of the century stuff. The screen read:

Welcome to the Arcana Curiae.
Please enter name and/or case number.
Press F12 to activate Search Assistant.

Annie pushed the F12 key and a little cartoon pitchfork with eyes popped up and blinked at her. *"Bloop! It looks like you're trying to find a case file. May I help?"*

"Ooo, how cute! It's like the paper clip guy." she said, clicking it to cycle through the funny animations. "I always liked Scribble the origami cat. I wonder why they got rid of these?"

Devon stared at the time-wasting animations, and indulged her for about ten seconds before cracking the whip.

Chapter 13
The Story of Θ

Devon poured over the contract for nearly an hour, muttering only when he needed Annie to scroll down or back up. It was a long, protracted document that looked like any other contract Annie had seen, sprinkled with headings, sub-headings, clauses, and Roman numerals. To Devon, it was as if he was reading about the rest of his life. The contract stipulated the terms of his imprisonment, as well as the fate that awaited him if any of the terms were broken. It was grim reading.

"As I feared, I cannot allow myself to be killed in combat or by accident; that would bind me into a life of eternal… ingestion."

"Indigestion?" Annie asked, having become rather sleepy and bored.

"INGESTION," he stressed. "Being eaten, being

stripped of all vitality and crapped out, only to be devoured again when I recover."

"Eeew. What about suicide again?" she asked.

"If I die by choice, my soul will be bound to servitude," he sighed. "That might include any number of tasks, depending on the needs of the owning demon."

"Gothraxess," Annie said, remembering the name of the Spider Queen who spun the World Wide Web.

"For now," he replied. "She may sell my contract if she so wishes."

"So why is the punishment worse if you die fighting for your life? Why fight at all?"

"Hope," he said, "There is the hope that we might find a way out. Demons are individualists and gamblers by nature; most would try to avoid such a fate, as I am."

"Just like most people."

"Quite," he said, "Besides, if we keep fighting amongst ourselves, it only serves Gothraxess. She gets the souls of the defeated in a weakened state, but she will feed on them eventually."

"Maybe trapped demons should all like, put aside your differences and work together?"

"Yes, and maybe you humans should do the same with all your problems," he said. "Sounds simple, doesn't it?"

"Hmph. Yeah, I see what you mean."

"Anyway, there are very few loopholes, as one might expect." Devon tapped the 'page down' key a few times. "The spell that trapped me forms a binding contract between Gothraxess and the ones who used it…"

"The kids you killed," Annie reminded him.

"Yesss…" he drawled in annoyance. "So obviously, they cannot be coerced into fulfilling any of the special obligations that might-"

"Because you ate them."

"I know! Stop rubbing it in," he complained, taking a moment to smooth his feathers. "It seems that once I left the summoning circle, I accepted the 'freedom' provided by Gothraxess, even though that freedom meant being trapped as a duck. She used an ancient clause written into the Conjuration Proviso to justify it, and it seems to be legally binding…"

"What about a loophole?"

"I can attempt to make a counter-offer that would be more appealing to her, although that would have to be something long-lasting and potent. A media sensation, so to speak." Devon brooded in silence.

"Okay," said Annie, "enough about you, what about me? I want to see if some demon has my soul under contract." She nudged the duck in her lap.

"Hmm, yes," said Devon as he cleared the form field. Annie typed in her name and answered a few questions to narrow down the search. Her name indeed came up, causing her breath to catch in her throat, and her pulse to quicken. *Shit. There I am.*

"Shit," she said, "There I am."

"Let us see what we have," Devon said, sounding casual, like a dentist poking in her mouth, as Annie scrolled nervously down the page. "Upon turning eighteen, the legal age of consent in your area, you signed up for a credit card."

"Is that a demon contract?" she asked quietly.

Devon scoffed, "What do *you* think? It seems that you were responsible enough and paid your balance… Yes, and canceled it before the terms came to pass. Lucky you."

Annie let out a sigh of relief.

"And here, we have a video rental membership… boring. Nothing but classic foreign films… no problems there," he said.

"Bueller Big Video's membership is a demon contract?" she cried.

"How do you think they kept the corporate competition out for so long?" the duck replied. "Don't worry; according to the terms, you'd have to be *weeks* overdue to invoke the contract… Unless it's a Madonna film…? Interesting."

"Wow," she said, "I'm canceling that like, today."

"Let's see… there is a long list of websites, but nothing binding; you are on the mailing list for several demonic entities however. Ah, here we are; you joined a website called 'Hung-Dynasty' a few years back…"

"Hey, I can explain that," Annie said, jerking upright. "A friend of mine in Phoenix was in a band called Hung Dynasty, and I just entered their web address wrong. It came up with-"

"Gay Asian porn," Devon said, as he read the screen.

"I didn't know!" she complained, "I was looking for the band!"

"And you had no choice but to enter your credit card information and purchase a membership," he said.

She glared for a moment before snapping, "Don't you judge me, duck!"

"Oh, we demons don't judge, Annabelle Puckett. We like you just the way you are." Devon replied, smiling as much as he was able. "According to this, you never purchased the platinum membership; it seems you are safe. Cheapskate."

"Well, it wasn't as 'hung' as I thought it would be," she moped. "So I'm in the clear?"

"So far," The duck nodded and scrolled down. "Hmm, here's something."

She looked at the screen, "Oh no. Tell me they don't have me over that."

"Time Vampires?" asked Devon.

"It's a computer game, the Massively Multiplayer Online kind, real addictive. You either play as vampires, or time-traveling vampire hunters. I was on that for like, four years." Annie looked sullen, then brightened a bit as she got nostalgic. "I played an Egyptian vamp named Desdemona; she was so awesome. I got her to level 80 in Victorian England, then the Carpathian expansion came out, and all my purple gear was like, worthless…"

"Yes, I'm sure it was a tragedy. Total time played: nine months, two weeks, four days, twelve hours and seven minutes." Devon commented as he read the text, "Impressive, I suppose."

"So I'm going to Hell?"

"According to the terms and agreements, only certain players invoke the demon contract based on their in-game actions." He read further, "Insulting someone's mother, spreading jokes about recently deceased celebrities, 'griefing' or starting a 'flame war' whatever that means, taking the name of Chuck Norris in vain… hmm, *him* again…"

"O-M-G, most gamers do all of that at least once." Annie paled. "My whole guild, all my online friends… going to Hell."

"Not necessarily. This particular contract is bound to the game, so the contractual agreement lasts only as long as the game does."

"So, if Time Vampires gets canned, we're all free and clear?" she asked hopefully.

He nodded, "Unless you die before then."

"Well, that's good news isn't it? All I have to do is outlive a major MMO. No problem; those things tank all the time." She sagged in her chair, thinking of all the times she almost died in the last few days. "I suppose that's the easy way?"

"Well, no," Devon said, "You can try to refer five new subscribers in an attempt to buy out your contract, but only if you request form A-5790 from the customer service department…"

"I'm not sacrificing others to get me out of trouble," Annie said defensively. "I'd rather try to take down the whole game and save everyone."

"Very noble, Annabelle Puckett," he deadpanned, "You are my hero."

"Shush, duck."

Annie and Devon didn't bother to return to the law office; they had gotten what they needed, and there was no reason to hang around. Besides, the douche paralegal might try to get on her good side, and she was too tired to deal with him now. As for her father, she doubted he would take it hard if she ducked out on lunch. If he dared to make an issue out of it, she had years of bitter, emotional ammunition to unload on him on that front. He likely wouldn't; not because he was decent or sorry, but because he favored ignoring such things rather than being hypocritically indignant.

She donned her sunglasses, leashed the duck, and let him push the Up button before leading her out of the elevator past the security guard. She waved in the man's general direction on the way out. *Seeing-eye duck*, she thought. *Awesome.*

The Douche was apparently on his lunch break, for she

heard the chirp of a car alarm being deactivated, and saw him talking on his earphone as he swung the door open and got in with one smooth movement. It would have been graceful, if not for the slippery duck shit on his tan colored bucket seat.

Annie grinned wickedly, *Revenge is mine, sucka.*

Annie decided to spend the rest of the day at home, even though the mall was beckoning her and she had her dad's credit card. Knowing that a demon had her soul under contract had taken the fight out of her, and she just wanted to sleep, letting her troubles soak into her pillow with the drool. Shopping, her normal therapy, just sounded like work. Besides, she had at least three weeks to visit the local malls and spend herself into happiness. Her stay in Scottsdale would be long and grueling, but it was better than having TV cameras in her face and reporters haunting her every step.

Devon's eyes had grown tired from staring at computer screens, and his feet hurt. Waddling on concrete was not comfortable at all, and he suspected he might be developing corns. He would have asked Annie to carry him during their excursion, but she was adamant about 'leash laws' and the need to keep him tethered like a pet. He resolved himself to look up the city's ordinances later.

Before letting her collapse on the bed, he bade his minion to set up the entertainment system to keep him entertained. He needed a distraction to take his mind away from his dismal fate. Annie picked out a selection of movies from her father's DVD library and loaded five of them into the machine. Apparently they would play in succession, keeping the big screen active for nearly ten hours. If that didn't take his mind off of things, nothing would.

The first movie began, and the title appeared over a large airplane landing at night. *'Die Hard' is it? This should be interesting*, he thought. The protagonist seemed to have a fear of flying, to which Devon could relate. The man seated next to him on the crowded plane then offered advice to calm his nerves: go barefoot on the carpet and make "fists with your toes."

Devon looked down at his webbed feet and sighed. *Must be an ape thing.*

The next two weeks were a drudgery, albeit a luxurious drudgery. Annie's father made little daily effort to check on her well-being, mostly leaving her alone and keeping meal conversations neutral and non-invasive. This was supposed to be a safe haven and retreat after all; an escape from the horrors of her recent experience. Amanda made a habit of asking Annie about her day at dinnertime, to which Annie would respond with practiced courtesy. It was like she was an exchange student living with a host family in a foreign country; there was little she had in common with these people, and they would hardly understand her if she decided to share. At least the food was good.

Estela was an excellent cook, though she was growing more and more suspicious of the duck that sat and watched movies all day long. Annie would go out daily, walking around Old Town, or visiting different malls, seeing movies and shopping with her dad's card. Devon was neither needed, nor inclined to go out, so he sat down in the basement and played movie critic for the films Annie set up for him. Estela would watch him out of the corner of her eye while she cleaned or did laundry. Taco was always present as well, sitting on the opposite end of the couch when he was feeling particularly brave.

When Annie would come home from her day's adventures, she would set Devon up with the computer, close the door, and quickly fall asleep. The duck would spend the next few hours doing research, pecking on the keyboard and nudging the mouse with his bill. His suspicions had been confirmed; there were no laws requiring ducks to wear leashes in public, and he confronted his minion when she woke up.

"I don't know what to tell you," Annie had said in her defense. "They must have loosened restrictions... it's been years since I lived around here..."

"Do not try to deceive me, Annabelle Puckett. The laws only apply to dogs and other potentially vicious creatures-"

"Hey, you freaking qualify as vicious, pal!"

"Ducks are not even listed as livestock! They are beneath the notice of your *leash laws*," he sneered, "and they roam freely in public, be they wild or tame! There are two in the swimming pool right now; your step-sister calls them 'Plucky Duck and Shirley McLoon'!"

"Clever," she scoffed. "I bet she still watches cartoons..."

"*You* watch cartoons."

"That's anime! It's *different!*"

"No more leash, Annabelle Puckett. I forbid it. You will carry me about if we must go out in public together and not in that fiendish 'pet carrier' either. Do I make myself clear?"

"Yes, *master,*" she snarled.

"Take care that you remember your place," Devon

said. "It may save your life one day." She stormed off in a huff, slamming her bedroom door. The girl was defiant and unruly, that was certain, but Devon was sure he could bring her to heel.

For the next week, the DVD player showed the original *Planet of the Apes* movies. Charlton Heston, upon learning this upside-down world was a product of his own people's folly, shouted "Ah, damn you! God damn you all to Hell!"

Oh touché, Annabelle Puckett, he thought grudgingly. *Touché.*

The two week vacation was almost over, and Devon was at a loss. His nights were filled with web searches for the spider queen, and his days were spent in front of the big screen TV, nodding off occasionally. One afternoon, he awoke from his couch nap to find the TV and DVD player off. Had Annie come home? It was rather early for that; she usually stayed out until around dinner. He called for Annie, but snores from the bedroom were her only reply. Estela was vacuuming somewhere upstairs; she seemed to avoid the basement if possible, and bits of down were starting to collect around the couch.

He sat quietly, examining the remote control on the end table. He had been rather intimidated by all the little buttons, but there was little else to do, so he began to experiment. It had a button marked 'TV/Cable' and one marked 'Power.' Easy enough. He pecked the buttons and the screen powered on. Next, he studied the volume and channel buttons. *It seems most of these buttons are unnecessary*, he reasoned. Soon he had the volume to a comfortable level and began channel surfing.

Taco the Chihuahua eyed him warily from the corner of the room, unsure of what to make of the duck that could command the moving pictures like a human. The little dog whimpered and curled nose to tail, not taking his eyes off him.

There was a vast array of mindless programming on hundreds of channels, very little of it interesting enough to distract Devon's thoughts. One channel featured a plucky cartoon duck getting blown up by a smug rabbit. Ugh. Bad memories.

Click.

A tiny, beautiful woman with a huge smile was demonstrating how to cook rich Italian food that she didn't look like she ever ate. She made the process strangely appealing though... and he was getting hungry.

Click.

A silly-looking, winged, snake-headed centaur was attacking a pair of actors whose careers had probably seen better days. To Devon's disappointment, neither actor was eaten immediately.

Click.

Young, attractive idiots were engaged in a sleazy, drama-ridden courtship, sprinkled with rambling cast interviews about how sleazy and drama-ridden it all was.

Click.

According to 'The History Channel,' aliens *may* have been responsible for just about everything. Even the Nazis. And Bigfoot. Why not.

Click.

There was a movie set in modern times, with cars, machine guns, and tanks, but Devon recognized the dialog as Shakespeare's 'Richard III.' *Oh, damnation.*

Click.

Zombies.

Click.

Sports.

Click.

Sports commentary.

Click.

Sports zombies.

Click!

A pleasant looking, middle-aged woman with dark skin and wide-set eyes filled the screen. She was choked with emotion, speaking to an audience, as a female voice narrated the scene.

"...will be ending her long running television talk show next season, bringing an era to a close. The announcement came as a surprise to her millions of faithful viewers who had come to depend on the show as a vital part of their daily lives..."

Devon moved to peck the channel button, but something stopped him. He looked back up at the vast screen as the montage continued.

"...a career spanning decades, from her early days in local news and acting, to building a vast media empire based on kindness, charity and understanding. Her influence could make instant careers, and her book club's featured picks could be guaranteed a top spot on the New York Times Best Seller's List..."

He blinked at the screen, his bill agape. He turned up the volume.

"...their long-time romance had teetered on the brink of marriage, but both insist that they share a 'spiritual union' with no need to make it official. When asked about having children of her own, media's reigning

queen turns attention to her South African school for underprivileged girls, calling the over 400 students enrolled 'her daughters'…"

Devon began to shiver and Taco started to growl.

"…so influential that her endorsements helped to elect the first African American President of the United States, likely delivering over a million votes. News of her fledgling worldwide media network, called 'OWN', continues to spread, promising that her work and influence will go on into the future…"

Taco rose to his feet and barked. Devon quickly turned off the television, lest the woman see him through the screen. He heard a muttered curse behind him, and he turned to see Estela at the top of the stairs, staring at him horrified.

"El pato del Diablo…" she said in a hoarse whisper, crossing herself and making warding gestures as she backed up the stairs. Taco bounded to Devon's side, baring his teeth and yapping at the frightened woman. Devon flinched as the rat dog stood beside him, then he flapped off the couch and went to wake Annie. He would worry about the maid later.

"Annabelle Puckett! I have found her! I have found Gothraxess!" he cried, beating his wings about her head, making her wake with a jolt.

"Whhaagah! Dammit duck, what's the big deal?" Her cheek was glistening with drool and her pigtails were askew.

"Gothraxess! I have found her earthly form!" he stammered with excitement, "She… the TV… I saw it, I saw it! She holds millions of minds in her sway! She makes people famous with a wave of her hand! She has hundreds of adopted daughters, but will not take a mate, lest she devour him!"

Annie sat up alert, wondering what shape the demon had acquired and how they had missed it. And why was Taco on her bed? "So who is she?"

"I cannot speak her name, or she will know it," Devon said in a hushed voice, "She must not be named!"

"Okaaay," Annie said, "Can you give me a hint? Who is She-Who-Must-Not-Be-Named?"

Devon looked about the room as if the walls had ears, and whispered, "Her initials are O-"

"*Oprah?*"

Devon hissed in alarm, ruffling his feathers. At that moment the television in the bedroom came on. "Coming up next, the Best of the Oprah Winfrey Show..." Devon squawked, and Annie looked for the remote. Taco was sitting on it innocently, looking as surprised as the rest of them.

She took it from under the dog, sniffed it, and hit the power button with her fingernail. The screen went blank, but Devon was more frightened than ever.

"She knows! She knows we know, and she knows we know she knows it!" He hopped about in little circles, "Ooooh, she will have her eyes upon us, she will see..."

"Look," Annie said, "It's O-" Devon hissed. "Um sorry, Gothraxess we're talking about, not like, Sauron or something. There's no unblinking, flaming eye over her house."

"You are right," Devon said, "She is not like Sauron. He is fictional; she is real. Her senses extend through a web of influence that spans the world. She calls her new media network 'OWN.' *OWN!* The gall of it!" He shook his head, "And by the by, Sauron had only one eye; she has eight."

"Oh right," she said, "spider queen. So, like what, we're supposed to avoid all contact with her fans? Not read *O Magazine*?"

"Her fans are legion," Devon said gloomily, "so that will be difficult. As for her magazine, I seriously doubt you read it anyway."

Annie frowned for a moment. "Was that a cheap shot?"

"I simply meant that you are very much your own person. From my observations, the standards of society and fashion have little hold over you."

Annie frowned again. "Was that *another* cheap shot?"

"Take it as you will," Devon said, regaining some of his calm. He fluttered off the bed and into his playpen, where he began to preen his ruffled feathers. Taco tried to follow, but was thwarted by the high sides and netting.

The cathedral doorbell rang upstairs, and Estela could be heard muttering as she went to answer it. She conversed briefly with whomever it was, her high voice mixing with lower melodious tones. The front door closed, but the voices remained. *Were they both speaking Spanish?* Annie lay back on the bed as she tried to gauge the depth of the shit-hole she was in. *Media mogul She-Who-Must-Not-Be-Named. Could anyone beat these odds?*

Estela called from above, "Mees Annie?"

Then the new voice spoke briefly, and there was nothing further from the maid.

Annie called back, "Yeah?" No answer. She got up and left the bedroom, turning towards the staircase. Standing above her at the top of the stairs was a familiar presence; thin and lanky, pale and gorgeous, with mused hair and a charming half-smile. Estela was lying on the floor behind him, possibly asleep, possibly dead.

172

Annie paled, "Fake Blake!" she gasped, loud enough for Devon to hear.

"Hello Annie," said the demon within the college boy's body. His eyes glowed red with a faint inner fire as he smiled.

The shit-hole just got a lot deeper.

Chapter 14
Battle of the Basement

Fake Blake slowly descended the stairs, his fingers playfully brushing the handrail. The demon seemed to have a certain confidence and style that the real Blake lacked, making the change eerie to behold, but kinda sexy. There really *was* a different person in there. He looked James-Dean-cool in his jeans and light jacket. He wore a black concert tee covered with skulls; Annie couldn't make out the band, not like it mattered.

She backed away, moving towards the middle of the large space, away from the guest room where Devon was trying to stay hidden. In his weakened state, he would be easy prey for a demon that possessed a human voice, and could cast magic spells. All Devon could do was quack; although he could be understood by other demons, it wouldn't do for using magic. Now the tables had turned, and Fake Blake held all the chess pieces. The shoe was afoot, the game had dropped, the fox had crossed the chicken, and the metaphors were mixing hopelessly. Annie's mind raced for a plan and kept coming up with one word: Panic.

"Where is your fowl companion?" the demon asked, reaching the foot of the stairs. "I expect you took him with you when you fled Bueller, being his minion and all. Is he still using you like a familiar?" Fake Blake looked around, his eyes wandering towards the doors to the laundry and guest bedroom. "It takes some getting used to doesn't it, having all that raw power coursing through you?"

"Yeah," she said, grasping at a desperate lie, "he keeps having me redo that protection charm… hurts like hell every time."

"Oh Annie dear," said Fake Blake in honeyed tones, "You have no idea how much Hell can hurt." He sniffed the air deeply; "The duck only made you do it once. I sense your protection is fading even now; the minor spells on the house could barely distract me as I entered." He moved to the door of the guest room and looked in. "Ah! There you are, my web-footed friend. That's quite a charming enclosure you've been set up in. Very festive, what with all the little dancing sheep."

"Yes," said Devon, "I chose it out of thousands. It's the little details that count, isn't it?" Taco the Chihuahua yapped menacingly at the figure in the doorway, as Devon made ready to flap out of his playpen.

"I agree," said Fake Blake, "which is why I'm here. There was one little detail that went unresolved during our last meeting."

While Fake Blake's attention was on Devon, Annie searched for anything to use as a weapon. Unfortunately, the home theater was made for comfort, not self-defense; the plush pillows and remote control would make poor missiles. The wet bar across the room though, now *that* was an arsenal; thick shot glasses, heavy bottles of booze that could be lit on fire, all behind good cover. *Would fire hurt him? Probably not.* She began inching towards the wet bar.

Fake Blake turned on her, and stretching out his hand, spoke a phrase in some strange language. It might have been ancient Sumerian, Aramaic, or Esperanto for all Annie knew, but the effect was terrifying; she was lifted off her feet by an invisible hand that tightened around her neck. She reached for the phantom hand; her frantic fingers felt pebbly skin, bony joints, and tendons like steel cable. She felt sharp talons at her throat, but could see nothing at all. Her boots kicked helplessly in the air as she gasped for breath.

Devon flapped out of his playpen and over the bed, dodging as Fake Blake uttered a smiting spell, shattering the TV screen. Taco scooted under the bed while Devon formed a plan. His minion was no good to him dead, so the first phase was to rescue her. He charged and took to the air, flapping towards Fake Blake's face while Taco lunged at his ankles. The demon sneered at the distraction, kicking the small dog away as he grabbed Devon by his long neck. The duck ignited himself, searing Fake Blake's hand and forcing him to release his hold. The young man's grasp on Annie vanished as well, and she dropped to the floor, gasping. Devon darted between Fake Blake's legs and hid behind a couch, and Annie crawled behind the wet bar.

"Pathetic, really pathetic," Fake Blake said. "You're just delaying the inevitable, you know. I've anticipated every possibility. You will both die here." He positioned himself before the stairs, blocking any escape.

"Perhaps we could come to an accord," Devon called from behind one of the leather couches, "We have important information about Gothraxess and her identity on this plane. We could work together to free ourselves." He waited for a response, adding, "We also know the specific terms of the spell that entrapped us. You could be free to return to Hell without consequence."

Green flame sprung from Fake Blake's hands as he prepared to attack, "If you two geniuses uncovered that, I'm sure I can do the same without much trouble." He circled slowly around the couch, searching for a glimpse of white feathers. "You'll have to do better than that."

"Annabelle Puckett, do you remember the protection spell?" Devon called hopefully.

"Uh, not really," she replied. "The pain kinda wiped out little details like that." She peeked over the bar and saw Fake Blake preparing to fling a green fireball over the couch. She grabbed a bottle of scotch and threw it with all her might, hoping it wouldn't scar him too badly. She wanted to hurt the demon, not the cute guy he was possessing. Fake Blake ducked under the bottle as it hit the wall, but the potent booze splashed on his back and shoulders. Snarling, he shook out the flames in his hand before they could ignite the alcohol.

"Quickly, you must cast the spell!" Devon called, as he moved towards the wet bar. "Repeat after me…"

"Duck!" Annie cried.

"What?"

"DUCK!"

"WHAT??" he shouted, as Fake Blake threw a plush pillow and hit him with considerable force, knocking him off his webbed feet. Feathers flew into the air.

Annie winced, "I meant 'Devon, duck!' Sorry…" It would have been funny if it weren't life and death. Hell, it was *still* kinda funny. The demon leaped on the couch and made to pounce on Devon, but Annie countered with a barrage of heavy scotch tumblers, scoring a hit on Blake's head. Of course, the other four glasses missed smashing into the enormous TV screen.

His scalp bleeding, the demon flung a smiting spell as Annie ducked reflexively. The spell hit the mirror behind her, causing it to shatter and shower her with broken glass. Fake Blake let out a deafening roar, causing the wet bar to shudder, and Annie's nerves to become totally frazzled. It was like shell shock; the power of the sound made her unable to think straight. She couldn't even hear herself scream.

Devon's eyes flared red as he regained his wits, looking up at the demon standing over him. He could feel the power churning within his feathered body, unable to be released due to a lack of vocal chords. All he could manage was a few parlor tricks, unless his minion could be used to channel the magic. Unfortunately, she was curled in a ball and screaming, not being of much use to anyone. She didn't look injured, but it was only a matter of time before Fake Blake flouted the demon rules of conduct and killed her outright. Devon twisted to his feet and stood, extending his wings to touch the young man's blue jeans. A blue blaze sprung from his feathers, catching on the denim as Devon fanned the flames. The fire leaped up his pants, igniting the scotch on his back as it spread rapidly about his torso. Fake Blake cried out in anguish and pain, spinning as he tried to get out of his jacket. Devon scampered to Annie's side, pecking her cheek to get her attention.

"Annabelle Puckett! The spell! Repeat: *a posse ad esse...*"

"Apsswwuh," she muttered. She was bleeding from numerous minor cuts, and her eyes were unfocused. In her present condition the protection spell might kill her, and Devon wanted to avoid that if possible. After all, she was the only human he knew that could understand him, and she was already trained, sort of.

Fake Blake tossed his jacket on the tile floor of the laundry room as he patted out the flames on his legs. The theater reeked of booze and burnt hair, and the smoke alarm began shrieking, adding to the bedlam. Devon peeked out from cover, fanning Annie with his wings as she regained her wits. They had precious few seconds to do something clever. The wet bar was hardly a safe place to hide; they were surrounded by alcohol that could be ignited with one well-placed fireball, Annie had thrown most of the tumblers, and unless they could get a priest to bless the soda water, they were out of options.

Blake had finally extinguished the flames with a spell, but his eyes were now glowing fiercely with a red fire of their own. He was chanting to himself in low tones, his hands held out to his sides. Devon felt the deep magic being invoked and knew that whatever was coming, it would be impossible to escape.

Annie groaned and looked around. "Is he gone? Did we win?"

The wet bar flew to pieces, scattering about the theater and exposing them. Before either could move, they were imprisoned in a sphere of fiery energy that glowed where it overlapped the floor and wall; the smell of brimstone filled their lungs, stinging their eyes. *Trapped.*

Fake Blake smiled devilishly as the sphere closed on them, becoming more and more confining by the second. "Not bad for a duck," he said, "You lasted a full minute longer than I thought you would. As for dear Annie, I think I'll save her for later. Imagine the fun we could have."

Annie whimpered, "Is it too late for that protection spell?"

Devon sighed, "Kind of."

From behind Fake Blake, Taco the Chihuahua crept from the bedroom. His eyes glowed with a feral light, and he bared his teeth soundlessly. His fur trembled, parting to reveal a scaly, reptilian hide of black and violet; his body grew rapidly, as venomous slaver dripped from his large fangs; soon, he was the size of a Rottweiler hound, but with a distinctly more hellish appearance. Devon and Annie watched with widening eyes as the creature readied itself to pounce.

"What... the.... *fuck?*" Annie exclaimed, beginning to tremble. "*That* is no Chihuahua."

"It is a Hell Hound, albeit a rather small one," Devon whispered. "I was wondering what Blake meant about the minor spells on the house…"

Fake Blake sensed something behind him just a moment too late, as Taco the Hell Hound leaped upon him, sinking his fangs into the lad's shoulder. He struggled briefly, but soon sank to his knees, his body going limp within seconds. The energy bubble surrounding Devon and Annie vanished with a pop as Fake Blake lost consciousness.

"Paralyzing venom," Devon explained, waddling towards the limp form and the beast standing over him, its forked tongue lolling as it panted. "Demons are immune, but not the bodies they possess. I imagine he is in there now, wondering what I am going to do with him." The duck peered into the unfocused eyes of Fake Blake, a quacking laugh escaping his bill.

"Suddenly the tough guy," Annie smirked. "He almost had us, Devon. He almost walked in and killed us both." She turned off the smoke alarm so she could hear herself think. "We're frickin' lucky that Taco here is on our side… which makes no *goddamn sense*, by the way! Why is there a Hell Hound in my dad's house?"

Devon looked at the top of the stairs and said, "Ask your stepmother."

Amanda and Tiffany were looking down upon the scene in shock, arms full of designer shopping bags, ignoring the poor housekeeper laying at their feet.

"Annie, honey…" Amanda began, "What's going on here?" Her voice was uncertain, as if she was deciding how much ignorance to feign.

"Succubi," Devon said. "That makes sense. They are attracted to wealthy, powerful men of great virility, although their victims don't last very long…"

"Succubi?" Annie cried, looking from mother to daughter. "Both of them?"

Tiffany whispered to her mother, "I think she's talking to the duck."

"Aren't you wondering why there's a Hell Hound in your basement?" Annie asked accusingly, but Taco had reverted to his pocket-sized form. "Hey, don't you even pretend, you 'Ghostbusters' reject!" she scolded the innocent-looking animal, who yapped in protest.

"Annie dear, I can explain… I think you and that young man had a little too much to drink." Amanda set down her shopping and came down the stairs, her voice became alluring, convincing in an unearthly way. "Too much drink mixed with watching scary movies on a state-of-the-art entertainment system, that's all it was…" She winced as she saw the damage to the big screen and surrounding walls.

Devon said to Annie, "She is attempting to charm you. Repeat the spell: *A posse ad esse, absolutum dominium.*"

Annie repeated the words, bracing herself for a mind-numbing pain, but felt only a rush of muscle soreness from her head to her toes. Apparently Devon had dialed back the intensity.

"Annie dear," Amanda said with disapproval, "have you been dabbling in the Dark Arts?" Her voice held a hint of threat, and Tiffany descended behind her mother, a cruel expression on her fashion-model face. "Your father always said you were such a good girl, despite your morbid fashion sense."

"Yeah well, don't you ever watch movies?" Annie said with bravado, "Goths and gypsies all know magic. Mess with us at your own risk."

"It's the duck, mother." Tiffany said, her face radiating cold, petulant beauty, "He's a demon familiar. He's giving her the power."

"Not quite, silicone sister!" Annie barked, "The duck is dynamite."

"Quack wack waack wack." Devon said.

Annie nodded, "He's a genuine demon, and so is this kid here. They had a little problem with a summoning gone bad, and they're trying to get back to Hell. That's why I'm in the middle of a murder scandal back home, and that's why your little Taco here was so eager to help us."

Devon, The Demon Duck From Hell

"Quack quack wack wack!"

"And Devon says Hell Hounds serve the most powerful demon first. That means him, so back off!"

The Chihuahua stepped between his new master and the succubi, emitting a threatening little growl that wouldn't frighten a bunny. Amanda and Tiffany stared at Taco, fear in their eyes as they backed away.

Annie, Devon, Amanda and Tiffany were all sitting around the dinner table as Estela served coffee, apologizing again for her fainting spell. She hadn't been allowed to see the disaster downstairs, or the young man who was bound, gagged, and unconscious on the couch. Amanda gave her the rest of the day off to go home and sleep, although the little woman warned her employer about 'el pato del diablo' before she departed. Once they were alone, they had their first real talk.

"So why are you with my dad?" Annie asked accusingly.

Amanda sipped her coffee and shrugged, "The usual reasons; financial security, stability, a nice zip code, unlimited credit."

"But you're a succubus, right?" Annie asked, "Aren't they like, sex demons or something? Don't you feed off men?"

Tiffany smirked and Amanda said, "We have our needs, like everyone, dear. But don't worry about your father; he's not my only source of sustenance."

"So you cheat on him." She shook her head. Poor dad. She wasn't his biggest fan but still... kinda served him right, actually.

Amanda laughed, "If I didn't, he would dry up like a mummy, the poor dear. I love your father, believe it or not. You have no idea how hard it is to find a good man who knows how to turn a blind eye despite his ego."

"Yeah, dad's got a soulful pair of blind eyes," Annie said. "You know he cheated on mom, right?"

"Oh, he doesn't cheat on me, dear. I keep him happy, and I can't go sharing my food source with other... women."

"Quack," Devon commented.

"You use a spell on him to keep him faithful." Annie repeated.

Amanda shrugged, "A girl does what she has to. Besides, I need to mark him as mine, lest others try and take advantage of the poor dear."

It took Annie a moment to understand. "You mean there are more succubuses-"

"Succubi," Tiffany corrected.

"Whatever. There are *more* of you in Scottsdale?" Annie asked.

The mother and daughter shared a laugh, and Amanda replied, "Oh my, yes! It's perfect! The posh lifestyles, everyone trying so hard to impress each other, the superficial relationships... the summer heat."

"Oh, the heat is wonderful," Tiffany said. "Check my tan." She pulled at her collar to expose golden skin and a pink bra strap. Annie smirked, folding her arms in a vain attempt to hide her pale skin.

A thought struck her and she asked Tiffany, "So you like, hunt elsewhere, right? I mean, there's no 'Jerry Springer' shit going on, is there?"

"Gross!" Tiffany said, offended, "This isn't Arkansas, sweetie! I can find my own guys, thank you very much." She might have been a junior demon, but she acted just like a typical teenage girl. Go figure.

Amanda said, "We're not exactly monsters by most standards. In fact, some guys even find the wings and tail kind of kinky."

"Whoa, TMI." Annie said. "I don't need to know the details." Devon chuckled in his ducky way. "I just want to make sure my dad is gonna be safe with you two here."

"Safer than without us," Amanda said. "There are spells on the house to ward off those with evil intent. Although they weren't strong enough to stop a demon-possessed young man, or even a duck, they work fine with mortals. Besides, security is usually very good."

"Some cute guys, too." Tiffany added mischievously.

Annie smiled uncomfortably at Tiffany, then asked her stepmother, "Is his soul in danger because of you?"

"He's a lawyer, dear." Amanda chuckled, as if that answered everything. "Anyway, we don't trade in souls like the greater demons. We deal in more earthly, tangible commodities."

"Yeah, I'm sure you both have ATM cards for the sperm bank," Annie quipped. The women were not as offended as she'd hoped. *Ewww.*

"I'm sure you of all people know what it is to be prejudged," Amanda said, reaching for Annie's hand. The girl tensed, but didn't pull away. The woman's perfume was subtle and heady, or maybe it was her power to put mortals at ease. "We just want a good life, without any complications. And we had that until you arrived," she smiled gently and sat back. "Now, what do you intend to do about the boy in the basement?"

Annie looked at Devon, who quacked a little sentence for her to translate. "I guess we're gonna take him back to Bueller and try to find the others in his coven who helped with the summoning. Devon says we can try to exorcise the demon, since I won't let him eat Blake."

Amanda nodded, "I can arrange for a flight back if you like."

"Quack." Devon quacked.

"That'd be great," Annie said.

"*Quack!*"

"Don't be such a baby!" Annie told him. "It's safer to fly."

"You might want to take Taco with you," Amanda said sadly. "We'll miss him, but you'll need him more than we will."

"Thanks," Annie said. "How are you gonna explain the basement to dad?"

Amanda and Tiffany just smiled at each other. "The two of us can convince a man that day is night. I wouldn't worry about the mess in the basement."

Annie decided she didn't need to know the specifics. Either way, her dad was probably luckier than he deserved.

Then she wondered if he was one of those freaks who liked the tail and wings. She shuddered at the visual, wishing she could poke out her mind's eye and scrub her brain clean.

Chapter 15
Deals Are Made To Be Broken

Mr. Puckett got home late that evening as the workmen were leaving; both of them smiling guiltily as they tipped their hats and drove away. He entered the house, following the sound of voices downstairs to the home theater. He found his wife talking to Annie and some college kid he had never seen before. The kid was looking strangely uncomfortable with the tiny family dog on his lap. The basement was a bit of a disaster; wood splinters were lodged in the walls, the leather couches had been scorched and nicked by debris, and there were stains everywhere. The room smelled like smoke, burnt fabric, and booze. His eyes darted in panic to the bar, but aside from strange marks on the wall and carpet, the bar looked perfectly fine. It even looked a bit… new.

"What... the... hell?" he asked, noticing the bits of glass in the ceiling. "Was there an accident?" he checked over Annie and the new kid for signs of injury, more out of concern for his liability that anything. Annie looked fine, but the kid had his shirt torn at the shoulder, stained with a little blood and some yellow-green discoloration. His jacket, which was bundled on the couch next to him, looked burned.

Amanda greeted him with a kiss on the cheek. She was wearing 'factory distressed' jean shorts, an old college tee, and a baseball cap. She looked like a do-it-yourself housewife in a late night hardware store commercial. "Oh darling, you missed all the excitement!" she said perkily. "There was some freak accident with the carbonation tank and *boom*! No more wet bar. But I made it all better. The men came and replaced it free of charge, and they're paying for all the repairs to the walls and furniture. Isn't that nice?"

Her voice was so alluring that even Annie almost believed it. *Wow, that's a wicked power. She must never get a speeding ticket, like, ever.*

"What... is that a burn mark on the carpet?" Mr. Puckett's eyes went immediately to the big screen plasma TV, as if it was his baby. There were three cracks in the glass, as if several objects had been flung at it, probably by the explosion. He ran his hand over his face, as if the scene might disappear or change. "Where's Tiffany?" he asked absently, his voice shaking.

"Upstairs, taking a shower," Amanda said. Tiffany the demon slut had done her part in the deal, and thinking about it made Annie's skin crawl.

"Okay, okay..." he looked at his bio-daughter again, this time concerned for her well-being. "Annie, are you

188

all right? You look terrible."

Annie felt terrible. Devon had used her to cast a protection spell on themselves, and a binding spell on Fake Blake, temporarily keeping him from using magic. The two spells were powerful and hurt like mad, but Annie just answered, "Cramps." That always made dad change the subject.

"Who are you?" Mr. Puckett asked Fake Blake, who looked down at the tiny dog in his lap as if for permission to speak.

"This is Blake, daddy. He's from Bueller too. We were gonna give him a ride back tonight." Annie said.

"Are you hurt?" he asked, looking at the torn shirt.

Fake Blake shook his head and managed a "No," before Taco yipped at him, making him jump. That was good enough for Mr. Puckett, legally speaking.

Amanda said, "I was hoping you would take Annie and her friend to the airport tonight. Oh, and our little Taco is going with them. Say, nine o'clock?"

"Tonight?" dad said distractedly. "Tonight at nine? Uh, yeah sure, no problemo. Taco is going with? I thought you liked Taco." He didn't seem too upset about the dog. *Or me*, thought Annie.

"Oh, Taco's been rather stressed lately. I was thinking of taking him to the pet psychiatrist, or schedule a stay at the doggy spa, but I think maybe some time in the mountains would be better, don't you?"

"What? Yes!" Dad exclaimed, unused to his wife suggesting the cheap option, "Yes, yes I do."

The ride to Scottsdale Airport was uncomfortable for everyone, Annie sat up front next to her dad, and the both of them struggled for things to talk about; Devon was in his pet carrier, annoyed that he could not roam free; and Taco the Hell Chihuahua diligently guarded Fake Blake, who rode with the dog on his lap.

The weather had gotten cooler, thankfully. Restaurants and nightclubs were hauling out the gas heaters for their outdoor tables, and patrons would start wearing their winter jackets once the temperature dipped below sixty-five degrees Fahrenheit. Annie had lived in northern Arizona for almost fourteen years, and considered herself a hardier breed, braving single-digit winters and the occasional blizzard. In truth, she was just weeks away from becoming an acclimated wimp.

"So, you two uh, went to school together?" Dad asked, looking at the silent boy in the rear-view mirror.

"No dad, he's still at BCC. We just ran into each other down here." Annie said, wondering if he was just making small talk, or actually showing interest in his daughter's life.

"Ah. So, you're *friends* up in um, Bueller?"

"We're madly in love, dad. Our wild sex destroyed your basement." Annie said, getting his suspicions out in the open. Fake Blake kept his expression neutral, glancing at Taco.

If dad was embarrassed, he barely showed it. He cleared his throat and said softly, as though to a client, "Well, if you guys are ah, *seeing* each other, don't you think he's a bit young?" This made Annie's eyebrows shoot up. Dad continued, "I mean, are you at least, you know, being safe, with the *safety* thing?"

"I was joking dad. We aren't an item. Blake is just a guy I see around town, a friend of a friend." She folded her arms and said, "I'm single because I don't believe healthy relationships exist… something to do with early life experiences."

Dad paused for a beat. "How's the job? I mean, you know, since the incident?"

God, he just sails on past, thought Annie. "I don't know if they'll take me back in light of the recent horrific deaths. Mr. Hollis gave me some time off, but it might end up being permanent."

"Well, if you think you're being treated unfairly, don't be afraid to drop my name. It doesn't hurt to have a trial lawyer in the family."

Don't even think of giving me your card, she thought.

Devon was grumbling as the plane took off, his claws scratched the plastic pet carrier, trying to steady himself against the acceleration. When the seatbelt light went off, he squawked to be let out of his cage.

"Jeez, you're such a baby." Annie complained. Devon settled himself across from Fake Blake and Taco. The Hell Chihuahua was pretending to sleep, curled in a ball in the chair next to the captive demon.

"So what do you intend to do with me, exactly?" asked Fake Blake, keeping his voice even.

"Well, Devon here wants to kill you and eat your soul…" Annie started.

"Which you can't do without destroying dear Blake." the demon reminded her.

"Exactly," she said, "so I want to find a way to separate the two of you so you can both go free. He gets his body back, you go to Hell where you belong."

Fake Blake blinked, his eyes darting between Annie and Devon. "You intend to release me, to free me from this trap? Why? Surely not just because you are attracted to this… collection of gristle and hair gel." He indicated himself with a sweep of his hand.

"Because I'm not evil and I don't want anyone else to get hurt," Annie said fiercely, "Because I've seen too many people die lately; because I'm trying to avoid going to Hell myself, and a good way to start is to save Blake's soul from the both of you."

Fake Blake turned to Devon and smiled, "I can see why you keep her; she is a remarkable specimen of human goodness. I'll bet her soul will be delicious." Taco growled at the threat in his tone.

"I have no designs on her soul," Devon explained, glancing at Annie, "Once our arrangement is concluded, she may go her own way."

"What is the nature of this arrangement, if I may ask?"

Annie said, "I watch his back and help him get information about the spell that trapped him, and he helps release me from my demon contract. And I don't help him kill people or get revenge."

"Oh? What demon contract did you invoke?" Blake asked.

Annie sunk back in the chair and sighed, "I was a subscriber to a video game called *Time Vampires*. I insulted someone's mother once, I took the name of Chuck Norris in vain, and got into several pointless, angry arguments. So unless the game tanks before I die, or I recommend five new players and request form A-5790…"

Devon did a double-take and blinked at her.

"Hey, it's my soul we're talking about," she said. "I remember the little details."

"So…" Blake smiled, "You got locked into the old 'Scorpion and Frog' contract."

"Huh?"

Devon explained, "The scorpion asks the frog to take him across the river, but the frog refuses, fearing the scorpion's sting."

Annie perked up, "Oh! I know this story. The scorpion tells the frog 'But if I sting you, I drown too.' So the frog agrees to carry him."

Blake said airily, "And the scorpion stings the frog anyway, because that is its nature."

Annie understood. "So gamers only invoke the contract if they do what's in their nature to do. Bummer."

Blake nodded, "I believe you people call it the 'Online Dis-inhibition Effect."

She looked a little embarrassed, "Yup, also known as 'John Gabriel's Greater Internet Fuckwad Theory."

"GIFT," Blake grinned. "And indeed, it is."

"Hmm…" Annie imagined herself delivered to Hell, wrapped up in ribbons with a bow on top. "Not funny."

They sat in silence for a few moments, then Fake Blake said, "It seems Devon got the better end of your deal, to be sure."

Annie frowned, "Huh?"

"Well, you are required to protect and serve him, while he takes his sweet time solving *your* problem. It also seems that he doesn't *need* your help to kill or get revenge." He let that sink in before continuing, "Say you help him get back to Hell; how much interest do you think he'll take in poor little Annie then? He only has to wrap himself in bureaucratic red tape until you die, or you solve the problem on your own." He chuckled again, stopping only when Taco raised his head and growled.

Annie looked at the duck accusingly.

Devon got defensive as he returned her glare, "What?

I'm obviously not dragging my feet on this. We learned about your contract and how to get out of it. *You* are the one who wants to do it the hard way," he mimicked her, flailing his wings about, *'I'm not sacrificing others to get me out of trouble!'* Don't blame *me* if you feel inconvenienced."

"Hey, stuff it, duck! You call being in the middle of two murder investigations an *inconvenience?*" She shifted in her seat to face him, "I don't need your help to fix my problem, and I've *more* than done my part for you!" She felt the resentment that had been building within her come bubbling out. "Consider our deal finished! You helped me, I helped you. You're on your own!"

Devon settled down in his chair. "Very well. Our initial arrangement is at an end... There is still the matter of your minion-hood, however."

She'd forgotten about the particulars of *that* deal. "You little *shit-loaf!*" Annie snarled, "You... you wouldn't dare hold me to that!"

"See if I don't! Seven years, Annabelle Puckett. Even if you negate your demon contract, you still have obligations to me whilst you live. I will not relent on the matter, not while I am in such a miserable state!" He spoke with authority, brooking no argument.

Annie fumed in her seat, wanting to pluck his feathers and wring his neck, but there was nothing she could do. Besides, she knew he could hurt her if he chose. She had made a deal with a demon; what did she expect?

Fake Blake turned to Taco, "Don't you hate it when mommy and daddy fight?"

Taco only snorted in reply.

Devon, The Demon Duck From Hell

Mom met them at Pulliam Airport outside of Flagstaff, her bundled frame visible in the cozy waiting area overlooking the tarmac. The sky was clear and chill, and the moon shone down coldly from above. *Ah, mountain air*, Annie thought, taking a sharp, deep breath, and feeling a little better. The breeze smelled of pine trees and burning firewood, and she welcomed the sting of cold on her cheeks.

She held Taco in one hand and Devon's carrier in the other as she came down the steps of the private jet. *I bet I look like a freakin' heiress back from rehab*, she thought. Fake Blake reluctantly took her bags from the steward, having none of his own.

Mom waved from the terminal, but her wave became hesitant at the sight of her company. She gave Annie a hug once they were inside, her eyes going to the young man behind her daughter. "Welcome back, sweetie! Who do we have here?"

Annie had been wondering what to say to her mom about Blake, since it was Annie herself who had all but implicated him in the dorm murders. She decided to come clean and hope for the best.

"Mom, this is Blake. He's a student from BCC. We ran into each other in the valley, so... we gave him a ride back home."

"Blake... Kingsley is it?" said mom with mild surprise.

"Yes, ma'am." Fake Blake said charmingly. Taco squirmed a bit. Annie mouthed a silent '*shit.*'

"Is-is this his dog?" mom asked, pointing to Taco. Mom had a problem with pets, Annie knew.

"Amanda is letting him stay with us... for protection," Annie explained. "It seems he's taken a liking to Devon here."

"Devon?" Mom glanced around, seeming puzzled.

"Mom, Devon is the duck," she said, raising the carrier. Devon made an unhappy noise at the sudden motion.

"Oh, that's right. That duck of yours," mom said, a bit of worry on her brow as she led Annie and her entourage to the parking lot.

Mom caught them up on local events during the ride home. "The news vans left soon after you did, since there isn't much else happening. Chief Wagner is looking into the survivalists at the Parker Compound; some of those boys are a bit unhinged, and one of them had a beef with that poor Tommy Banks boy you didn't like. I don't think they're on the right track though, but the cops have to do something." Her eyes flicked to Blake in the rear view mirror. "They questioned Maurice, that big biker who marked you up and poked holes in you."

"Maurice? Is he a suspect?" Annie asked, concerned. Maurice's only crime was in recommending a cool-looking tattoo that turned out to be a demonic translation sigil. "He had nothing to do with it."

"Maybe not, but I'm sure he's guilty of something," mom remarked.

"Mom!"

"Well, Sally at the bar says he's always talking about blowing people away…"

"He plays shooter games, mom. He blows people away on his computer all day long." Annie groaned.

"Video games," mom huffed, "They're sending people to hell in a hand-basket, mark my words."

"Yeah," Annie sadly agreed. If mom only knew the truth, she'd flip out again. "Any other developments?"

Mom looked in the mirror again at the passenger in the back seat before answering, "Mr. Hollis called; he wanted to talk to you about coming back to work. The store looks nice after only two weeks."

"Yay," Annie said. She was not keen on returning, since discovering the demon dealings in the video membership, keeping the corporate competition at bay. "I'm not so sure I wanna go back."

"You have to work somewhere, Annie." Mom scolded her as they turned onto the home stretch. "And you're lucky that Mr. Hollis wants to take you back, after all the trouble…" She broke off before mentioning the deaths and damage.

"I'm the victim here, mom."

"I know dear, I know." Mom sighed, "But people are talking and… well, have you thought about maybe not dressing like that all the time?"

Here we go again, Annie thought. "You think if I went all 'Stepford' then people would stop talking? That'd make it worse. Besides, I'm not the sun-dress type."

"You're whiter than I am," Devon said from his box. Fake Blake smiled, but all mom heard was "Quack."

"So how's your father?" she asked absently, changing the subject to an awkwardly more comfortable one. "Did you guys spend much time together?"

"You mean at dinner? Yeah, almost every meal."

"Same old Bill," mom smirked. "Is Amanda still a succubus?"

Annie's head whipped around, and Fake Blake, Devon, and Taco sat at attention. "How do you know about… those?" Annie asked carefully.

"I watch *Charmed* and the SyFy Channel," mom answered. "I'm not as square as you think."

Annie relaxed and started breathing again, "I don't think you're a square, mom."

"I never liked her. She has a predatory vibe, she and that little tramp of a daughter," she remarked. "Still, I suppose she and your father deserve each other…"

"Mom, I don't want to talk about dad. I just wanna go to my room and take a nap." Annie rubbed her eyes, "Do you mind if Taco and Blake sleep on the couch? We have a big day ahead of us."

"Er, no, not at all," mom said, as she pulled into the driveway. "That'd be peachy."

Mom had gone to bed, leaving Annie and Blake alone with the dog and duck. They sat on the couch in the illusion of comfort and relaxation, but in fact, the tension in the air was electric. Or maybe the ion air freshener just needed cleaning.

"Okay, you are a guest in my mother's house, so I expect you to be on your best behavior. The last thing I want to explain to mom is why the rat-dog or the duck devoured you." She didn't trust him at all, not even with the promise of letting him go free. *Maybe it's because I wouldn't trust us either*, she thought. *Or Devon. Mostly Devon.*

"I am too weak to do much, even if I wanted to," Fake Blake said, putting on a feeble smile.

"Bullshit. You have thumbs; that makes you worse than Devon. Your powers might be on hold, but you can still cause plenty of trouble."

"We could remove his thumbs," Devon offered.

"Not helping, duck." Annie huffed.

"Just how do you plan to pull off this little trick," asked the demon in the boy's body.

Devon, The Demon Duck From Hell

Devon replied, "You know full well that Blake Kingsley was not the only one to summon you that night. There must have been two others; two who are still bound by the spell, bound to you."

"Yes, the power of three. Lucky for me, I didn't hunt my summoners down and kill them, like you did." Fake Blake smiled, waiting for the angry retort.

Devon gave himself a moment before replying, "I admit, I acted in error. It was rash and foolish. I should have trusted Annie to find a way to help me, as she has done with you. I trust her now. Live and learn."

Annie stared at the duck. *He said he was wrong? He trusts me? He called me Annie, not Annabelle Puckett. Well, shit.*

"Nevertheless, my fate is sealed, but yours is not, and I think we would both feel better if you were back in Hell where you belonged. Would that I could join you, but I must find my own way, with Annie's help." Devon lowered his eyes to study the garish, stained upholstery.

"Excuse me if I can't believe that a demon could be so... altruistic," Fake Blake said. "Here I sit, a Possessed, at your mercy, and you can't bring yourself to consume my soul and take more power. Tell me, is it the bill? The webbed feet? Would you be as kindly if I were a worm, or a frog? Or has your new body made you soft, like a downy pillow?"

I wondered that too, Annie thought. Devon just shook his head. "I have never been fond of raw souls. I prefer the taste of finely aged adoration."

"Ah, you must be in the entertainment business," Fake Blake said. "Let me guess... musical contracts?"

"Literary. And I haven't pursued it for some time." Devon said. "I prefer the classical style of the

Renaissance."

"Well, whoever you are, you obviously didn't get Shakespeare. *His* demon would have been able to buy his way out of this entirely. He even owns a mansion in the Karrkan Pits-"

"I KNOW!" the duck shouted, leaping at Blake with glowing, red eyes. The young man flinched, Taco got to his feet, and Annie winced, trying to position herself defensively if things got violent.

But Devon managed to collect himself with a few deep breaths. His eyes lost their glow, and he hopped off Blake's chest and onto the couch.

"I know," the duck said. "Suffice to say that I am of a different class. Take it for what it is, and count yourself lucky."

Taco's new master was unsettled, so he growled and yipped at the possessed boy. Venom dripped from his tiny canines.

"Annabelle! Please keep that racket down." Mom's voice came from beyond her bedroom door. "This isn't a petting zoo."

Annie huffed, "Okay kiddies, off to bed. It'll all be better in the morning."

Chapter 16
It Was Not All Better In the Morning

Annie awoke to the sounds of radio chatter. Thinking her alarm clock had been set to one of those boring chat shows, she hit the snooze button. The chatter continued, then she heard the whoop of a siren nearby. She raised her head, her cheek wet with drool, and looked about the darkened room. It was six in the morning and the sun hadn't come up yet, but the walls were colored by flashing lights of red and blue. *Did mom put up Christmas lights?* She thought blearily, *it's not even Thanksgiving yet.*

Devon came out of the bathroom where he slept in the tub, his eyes wide. "Annabelle Puckett. Something is wrong."

Annie sat up and heard a commotion downstairs, and a realization hit her. *Police lights are red and blue. Blake Kingsley was a wanted man because of me. What about mom? Oh shit.*

She got out of bed, pulled a pair of warm-ups over her panties, and raced down the steps. *If the TV crews are there, I'm not gonna be in my underwear at least*, she thought.

Mom was at the bottom of the stairs to meet her, as Chief Wagner and his men led Fake Blake out in cuffs. The demon gave her a blank stare as they ushered him out the door without a fight, Taco the dog yipping at their heels.

"Mom, what the hell?" she knew at once what had happened. Mom had a way of getting demons locked up without knowing it. Springing Devon from the pound had been a piece of cake, but this would be a bit harder.

"Annie honey, he's a suspect in the dorm killings! I thought you knew! I couldn't have him in the house, or we might end up like those poor kids." Mom was scared, but felt she had done her civic duty.

"Mom, we were gonna straighten this out tomorrow, er, today! He didn't kill anyone in the dorms..." she blurted it out before she could think.

Chief Wagner came over at that instant, a serious look on his face. "Annie, if you know something else about this case, maybe you'd like to share it down at the station." It wasn't a question. "I'll give you a few minutes to get dressed."

Big damn mouth, Annie cursed at herself. She went upstairs and tried to pick out something good for a police interview. *I ought to keep a frickin' bag packed*, she thought bitterly.

"What is happening? Are the authorities here?" Devon asked. He was rightfully concerned, for the spell that bound Fake Blake would wear off in jail eventually and

202

he would escape. "They took him didn't they?" His eyes narrowed, "It was your *mother* again, wasn't it? She likes to turn in her houseguests. I'll bet she was a Nazi informant in a past life…"

"Hey shut up about my mother, duck! She's concerned for our safety. Blake is a suspect because we-"

"You."

"*I*… Because *I* told the cops he was suspicious. Now *I* have to go down to the station and make some shit up about how he didn't do what *you* did!" she pointed accusingly at his bill.

"Well, I would love to go with you," Devon said, as she scrambled about. "I do enjoy watching you improvise." She shot a pair of soiled panties at him, catching his head. He shook them free. "Yes, very mature."

"It's only because I don't have any plastic six-pack rings. They'd fit you beautifully." She put on a sweater big enough to hide in, and dug out her boots.

It was far too early in the morning to be sitting in a cold metal chair at the police station. The little white foam coffee cup mocked her with its inadequacy, and she wished instead for the T-Stop Bladder Buster the chief had in his hand; the aroma of house-blend convenience store coffee making her nose twitch for caffeine and sugar. It covered the scent of bleach and pine cleaner coming from the temporary holding cells down the hall. Blake was back there, figuring she had betrayed him.

She had all of half an hour to come up with something plausible, something that would clear Blake for Devon's dirty deeds, and lessen his crimes to animal snatching, something that would mesh with her previous stories and not make her look like a colossal liar or a lunatic. The best she could come up with sounded so cliché; *Yes officer, I know he didn't do it, because he was with me all night.* It sounded like a load of dramatic horse shit from a TV cop show, and it would sound worse coming from her lips. *Is a sex lie the best you can do, you post-feminist bitch? Why not claim he has an evil twin brother? God, I suck at this.*

She tried to go over the facts in her head. Blake had gotten the demon tattoo and left Maurice's shop about forty minutes before she got there, plenty of time for him to get to campus and kill the three students; that left nearly an hour between Blake's last sighting at the tattoo shop, and when Annie called the police to report the murders. Witnesses could place her at the bar alone that night, *and* at the tattoo shop, *and* the time she spent looking for Devon at the dorm party. That left maybe three minutes where she and Blake were unaccounted for at the same time. That didn't exactly make for an airtight alibi for him. Didn't make for much of a sex fling either, and Annie wanted to give him the benefit of the doubt. *He better be good for more than three minutes, or I'll kill him myself. Oh, shut up Annie.*

"So you want to fill me in on the details, Annie?" Chief Wagner asked over his coffee jug. "You seemed pretty sure that Blake was innocent of the killings."

"I figured he was guilty of animal kidnapping, not murder," she said. She left out the whole demonic sacrifice thing; that wouldn't have helped.

"You realize you were harboring a fugitive in your home?" he asked grimly.

Annie had watched plenty of crime television and had a fair grasp of the legal system. She hoped. "I thought he was wanted for questioning as a person of interest, not as a suspect."

"We found evidence that points to more than that," he said. "An e-mail was sent to the murdered students, asking them to meet the sender that night, in that room. The sender was Blake Kingsley."

Fake Blake, she thought. *He knew Devon would search the dorm and just made it easy for him. Well, he got himself trapped in his own web, didn't he?* "Look chief, I didn't harbor him. All I did was give him a lift back home on dad's plane. I don't know what he was doing in Scottsdale, or how we crossed paths; I just figured he was innocent of the murders and I wanted to help." She was grasping for time now, answering but not saying much. She could almost hear her dad whispering legal advice in her ear. *Ewww*, it made her feel unclean.

"How did you figure he was innocent?" asked the chief with finite patience. He liked Annie, but that would only go so far.

Annie took a breath. "I discovered the bodies while looking for my duck. I saw the blood under the door and rushed outside. I found the duck outside the window, and the screen had been torn out. There were no footprints in the mud, and no bloody footprints in the hall."

"In fact, the only footprints in the mud were yours," said the chief.

"And my puke," said Annie, not liking where he was going with this. "I mean, with a mess like that, you'd think there would be a trail of blood, but the only one splattered with blood was poor Devon."

The chief looked at his notes wearily. "Devon. The duck," he confirmed. "I'd also like to know why this duck was in the room at the time of the murders. You said in your earlier deposition that you decided to look for the duck on campus, because your theory was that students had stolen them. Something about a pattern..."

"A spiral pattern," Annie offered.

"Right," he said, "and your duck ended up in the room where the students were murdered that night."

"Heh, you don't think the duck did it, do you?" Annie hoped he'd laugh, or smile, or smirk. Nothing. *Not good.*

"I think he found the person who kidnapped him alright. He maybe even followed him or was carried into that dorm room, and got locked in after the deed had been done. The window screen was torn, but the hole was too small for the killer to exit through; it must have happened in the struggle. So he left through the door, before the blood pooled too far. Maybe he carried his bloody shoes and walked away on clean socks. No one would have noticed someone splattered with blood on Halloween, especially if he was in costume. The e-mails point to Blake Kingsley luring them all to the room of one of the victims, and viscously murdering them."

Annie had no answer for that one. "I have no answer for that one," she said. "But Blake didn't kill those kids, I'm sure of it. There might be others involved though, like, a cult or something. I don't have proof; I'm just following my gut instincts. I mean, what do your gut instincts tell you?" She almost didn't want to know.

The chief said pointblank, "I think you know more about this than you're letting on, and that really bothers me, Ms. Puckett."

"I'm just confused is all," she said, and decided to tell the truth just for shits and giggles, "It's like, the evidence might also point to the duck being the killer, and that's just stupid."

Devon, The Demon Duck From Hell

Chief Wagner jotted down some more notes and looked hard at Annie. She looked back with her best innocent-and-eager-to-help face. Finally, he shook his head and got up from the table. "Blake Kingsley is going to be held for questioning. Any of his school associates will also be brought in, providing they're not already in the hospital."

"In the hospital?" she asked. *Had something else happened while I was away?*

"There have been some… illnesses in the last few days since the killings. Doctors said it was stress, but it's looking like something more serious. We're putting the dorm under quarantine until they figure it out."

"Wow," Annie said fearfully, both worried and relieved that something bad had gone down that she wasn't in the middle of. "Are they gonna be alright?"

"We don't know," he said. "More kids are coming down with it, whatever it is. Shee-it," his old southern accent came out when he swore, "it's like this whole damn town's going to hell right in front of us."

Annie just nodded blankly. *You said it, chief.*

It was late in the morning when Annie got back from the police station. She walked home, said three words to mom ('I'm going out,') and took Devon for a walk down to the cafe where she used to work. It was the center of the town gossip and she needed her ear to the ground, as the ancient Hollywood Indian saying went. Luckily, Devon was in the mood for a walk, so he didn't complain about not being carried.

The Mountain Perky Bean was a typical college town cafe, non-corporate and not worried about driving away the wrong sort of people. The most socially volatile topics, the top three being politics, religion, and Mac vs. PC, were vocally debated by the staff and patrons with no fear of being silenced by sensitive ears. 'This is a free speech zone' was a sign that hung above the Visa/MasterCard logos and business hours. Annie had managed to push her free speech to its limits once, resulting in her being fired by an uptight supervisor. Coffee could be such a dramatic business.

She opened the door, expecting the familiar bell chime overhead, but she heard an electronic 'moo' instead, like a robot cow was watching the door. Devon was struck by the aromas of roasted beans and steamed milk, and followed his nose to the counter to peruse the baked goodies on display. Annie trailed behind him, noticing that some customers had their eyes upon her, and not in an appreciative way.

"Annie!" called Wendy, one of the old-time baristas. She was a coffee lifer, destined to die behind the espresso machine someday. Her lined face and fading blond hair made her a child of the 1960's. "Long time, no see. I hear you're a media sensation."

"Er, yeah, kinda," she said hesitantly. "It's not the sort of press I want. I stepped into something I can't scrape off."

"No offense taken, wench." Devon said with a series of discrete quacks.

Wendy leaned over the counter at the noise, "Nice duck!" she remarked. "Where'd you get her?"

"It's a *he*," Annie replied, "and I found him walking alone near campus, the night before all this trouble started. I think he was involved in something sinister."

"Hey Puckett," came a deep male voice from out of the back room. Wayne Yazzie was a Navajo boy in his late teens that started weeks before Annie was fired. He had buffed up since Annie had seen him last, no doubt a byproduct of being on the BCC wrestling team. "How's the whitest girl on the planet?"

"Ya-ta-hey, kiddo," she said, noticing his rounded shoulders and broad chest behind the green apron. "Why are you working the morning shift? Getting out of chores on the Rez?"

Wayne pointed with a nod to a group of tables in the corner. "Cute Asian Girl Hours. They come in early to study." He smiled and waved to the group of college girls who were talking quietly amid their laptops, books, and hot tea, mostly trying to ignore the attention. Annie noticed a few were smiling behind their curtains of black hair.

"Figures," Annie smirked. "Gotten any phone numbers yet?"

"I don't ask anymore. Learned my lesson." Wayne had pestered a girl for her number once and gotten it, later to find he was ordering a pizza. "I let the bees come to the honey, baby."

"Good gawd," Annie groaned, but she had to admit, he was looking pretty sweet.

"Annabelle Puckett, I would like one of those gingerbread biscotti, if you are so inclined." Devon quacked.

Wayne looked over the counter. "Nice duck," he said with amusement. "What's her name?"

"Devon, and she's a *he*." Annie frowned. *That was twice.*

Wayne smiled, "I don't think so. Females quack like that, males grunt."

"Go figure," Wendy remarked.

Devon just looked up at them with an unreadable duck expression. He might have raised his eyebrows if he had them.

"Well, I've never exactly checked..." Annie said.

"Nor shall you," Devon warned. "The gender of this body is immaterial."

"Oh Em Gee," Annie said. "Is my little Devon a girl ducky? Ow! Dammit." A piercing pain hit her between the eyes and she winced, inhaling sharply.

"You okay?" Wendy asked.

"He just gives me a headache sometimes," Annie said. *The little shit-loaf is touchy today,* she thought. *I better buy him his biscotti.*

"So," Annie said, rubbing between her eyes, "I hear Wilson Hall is being quarantined? What did I miss?"

Wayne was a part-time student and helped in the admin office, so he heard the news firsthand. "Some kind of epidemic, I guess. They aren't saying much because they don't wanna cause a panic, but a few students have been hospitalized. Dehydration, fever, hives... I heard they contacted the CDC about it."

"What is the CDC?" Devon asked while waiting as Annie paid for his biscotti.

"The Center for Disease Control?" she asked, in an expository way for the duck's benefit. She hoped Wayne stopped using acronyms; she hated talking like she was in a dumb movie.

Wayne nodded. "They got doctors processing the residents, looking for signs of contagion. It's like that one movie with the plague monkey."

Annie pictured herself saying, *"You mean 'Outbreak,' starring Dustin Hoffman, and directed by Blah McBlahblah?"* Instead, she said, "Yeah, the one where they almost bomb the town to destroy the virus." Annie had seen it as a teenager, having recently moved to a small town, and it scared the crap out of her. "That's all we need: a murderer on the loose and a plague to boot."

"Personally, I think it was infected blankets," Wayne deadpanned.

Devon pecked at her leg, asking, "Did he say plague *monkey?*"

Annie looked down and nodded, hoping no one would find it odd. The duck looked thoughtful as Annie ordered a latte for herself.

"Any news on the murders?" she asked.

Wendy shook her head, "Nothing solid. They suspect either a current or former student. The police have been asking about a few characters in the Parker Compound, but they're closing ranks like you'd expect."

The Parker Compound was a survivalist camp in the mountains where the members prepared for the inevitable foreign invasion, civil war, robot revolt, zombie apocalypse, or whatever calamity might befall modern civilization. The people there were nice and friendly, so long as you never mentioned gun control, Congress, or liberals. Some were rarely seen in town, and so much the better. The police handled the compound folks very diplomatically, since neither side wanted a confrontation. The survivalists often claimed they could hold off the National Guard for months, if it came to that. When a 'Parker Barker' made such claims, the townsfolk would smile, nod politely, and wait for camo-pants to get in his military surplus Humvee and return to base.

"What about Tommy Banks? Did they name any suspects?" Annie knew the demon bunny responsible had been destroyed and consumed, but that wouldn't do for human justice.

Wendy replied quietly, "They said it was either an animal attack, or someone using a sharp instrument, like a woodworking tool. You didn't see anything at all? I mean… you were *there*."

It was bunny incisors, she thought, *wrap your brain around that one*. What she actually said was, "I only saw the blood on the window. It all happened so fast."

The baristas exchanged a look, wanting to believe that their friend was not mixed up in it somehow. Annie was a flake in a town full of nuts, but that didn't make her a murderer. It might not make her entirely innocent however.

"Someone tied explosives to all those rabbits too?" Wayne had heard the story but found it incredible to believe. His truck had been in the destroyed parking lot that night, but suffered only minor damage; he saw Annie in the middle of it with a duck and a shotgun. It was a surreal evening.

Annie just nodded blankly. She had nothing more to say on the matter, even if her friends had questions. They would either have to believe she was innocent and sane, or follow her into the world of demon-possessed, murdering animals and take their chances. She would rather convince them of the former than introduce them to the latter.

After making more small talk with the baristas, Annie and Devon sat outside with their snacks, ignoring the suspicious stares from passers-by. She dipped the biscotti in her latte and broke it up on a plate for Devon, who devoured his treat like it was an enemy demon soul soaked in blood. *Nom nom nom.*

"What are we gonna do now, ducky?" she asked, sipping her frothy drink. "Fake Blake thinks we set him up, so the truce is off, I suppose. If we bust him out, then we're accomplices. If we don't, then he comes looking for revenge, and not just on us, but mom too, since he knows where we live. This sucks."

"Indeed," said Devon, before shuttling the soggy pastry down his throat. "I can use you to invoke more protection spells if you like, but that is only a precautionary measure. He will eventually catch us off guard."

"The fewer spells you can pass through me, the better. Makes me feel like I'm taking a bath with a toaster." She liked that element of their relationship the least, but had to admit that doing magic was kind of cool, even if it felt like she was one giant cramped pair of ovaries afterward. *That was an interesting visual*, she thought. *Attack of the Giant Cramped Ovaries, coming to a theater near you.*

"Well, if I am correct, Fake Blake might be the least of our worries." Devon said. "This plague that conveniently started in Wilson Hall has the mark of demonic vengeance about it."

Annie choked on her latte. "Another demon? You think there's *another* demon on the loose?"

"I do," said Devon, "and if I miss my guess, he was the first one summoned by our little college cult, and has been building his power, biding his time." He looked dramatically towards the school and said with a heavy voice, "The wrath of the Plague Monkey is upon us."

Annie wondered if even Dustin Hoffman could save them now.

Chapter 17
How to Escalate a Crisis from the Comfort of Your Own Home

Annie and Devon had no time to lay low. There was a demon possessed monkey on the loose making people sick; there were only days before Fake Blake's powers returned, and he broke out of jail to pay them a visit; and they had to find the last remaining cult members so they could free Blake from his demon, and Annie could nurse him back to health like a sick baby bird, dabbing his glistening brow with a damp towel, running her fingers through his thick, unruly hair…

"Annabelle Puckett! Snap out of your foolish daydreams and help me." Devon had been testy since learning of yet another trapped demon. He had good reason to fear competition; since Hell's economy had tanked, demon souls were now a commodity, just like human souls had always been. It was

214

'demon-eat-demon' out there.

Taco yipped at his new master's dismayed quacking. The little Hell Chihuahua's eyes glowed red for a moment, before he curled nose-to-tail and resumed his nap in the morning sun.

"I'm not daydreaming, duck! I'm working our problem." She stared harder at the computer screen, searching for a combination of pixels that would vindicate her.

"You had a silly smile on your face, and there is nothing here worth smiling about," Devon replied from her lap. "We must find the lair of the Plague Monkey before he can do more damage."

"I don't understand how satellite photos are gonna help," Annie said, as she scrolled about the image. "The resolution sucks, because no one at NASA or the CIA cares about Bueller. And I told you already that these aren't live. These pictures are sometimes years old, and they're all put together like a jigsaw puzzle."

Devon sighed, "To defeat the enemy, you must learn to think like the enemy. This demon is trapped in the body of a monkey, therefore he must make use of a monkey's strengths."

"What, like throwing crap?" Annie scoffed.

Devon explained, "Like moving from tree to tree, climbing high out of reach, collecting useful tools and stashing them. Why do you think I asked you to help?"

"Because you don't have hands." Annie replied, "I've seen you push the mouse around and click with your bill; it's cute, but kinda pathetic."

Devon glared, "I asked because I was hoping you'd have some personal insight, being as you are the closest thing to a monkey in the room."

"Shit-loaf," she muttered, as she scrolled around the bird's eye view of the campus. "I'll monkey *you*, you little... wait a minute. How does he use magic to make people sick if he has no one to speak the words and act as a conduit? He can't actually talk, can he?"

Devon considered, "I imagine he bites them. Some powers are innate, like my ability to burst into flame. If he was powerful enough, he could make his bite into a pestilent curse."

"So we should be looking for monkey bites! The hospital must have a record!" Annie hopped in her chair, causing Devon's bill to clack on the edge of the table.

"Ow! Be careful!" Devon cursed under his breath, and then asked, "How will hospital records help us?" He jumped from her lap to the cluttered floor to avoid further outbursts of exuberance.

"We can find Patient Zero, the first person to come into contact with our demon monkey. Whoever that person is lived at Wilson Hall, because the dorm is under quarantine. I'll bet he even helped summon him!" Annie sat up proudly as she searched for the local hospital's phone number. "If we find more monkey bites, we might establish a pattern; you know, find out where he hangs out."

Devon settled down on the floor amid the laundry, "Not quite the monkey insight I was hoping for, but I suppose it will suffice."

"One thing puzzles me though," Annie said.

Devon smirked, "Only one thing?"

She ignored him, "If he was the first one summoned, then he's had time to get stronger and make plans; he's obviously not as revenge-happy and thoughtless as *some* demons I know..." Devon just glared at her, and she

216

continued, "Why cause a plague on campus, why not try to trick the ones who summoned him, like the snake tricked Blake? You know, get a better body with vocal chords and stuff?"

Devon pondered, "I've been thinking about that too, and the implications are dire. Blake the Snake was almost helpless before taking over that boy's body. He didn't even have limbs, and contrary to what you people think, snakes aren't a popular form for demons to take. But consider, what would a desperate *plague* demon do to buy out his contract, if he could not come by much more valuable demon souls?"

Annie blinked, "Start a plague?"

Devon nodded, "Yes, he already has everything he needs to unleash a hideous pestilence upon mankind, slaying hundreds, thousands, even *millions* with his power, rather than do it the hard way."

"Are you saying that he's gonna buy his way out of his contract with a world-wide epidemic?" The thought shook her to the core. This wasn't a *Planet of the Apes* scenario, it was *The Omega Man*. What was it about Charlton Heston anyway?

"A few million human lives ought to do the trick, I imagine," the duck remarked.

Annie's hand trembled as she dialed the hospital phone number.

She made her way through the automated menu, waiting, being transferred, and waiting some more, before finally speaking to a human. "Bueller General Hospital switchboard, how may I direct your call?"

Annie blurted, "Please don't transfer me or put me on hold; I need to talk to the doctor in charge of the community college dorm quarantine… I think I know what started this mystery illness."

Devon blinked at her. *She must know what she's doing*, he thought.

A half hour later, the Puckett house was surrounded by police cars, suburbans with government plates, and a white CDC van, while men in suits stood about looking imposing. Annie sat on her mom's couch, kicking herself for bringing more crap to encroach on her mother's fragile mental state. Mom was in her own bedroom, hopefully sedated, while the various authorities stood around questioning her about the ominous phone call to the hospital. How was she to know they'd send a goon squad?

"A plague monkey?" asked Doctor Thomas of the Center for Disease Control. "Like the Dustin Hoffman movie?" He shook his head in disbelief. "This is no joke, Ms. Puckett."

"She works at the video store," said one of the deputies from town, "probably saw it on the shelf hundreds of times. Guys, I told you she's an attention whor... er, hog." He tried to cover himself with a cough, "She's been jerking us around since these weird murders happened on Halloween, claiming all kinds of silly shit. Burning bunnies, my ass..."

Annie glared at the deputy, wondering if the chief would have been so crass with her. Maybe he sent this bozo so he wouldn't have to be fed up in person. *'Attention whore,' my ass. I'm trying to save you all from Hell on Earth.*

An administrator from the college, who had arrived hurriedly just moments before, shook her head and adjusted her large glasses. "The Rhesus monkey that was stolen from our lab was certified for *behavioral*, not biological research. It had a clean bill of health, and all the papers were in order. There is no plague monkey, gentlemen, at least not from *our* campus."

Doctor Hallek from Bueller General interrupted, "Ms. Puckett was right about the bite being the vector of infection; that's not information we've released to the press. Our working theory has been that this contagion was transmitted cross-species. We still don't know how it spreads, but the first victim had suffered an animal bite."

Doctor Thomas countered, "The infection may have started at the bite, but we can't conclude that it was *transmitted* by an animal. It could have been a secondary opportunistic pathogen or bacteriological sepsis…"

"Sepsis is not contagious, as you well know. We've seen twelve similar cases in the past week and a half, and only two patients had bite marks. I tell you, this has to be Hantavirus-"

"Have you ever *treated* Hantavirus, doctor? In my time at CDC, I've personally overseen field hospitals in Argentina, emergency clinics in Yosemite National Park, and the Four Corners…"

This began an argument that had obviously come up before between the two professionals; they were throwing around enough hundred-dollar words to pay off Annie's student loan. She broke in before they could whip out their PhDs to see whose was bigger.

"Look guys, I'm telling you what to look for, okay? It's the monkey from BCC campus! We have to organize a search and bring it in. If it's not the vector thingy you're after, then no harm done. If it is, then our butts are saved." They all turned to look at her as if she was the most unqualified person in the room. Oddly, she was not, so she pressed on, "The ones who stole it... I think they might have done something to make it sick. One of these creeps burnt a snake to ashes and he's in jail right now. Someone set a bunch of bunnies on fire and blew up a parking lot, *like I said*." She aimed that at the deputy. "These are sick people we're dealing with. Maybe they injected the monkey with something..." She turned to the college administrator, "I understand you have to cover your ass, but this is bigger than your school's reputation. The town could be at stake, maybe more."

The professionals looked at one another, their expressions ranging from abashed to exasperated. The deputy was the first to speak, "You know, another suspect was one of the local survival nuts; they live in a compound outside of town, planning for the apocalypse. They'd have access to explosives, firearms, and hell, maybe even uh, biological weapons or something. The kid we were looking for, Doug Parker, had a bad history with the first murder victim."

Annie sat in silence. *Hmph, another wild goose chase. They're going to go barking up the wrong tree again, running around like chickens with their heads cut off, following false leads like lemmings. Okay, that's enough animal references for today.*

Doctor Thomas looked at the ceiling for a moment before making a decision. "Deputy, inform the sheriff that we will need a search party to find this animal. I'll contact the FBI about the possible suspects at the compound. If this turns out to be a terrorist act, they'll take over from there."

Annie sunk into the couch as the deputy made for his patrol car. *Oh great, the FBI. I hope they send Mulder and Scully*, she thought bitterly. *They'd believe me. Well, Mulder would anyway.*

"So," Devon said, as Annie sulked on her bed, "with a single panicky phone call, you managed to bring yourself to the attention of the, what was it, Federal Bureau of Investigation? Quite a masterful stroke; perhaps you'd like to dance naked through the middle of town singing 'It's a Small World After All,' just in case you escaped anyone's notice."

Annie glared but didn't argue; she'd fucked up. "How do you know that song? It's a bit after your time, isn't it?"

"Everyone in Hell knows that song," he said. "And while you're at it, why not go on that... *woman's* talk show and bleat about your demon issues."

Devon's soul was the property of Gothraxess, currently in the guise of the reigning queen of all media, whose initials, coincidentally, were O.W. His chances of buying out his contract were slim to none; a snowball in hell. Ow.

"Look, I didn't mean to bring down this load on us, but maybe it's for the best," Annie huffed, "Having help to track down that monkey could save countless lives."

"And what if he's caught?" Devon snapped, "He needs to be destroyed, not kept in a cage and poked with needles. These doctors cannot cure *his* plague with their leech-craft!"

She began to argue that doctors didn't use leeches anymore, but then remembered that the practice had made a comeback. "What are you saying, Devon? Do you really think we'd do better all by ourselves? Are you gonna fly aerial reconnaissance while I search the ground for monkey crap? We're in it deep, ducky. We need help."

Devon settled down a bit before continuing. "I suppose if they capture the monkey, it will put one problem on hold at least," he said. "We can focus on finding the other coven members who summoned Blake's demon and try to get him free."

"There you go, now you're thinking positive," Annie said, "When life gives you lemons, make lemonade; that's what I say."

"Yes, you are the perpetual ray of sunshine," he smirked. "I suppose you have a plan to find the other students that doesn't involve a national news conference?"

"Well," Annie mumbled, "I thought we'd go ask Blake. The demon must know their faces, maybe even their names. He stayed in that dorm room as a snake for weeks."

Devon shook his head in resignation, "I suppose that's the best idea. The protection spells should still be potent enough. I just hope he's willing to trust you."

"Trust *us*," she corrected.

"Yes, yes, I meant us," Devon muttered.

Devon, The Demon Duck From Hell

Chapter 18
A Duck By Any Other Name

Blake Kingsley did not look happy. Rather, the demon possessing him twisted the boy's handsome face into a scowl when Annie and the duck entered the holding area. The deputy escorting her said, "Five minutes," before leaving them alone.

"Come to gloat, have you?" Fake Blake said from behind the bars. "I must admit, it was a clever ploy, using hope like that." He glared at Devon from his seat on the cold floor.

Annie set Devon down and said, "Look Fake Blake, this wasn't part of the plan. We still intend to find the other coven members and get you back to Hell, free and clear. We just need some information."

"Oh, is that all? I just tell you their names and you spring me, posting my $100,000 bail from your vast personal wealth, and we all go traipsing over to the college together, past the doctors and policemen and panicked residents who think I'm a mass murderer?" He looked at her with those pretty eyes, but the expression wasn't pretty. "Is *that* part of your plan?"

Annie slumped. "Well since you put it that way, it does look kinda bleak, Blake; but one thing at a time. If we can find the coven members, we can get things ready for the ceremony. There is a ceremony, isn't there?"

Devon nodded, "Yes, we will need supplies, but hopefully the students have a stockpile of such things."

"Good!" Annie said, "That just leaves their names. Who else summoned you, Fake Blake?"

He smiled and gazed at the gray ceiling of his holding cell. "There's just one thing I would ask of you first; call it a sign of trust." He turned to look at Devon, "If you find the students and learn about my summoning, you will no doubt come across my true name." He smiled as Devon shifted uneasily. "It would give you quite an unfair advantage over me, wouldn't it? If I am to give up the students who called me, then you must first give me *your* name."

Before Devon could reply, Annie said, "It's Farquatz, OK? Now, who summoned you?"

"He meant my *summoning* name, Annabelle Puckett," Devon said, and then he scoffed at Blake, "You could lay any number of curses upon me with such knowledge. The answer is a resounding *No*."

"Farquatz..." Fake Blake pondered, as if he didn't hear, "Of course! Farquatz of Agatha Christie fame! Oh, and you also represented that firebrand of a playwright with the branded thumb... Ben Jonson, was it?"

"Yes, jolly old B.J." Devon recalled, pleased to have his work recognized. He then explained to Annie, "He once impersonated a clergyman to avoid a murder charge. He escaped the hangman's noose, and only suffered a branded thumb."

"Swell," she said.

But Fake Blake wasn't finished. "You had an option for Shakespeare too, I understand. Oh, but you *passed* on the Bard, didn't you?" His voice dripped with honeyed sarcasm. "That blunder has become a legend in the business, did you know? To 'Farquatz a deal' is to pass up something that would have been amazingly successful, leading to regret and shame."

Devon stiffened. Annie's eyes widened and she took two steps back.

"But I'm sure Ben Jonson worked out for you just fine. Agatha Christie too, although it's a pity your investment was so long term..."

Devon looked about ready to burst, and Annie struggled with the wisdom of stepping between the two demons.

"I'll bet Shakespeare's demon could buy himself out of this mess without even liquidating his assets," Fake Blake said airily. "If not, he has that gorgeous mansion in the Karrkan-"

Devon erupted into flames, letting loose a flurry of quacking that would put an entire flock of ducks to shame. He rushed the bars, and Fake Blake jumped back with a devilish grin on his face.

"Devon! Calm down!" Annie cried, as her eyes darted to the dark surveillance bubbles on the ceiling. "We're on camera here!"

The duck extinguished himself, but did not relent in his wrath. "There will be no deals, snake! Tell us what you know, and I may let you live."

"Devon, his death wasn't in the plan," Annie reminded him sternly.

"Listen to your pet," Blake said. "She knows what's best for everyone, including dear Blake Kingsley. If you fear my power, you could have her channel another protection spell, just like the one keeping you safe now. I'm still powerless since the last one." Fake Blake held up his hands as if to show he was unarmed and harmless.

"You are lucky I value my minion so highly," Devon hissed. "Letting you live is better than you deserve, since you've tried to kill me twice already."

"Only once," Fake Blake complained. "The time outside the dorm doesn't count. You protected yourself before I could utter a single spell."

"You can rot here for all I care," Devon spat. "Or maybe you'll be killed trying to escape?"

"Don't bet on it," Fake Blake said. "I'm sure this body can take quite a bit of damage before expiring."

Annie didn't want to think about that. "Devon…" she began.

"You might be able to heal a few flesh wounds," the duck sneered, "but only if you can use your *powers*."

"*Devon?*" Annie pleaded. This was not going well at all.

Blake shot back, "You can't suppress my powers forever, and your minion can only take so much of your channeling before it drives her mad."

Drives me mad? She thought with a bit of panic. *This is so fucking stupid. I have to end this.*

Devon's feathers ruffled as he quacked out a new threat, "It would be a pity if this building were to burn to the ground with you trapped in that cell!"

"Oh fer crying out loud," Annie said, "his name is

Malgamadalard, OK?"

Fake Blake smiled broadly. Devon's bill dropped open as he did a double take at his minion. Annie rattled the bars, "Now give us the names, you snake!"

"Annie, Annie, Annie... what a precious human you are," Fake Blake said. "Very well, their names are Rhonda Bell and David Stevens. I believe David lives in Wilson Hall and Rhonda lives off campus somewhere. Good luck to you." He turned his head and smiled at the wall. The interview was over.

Devon gave her an earful on the way out of the police station; it wouldn't do to send her into wracking convulsions in such a public place. He would have to settle for verbal abuse until he could get his minion to the proper setting, preferably a room with soundproof walls.

"Of all the moronic, shit-witted, traitorous, double-dealing, mud sucking, back stabbing, idiotic things to do! You... you..." he grasped for another wilting adjective, and failing that, shouted "What in Heaven and Hell did you think you were doing? You gave him my summoning name! I forbade you to speak it to anyone!" Devon wanted to bite her, wanted to light her hair on fire, or make her fingernails swell and fall off. All he could do was quack like a damned duck while police officers grinned and made wisecracks. It was infuriating.

She tried to keep her voice low, "We needed that information Devon! Besides, he had a point. You would learn his name too, so it's only fair."

"Fair!" Devon quacked, "Fair! Demons don't play fair!"

"So cast another protection spell through me if you're

227

so worried. I hate it, but I can take it." Annie straightened her back defiantly. "How does it go? Ad possum something?"

Devon was exasperated, "Assuming he gets a modicum of his power back, he could use a counter-spell! Since he knows my summoning name, he will be better able to defend himself! Therefore, the power of any new protection spell must be increased, probably beyond what you could survive. Do you want to die to keep me safe?"

"Not really," she said. *Not at all, actually.*

"THEN DON'T GO BLURTING OUT MY NAME!" he shouted in a flurry of quacks, making people turn their heads from across the street. Annie just smiled sheepishly, quickening her pace towards the coffee shop.

When Devon figured out where they were going, he said, "Buying me biscotti will not help you, Annabelle Puckett. I am *very* angry with you."

"Yeah, I noticed the pressure in my head. If you pop my brain, whose gonna put up with your shit?" She rubbed her temples, "We need help, and I only know one student at Bueller Community right now. He might know how to find those kids, so lay off the migraine!" Annie exclaimed, feeling the demon-induced headache lessen slightly. Devon's wrath was on a slow burn, and she didn't want to think about what he would do when it was more convenient.

"Hey Puckett! Welcome back," Wayne Yazzie called, waving as Annie came through the door of the Mountain Perky Bean. The electronic chime mooed at her, as the espresso machine groaned and brayed like a sick mule. It was a busy time of day, and the cacophony of multiple conversations gave the shop a happy buzz. The scent of heavenly caffeine concoctions made her nose twitch.

As Annie returned the wave and wandered over, she couldn't help but notice some of the patrons giving her odd looks and whispering to each other. At first, she thought it might be the duck under her arm, but something told her it was her growing reputation as an attention whore and troublemaker. She was used to being an outsider, but this was different. People had died around her. In a different time, they would have burned her as a witch by now.

"Hey Wayne, how's the fam?" she asked, trying to sound more confident than she felt.

"Good, good; grandma's still keeping us on our toes," he said. "The doc has her on those… antidepressants? Now it's like she's a comedian. She says some funny shit. How's your mom?"

"Still frazzled," Annie said with a sigh. "I'm not helping much."

"Imagine that," he smiled. "What can I get you? Another biscotti for the duck?"

"Actually Wayne," she set Devon down so he could walk off some of his stress, "I've got to track down some students at BCC and I was hoping you could help."

He looked offended, "So what, you think we all know how to track people, is that it? You need my Injun tracking skills?"

She'd played this game with him before. "No idiot, I need your Injun computer skills to get some addresses from the student admin office."

"Jeez Puckett, if you're that hard up for a date, I'll go out with you." He snickered as he wiped down the counter. Annie was taken aback, but stopped herself before she could blush. At least she hoped she did.

"It's important Wayne. I have to find these people soon, or there could be a butt-load of trouble going down." She gave him a serious look.

"I'm afraid to ask what *you* consider a butt-load of trouble now-a-days," he said, his smile fading. "Things are crazy enough already."

She nodded, "They're gonna get worse, believe me."

"Okay, okay. I get off at noon. Want a drink while you hang out?"

Grateful, she relaxed her shoulders and said, "Sure. One blackberry java froth and a biscotti for the duck." It couldn't hurt to try a little bribery. Devon only grunted something unintelligible.

As Annie sipped her java froth, she took a new look at Wayne Yazzie. The kid had grown a bit in the last year, putting on a nice bit of muscle and a few more inches of height. His long black hair was pulled back in a ponytail for work, but he normally wore it down where it covered his shoulders. Now his shoulders were bare, his black tank-top showing off his sculpted frame. It was a little unsettling, since Annie had never thought of him as attractive before; he was always just the nice kid with the fun attitude. Now he was kind of hunky. She felt a twinge of guilt, as if she were somehow cheating on Blake for admiring Wayne. *No*, she reminded herself, *he is going to help me save Blake. If I can get that demon out of him, I can save what's left of his poor little soul.* She then wondered if Wayne had been half-serious about dating her. *That was just a joke, wasn't it?*

"You buy me a biscotti, but you don't even bother to break it up or soak it," Devon said. "Not good, Annabelle Puckett. Not good at all."

"Oh, sorry ducky," she said, hastily preparing his

snack. "Kind of distracted."

"I'm sure there are many worthy things spinning in your head to distract you... the secret to world peace, the meaning of existence, the nature of God... or were you just mooning over some addle-brained romantic fantasy again?" He spat the question at her.

"No..." Annie offered weakly. She decided to just shut up and feed him before she said something else she'd regret.

Wayne finished up by noon, bundling up his apron and waving goodbye to his mid-day replacement. Annie and Devon met him at the door, and together they went out to his truck which was parked around back. Wayne had a nice Ford 4x4 pickup with blue sand-scratched paint, a thumping stereo, and working AC. It was his pride and joy, and Annie was grateful that it hadn't been the victim of a burning bunny attack, unlike most of the cars in the theater parking lot that night. The day was quite cool and breezy, so they opened the windows as Wayne pulled into traffic, keeping his stereo off so they could talk.

"So what's this all about?" he asked with a smile, trying to cover his nervousness.

"There are two students who are involved in some weird shit, and I need their addresses. There's... frankly there's a few lives at stake."

"Is this about the Halloween killer and Tommy Banks?" he asked, suddenly very serious.

Annie looked at the duck in her lap and said, "Kind of... look Wayne, this is a really weird situation, weirder than most people think. Have you ever heard stories that you thought were true once, then you grew up and realized they were just stories... then something happens that makes you believe again?"

Wayne glanced at her as he drove around the campus towards the admin building. "I guess you don't know too many of us, yeah? There are all kinds of old stories we believe, even the ones who live outside the Rez. You might think they're just legends, but in the back of your head you still believe, even if you don't want to. It's our culture, you know? We keep it alive, even the scary stuff."

Annie heard the cry of a hawk overhead, and she looked up, expecting to see one circling the truck. She saw nothing but drifting clouds. Devon shifted uneasily.

She asked, "Like, what kinds of stories?" She only knew about Native American legends from the movies, and those were probably all made-up Hollywood crap, like the one about the mutated bears.

"Like uh," he began, "Like scary stuff we don't talk about. Shape-shifters, evil spells."

"Like skin-walkers?" Annie blurted. She'd seen a few werewolf movies that mixed it up by replacing the European legends with supposed Native American ones. Judging by Wayne's reaction, it was legit.

"Don't... don't go talking about it, Puckett!" He made a chopping gesture, swerving the truck a little, "Words have power, okay; you don't go talking about bad things unless you want bad things to happen."

Devon quacked, "Yes, she has a problem understanding that."

"Sorry," she squeaked. "But that is what you mean, right? Like werewolves?"

"Yeah, kind of," he agreed. "You'd call it witchcraft; not that New Age stuff, but the dark witchcraft they used to burn people for."

Annie didn't want to get into the particulars of history

232

that led innocent midwives and healers to be labeled witches, and persecuted by the male-dominated clergy, so she just nodded her understanding. Now was not the time for a feminist neo-pagan rant. Besides, she knew more about the history of the Galactic Empire than she did about Wayne's people.

"The beliefs are strong, even today. They say that if one wants to hurt you, he can use anything that's yours to witch you; your name, picture, hair, footprints, whatever. Not everyone believes it, but we don't like to take chances, you know? Just in case it's all true."

A hawk cried in the distance again. "Did you hear that?" she asked.

"I heard it too," Devon said.

"Hear what?" Wayne asked as he turned into the parking lot.

Annie carried Devon protectively, both of them looking skyward, as Wayne led them to the student admin center. The last thing they needed was a hungry bird-of-prey snatching the duck away; Devon could probably take care of himself, but Annie didn't want to see him further upset.

There were signs posted on the grass, warning about the quarantine and showing what parts of campus were off limits. There were very few students to be seen about; many had been pulled out by worried parents, or were staying off campus in cheap hotels until the trouble passed. They walked unhindered to the admin office, pausing only at the sign that read 'No Pets Beyond This Point.' Devon would have to wait outside.

"I shall be fine," he said, clearly annoyed, "Just hurry." He settled near a bush as they went inside.

Wayne led her to his desk, entered his password, and

logged on to the campus network. If he was doing anything he shouldn't, he kept that fact out of his body language. Annie envied that; she had a habit of fidgeting and casting nervous looks at people when she was trying to be sneaky.

"Names?" Wayne asked, businesslike.

"David Stevens and Rhonda Bell," she said.

"Ok... wait, David Stevens?" he pulled up the file and looked at the photo. "I thought so. He's the kid who started the whole disease scare. He's in the hospital now, last I heard."

"Crap!" Annie said. "Patient zero. Mister Monkey Bite. Figures."

"What, are you saying it *was* a plague monkey? John Wayne's teeth!" he exclaimed.

John Wayne's teeth? she wondered. *Whatever.* "What about Rhonda Bell?" Annie prompted, looking around. Some of the office staff were noticing their anxiety.

Wayne tapped the keys and pulled her file, "Let's see... She lives in an apartment complex behind the supermarket... nice location, convenient, good view of the mountains..."

Annie jotted down the address. "Sounds great. We've got to get to her immediately."

Wayne gave her a long look, "What's this about, Puckett? What's got you so freaked out? I thought you were like, a Goth creature of the night." He looked genuinely concerned, even as he made fun of her. "You dating a moody teen vampire or something?"

"No," she groaned. "Nothing like that." *Not that I'd complain*, she thought. "It's sort of, um... I guess you could call it the Occult, as in demonic rituals and animal sacrifices. I think these people were involved in something like that, and now it's come back to bite them. Literally."

"Huh," was all Wayne said. He didn't seem overly shocked or skeptical; maybe he could handle it after all? "You know Puckett, when people mess with powers like that, they usually get what's coming to them. Like what we were talking about before?"

She nodded. *Don't say skin-walkers*, she reminded herself.

"Well," he went on uneasily, "It's said that in order to get their power, they... let's just say they have to do something really evil."

"Like what?" she asked, morbidly interested.

Wayne shook his head, "I've already talked too much."

At that moment, Devon's heard a Red-tail hawk cry somewhere far above.

"Quack," he muttered nervously, waddling deeper under the bush.

Chapter 19
Help Me Rhonda

The trio drove to Rhonda Bell's apartment, located up the hill from the middle of town, only a mile past the theater where all those bunnies committed fiery suicide. As they passed the theater, Annie couldn't help but notice all the scorch marks in the parking lot, and the heat discoloration on the lampposts. It wasn't exactly her fault, but she still felt guilty. The theater had been closed until the smell of burning oil and rubber could be expunged. Oops.

Rhonda was not at home; in fact her roommate Angela had not seen her in a few days. She invited them inside, offering a seat on the couch.

"Do you know if she's okay?" Angela asked. "This is so unlike her…"

"We don't know for sure, but she might be in some serious trouble," Annie said grimly. "Did she ever talk

236

about someone named Blake Kingsley or David Stevens?"

Angela said, "David was over once or twice. Nice guy, kind of weird though. I think he was a D&D buddy; they were always talking about casting spells." She thought for a moment more, "Blake Kingsley... He's the one they think killed those kids, isn't he?" Her voice shook. "I know she mentioned his name more than once. I saw him on TV; he doesn't look like a killer, you know? Kind of cute actually."

"*Yeah*, he is." Annie said, with a bit too much gusto. Devon and Wayne looked at her with the same annoyed expression. "I don't think Blake is responsible for the deaths, but they might have been mixed up in something nasty. Where would Rhonda go if she were in real trouble? Her parents' house maybe?"

Angela shook her head, "Her parents are divorced, her dad's in Brooklyn and her mom lives in Los Angeles." Then, with a hint of distaste, she said, "The only family she's got around here is her uncle Jim and cousin Doug."

"Do you have an address?" Annie asked.

"Um... you know the Parker Compound? Where all the survival nuts hang out?" Angela asked.

Annie jumped. "Doug *Parker*? *That* Doug Parker? The cops are looking for him! Crap on a stick, this isn't good at all."

"Who is Doug Parker?" Devon quacked, "and what is a survival nut?"

Annie explained to the duck in her lap, "He's the one they think was behind Tommy Bank's murder and the burning bunnies. And a survival nut thinks he needs to stock up on guns and ammunition to protect himself when society goes to hell."

Wayne and Angela looked at her like she was a loony. "Um, great." Wayne said, "Does the duck have any more questions?"

Devon muttered to her, "Very clever, Annabelle Puckett. Why don't you address me as 'master' next time and *really* impress them?" Wayne and Angela only heard "whaa wha whaa whaak."

Annie blushed, "I uh, talk to the duck to keep things straight in my own head," she explained. "Come on, don't you ever talk to your pets?"

It was a slip-up, but it was bound to happen eventually. She thought of Devon more like a real person than an aberration of nature, and it became harder to remember that others couldn't understand him as she could. *Stupid tattoo.*

Angela stood up, "Well, um, if you hear from her, please let me know. I've been kind of worried." She moved towards the door to show the loony out.

Once back in the pickup, Wayne asked gravely, "You really want to go poking around up at the compound? They don't like visitors, Puckett. Plus, isn't it like duck season?"

Devon reacted, but didn't quack. Wayne gave him a suspicious look.

"We may have to," she said, buckling up and setting Devon back on her lap. "If we're gonna get this all straightened out, we need to talk to her."

Wayne pulled out into traffic. "So how is this supposed to go down, exactly? You just gonna drive up and ask her if she's a witch?" To Wayne's thinking, that was like accusing someone of murder, or worse.

"Something like that," Annie said. "I'll need to bring Devon with me, duck season or no."

Devon asked, "They wouldn't shoot me if you were holding me, would they?"

Annie shook her head. "Besides, they won't shoot him if I'm holding him."

Devon relaxed a bit, but noticed Wayne kept glancing at him.

"Why is the duck so important?" he asked.

"He's, um, evidence," Annie replied. "He was meant to be a sacrifice, but he escaped."

Wayne laughed, "Huh, he told you this, did he?"

"No," Annie said defensively. "That would be ridiculous. I just happen to be a natural detective with brilliant instincts."

"Wawawawawa!" Devon laughed.

"Shut up, duck."

The Parker Compound was a collection of poured concrete buildings and log cabins located in the hills outside of town. The buildings were surrounded by chain link fences and barbed wire, and it posted more "Danger" signs than a factory that made both fireworks and matches. The road into the compound was a winding, unpaved path of switchbacks through the pine trees, which caused the sun and shadows to strobe across the eyes, giving Annie a headache. The weather was getting colder and she regretted leaving home without a jacket, sunglasses, and a bulletproof vest. The survivalists weren't the shoot-on-sight type, but they did practice with live ammo. Accidents could happen, especially if they were circling the wagons around two of their own.

They reached the main gate, which was about a half mile up the road from the buildings. It consisted of a little heated guardhouse, and a heavy metal swing-gate that blocked the road between the chain link fences. It was hardly what you'd call fortified, but no one sought to test it. The sign that read "This is NOT a Gun Free Zone" was enough to discourage gatecrashers.

Wayne pulled his truck up to the gate and rolled down the window, nodding at the burly man in camouflage pants and a deer hunting t-shirt.

"Can I help you, chief?" he asked. He had his hands on his hips, just above a holstered sidearm.

Wayne eyed the gun and decided not to take offense. "I'm just driving, she's the chief." He thumbed over to Annie. The man made his way around the front of the truck to the passenger side.

"Thanks Wayne," Annie said sardonically. "You're my hero." She rolled down the window and smiled at the armed redneck. "Hi!" she said cheerfully, "We're looking for a friend of a friend from BCC. Her name is Rhonda Bell, and we heard she was out this way."

The guard just looked her over, lingering on her Egyptian eye makeup, pigtails and spider earrings.

"So, um, if you could like, tell her we're here, that'd be great. She doesn't know me, but my name is Annie, and I'm a friend of Blake and David." She shifted in her seat as the guard noticed Devon, frowned, and walked back to the little guardhouse to call it in.

"What do we do if he draws on us?" said Wayne under his breath.

"How fast can you drive backwards?" Annie asked.

"Pretty darn fast, until I hit a tree or something," he replied.

The guard came back a few moments later and swung open the gate, motioning them through. Wayne smiled and waved, driving slowly. Annie wondered if there were snipers watching them through cross-hair scopes like in the movies. Those at the compound weren't known to associate with hate groups or anti-government militia, but there were certainly a good number of paranoids here. Best not to make any sudden moves.

The truck pulled up the main drive where a few men armed with scary-looking rifles waved them to a stop. They walked over calmly, one to each side of the vehicle, with weapons slung but ready. After examining the truck, they motioned the visitors to step out, leading them into the main building. While the guards were polite, they said no more than was necessary.

This is not a small-talk situation, Annie decided.

She looked around nervously with Devon clutched under her arm. The compound buildings were nondescript and unlabeled, so it was difficult to guess what led where. She saw perhaps a dozen cars and trucks on a gravel lot, and people going about their business between the buildings, some watching carefully, others paying them little mind. It was actually kind of peaceful, rather like a camping retreat for people with boring taste in fashion and architecture. Then the stutter of automatic weapon fire echoed far in the distance, shattering the serenity.

Once inside the main building, her impressions changed drastically. They were ushered into a warm, wood-paneled hall decorated with American and Arizona state flags. Portraits of various right-wing political types adorned one wall, hunting trophies loomed nonchalantly, unaware of their present predicament; a pool table occupied one corner, balls neatly racked, and cues on display like spears in an armory; dozens of stacked, folded chairs flanked a podium on a little stage; there was a wet bar, a dart board, and an arcade-style video game for shooting zombies. It reminded her of the clubhouse her grandfather used to belong to before he died; the Royal Order of Mooses, or something like that. She remembered sipping a Shirley Temple and kicking her feet over the edge of her chair while the old people talked about who-knew-what.

They were met by a sturdy, almost squat-looking man with a weathered tan and close-cropped gray hair. Jim Parker was well-known in town, at least by reputation. He was former Special Forces, and he had gone places and done things he could only tell you about if he cut off your head and locked it in a safe afterward. No one crossed him; he had a steely glare that could kill a man at range, a piercing stare that was currently scanning Annie like a laser beam.

"I hear you want to talk to my niece?" he asked her in a way that sounded like a verbal poke in the chest. Annie flinched as if he had.

"Y-yes sir," she answered. She hadn't intended to call him 'sir' but felt rather compelled.

"What makes you think she's here?" Parker asked, hands on hips.

"Well," Annie started nervously petting Devon, "we know she's in trouble, and she hasn't been to her apartment in days. This would be the safest place to go if she didn't know who to trust." *Butter him up. Couldn't hurt.*

"What do you know about her trouble, exactly? She thinks someone's out to get her; maybe that someone is you?" he leaned forward, making her lean back. *So paranoia runs in the family*, she thought, then remembered, *it's not paranoia if they really are out to get you.*

Annie took a deep breath and said, "I kind of share her problem. I know about her extra-curricular activities and her school friends. Some of them are dead and some are going to die. I don't know how much she told you, because it's all pretty crazy, but if I can talk to her, I think I can help."

Jim Parker looked at her for a long moment, and then turned to Wayne. "And what's your story?"

Wayne just shrugged innocently, "She needed a ride."

Parker turned back to Annie. "If you share her problem, maybe you can tell me about it? What's she gotten herself into?" He crossed his arms and waited.

Devon quacked a suggestion.

Annie said, "It involves the Mystic Star and Circle."

A gasp was heard from across the room and a girl appeared from one of the adjoining rooms. Apparently, Rhonda had been listening in. She approached with shaky steps, her blond hair looking unwashed, her lovely figure not quite disguised beneath her sweatshirt and jeans. *So this was Blake's friend*, Annie thought to herself. *She's too pretty. Hate her.*

"It's alright uncle," she said as she came over, hugging herself. Then she saw the duck. Her eyes widened for a moment before she collected her wits. "I think we should talk in private."

Jim Parker frowned but respected her wishes. "Okay, Rhonda honey. You just give a shout if you need a hand, you hear? I got men at the door. I'll be in the kitchen." He walked off the way she had come in, his booted footsteps echoing through the hall, followed by the smell and gurgle of brewing coffee.

Rhonda pulled up a chair and sat across from them, her legs and arms crossed defensively. She was shaken up pretty bad, so Annie decided to take it slow. Besides, if she unloaded all at once, Wayne might flip out too. It was crazy shit after all.

"Hi Rhonda, I'm Annie, this is Wayne, and this," she nodded to the duck, "is Devon."

Rhonda's eyes lingered on the duck. "You aren't in the MSC," she said. "How do you know about... my trouble?"

Annie squirmed in her chair, "I kind of got involved in a secondary way. I found Devon here walking alone one night and... well, you see this tattoo?" She turned and presented the back of her neck; her black pigtails framed the demon symbol. "I got it because it looked cool, but it turns out that it's the symbol of Babel, the Demon of Many Tongues. I found out that it... lets me understand demons, even if no one else can. Like, say... if they were to get trapped in the body of a snake, or... or a duck."

Rhonda covered her mouth in horror as she stared at Devon. Wayne looked at Annie like she was insane, and he shifted in his chair.

"You mean, the snake we..." Rhonda stammered, "He was really a trapped demon? We thought we'd only summoned another snake! Oh god, and the rabbit too..."

"Yeah, Bingo the Burning Bunny," Annie cringed. "What was his name again, Devon?"

"Quack quack," Devon said.

Annie nodded, "Yeah Haggarath, Demon of Itchy Sores. You summoned him too?"

Rhonda's gaze was fixed on the demon duck as she answered quietly, "Yes, we didn't understand why the spell kept failing, making copies of the sacrifices. It was doing *something*, but not what we expected." She shivered and receded into her sweatshirt. "When I heard about the Banks kid and the burning rabbits, I freaked. I told Blake something was *really* wrong, that we had messed up somehow."

Annie smirked, "Understatement of the year. The bunny demon was defeated, but there are more out there. The one making people sick on campus is a monkey…"

"The first one!" Rhonda gasped.

"Yeah, and the snake; well, the snake tricked us and… managed to possess Blake." Harsh, but there was no other way to say it, really.

"Blake is possessed??" she cried, a bit too loudly. Her uncle poked his head out from the kitchen to make sure she was safe before disappearing again.

"Yeah, it's a real bummer," Annie agreed. "That's why I'm here, to see if we can help Blake. See, the demon claims that the ones who summoned him can release him from his contract and get him back to Hell."

"What contract?" Rhonda asked. "We never made a contract."

"Remember to read the fine print," Annie said sagely. "The spell you used formed a binding contract between you and the demon who provided it, in this case, a Spider Queen named Gothraxess. She now owns the demon souls unless they can get out of it legally. That's where you come in."

It took Rhonda a while to absorb this. She pointed to Devon. "So what's *his* story?"

Annie said, "Devon here unfortunately screwed up his chance, now he has to try and become more popular than Oprah."

Devon, The Demon Duck From Hell

Devon hissed in alarm.

Rhonda blinked, "Why Oprah?"

"She's the spider queen that wove the World Wide Web," Annie explained.

"Okaaaaay!" Wayne stood from his chair and edged towards the door, "You are officially the most insanest white people I have ever met. You're telling me you talk to evil spirits, Puckett? The duck is possessed? You hang out with witches and, and… Oprah is a spider who invented the Internet?? Count me out! You can invite all kinds of crazy shit down on yourselves, but this faithful Injun companion is getting out of Dodge, ya hear?" He started for the door.

"Wayne? We need your help, Wayne! People's lives are at stake."

Devon offered, "Tell him you'll put a curse on him if he leaves."

"No! Shut up duck! Wayne, please…" Annie begged.

Wayne burst through the doorway, making the armed men jump, but he was too upset to care. Annie set Devon down and followed as the truck engine started, but she was met by a cloud of dust as he drove down the road.

"Well great, there goes my ride," Annie complained.

Devon got comfortable on a chair and said, "Don't be too upset with him, Annabelle Puckett. You know, he's really the wisest human I've met so far. If you had screamed and ran away the night we met, instead of acting like an imbecile, you would have fewer problems now."

"Don't keep reminding me," Annie groaned, sinking into a chair.

Chapter 20
Lost in Translation

Rhonda talked her uncle into letting Annie and her duck stay the night in the safety of the compound, where they could make plans and discuss the depth of the shit they were in. Jim Parker was a decent host when he wasn't being intimidating or downright scary, and the other members of the survival group gave them their space. Annie, Rhonda and Devon shared a room in the 'barracks', which was spartan but cleaner than expected. Seems the rugged survivalists didn't like bugs in their beds either.

"…So that's how we met," Annie concluded, "I agreed to help him, and the next night I took him to work at Bueller Big Video. That's when the bunny showed up… Devon says the demon was after him, but Tommy Banks got in the way."

"So the bunny demon killed that Tommy," Rhonda moaned. "Now my cousin is being blamed, and it's all my fault."

Annie didn't argue. "The bunny multiplied, burst into flames and chased us down the road; it all ended in the theater parking lot. That's where Devon got him."

Rhonda sat numbly for a while. Annie felt a little pity for her, but not much. *Deal with demons and you're gonna get burned*, she thought. *Well, **summon** demons and you get burned. Yeah, that's it. Dealing is okay if you mean well. Isn't it? Sure it is.*

Rhonda lifted her head and looked at Annie with a haunted expression. "What about the three freshmen who were murdered? They were MSC initiates, just trying to prove themselves. Did... did Blake's demon murder them?" She wanted to know if that was her fault too.

"Um..." Annie began, *This is where it gets sticky*. "No, that wasn't Fake Blake." She motioned to the duck on the bed. "That was Devon's handiwork."

Rhonda flinched away from Devon, a look of horror growing as the blood drained from her face. The duck smirked, "Oh please, don't be so dramatic. They had it coming."

"What did he say?" asked the terrified girl.

"He says he's sorry about that, it was idiotic and he made a big mistake." Annie said.

"Quack!" Devon retorted.

"*Huge* mistake," Annie translated.

Rhonda was not comforted as she stood, backed away, and pointed accusingly at Devon. "*That* demon murdered them? He's the killer? Oh god, what about Blake? They're blaming him for it." She began pacing the floor, "Even if we get the demon out of him, they're still going to put him away. We can't say the duck did it." She was working herself into a frenzy and Devon was getting anxious.

"Yeah, it's a bit of a pooper, I know. Believe me, I've had this particular problem on my mind for a while now." Annie said.

Rhonda blurted, "Why do you still help this horrid little monster, after what he did? Does he have some kind of power over you? Why don't you just... kill him?"

Devon asked Annie, "She knows *I* can understand *her*, doesn't she?"

"What did he say? What did he say?" Rhonda cried.

"Calm down, Rhonda!" Annie pleaded, "He's just a smart ass. Don't lose your shit, OK? For now, he's on our side." She motioned for her to sit back down. "Please? Just hear me out."

Rhonda took several deep breaths before finally sitting across from Annie, away from Devon.

Annie began, "We um, we had an arrangement, but he broke it when he killed people," she glared at the duck. "His part of the bargain was to find out if I unintentionally made a demon contract on the Internet."

Rhonda frowned, "Did you?"

Annie nodded, "Yeah, ever hear of Time Vampires? It's an MMORPG."

Devon sighed. *The modern world and its love of acronyms...*

Rhonda gasped, "Oh my god! I played that!"

"Really? What server?" Annie asked.

"Bloodfang."

"Oh-Em-Gee, me too!" Annie said, "Hunter or Vamp?"

"Vamp of course!"

"What coven were you in?"

"Transylmaniacs," said Rhonda, relaxing a bit.

"Holy shit, me too! I was Desdemona!"

"Oh my god! I was Valinda Darkroots!"

"I remember you! You were on that raid against the Hunter Lord, where I got kicked into the garlic patch and aggroed all the clovelings…"

Rhonda laughed, "…and the blood healer freaked out and started screaming, and cussing you out over team-speak…"

Devon, having heard enough, babbled mockingly, "Oh-Em-Gee, Oh-Em-Gee, I remember that too! LOL! Why don't we order a pizza and braid each other's hair?" He got up and waddled to the window, "Can we please focus on our Blake problem now?"

Rhonda quieted down at the obnoxious quacking, looking to Annie for translation. Annie explained, "He's just being pissy; he wants us to focus on the Blake issue." Then to the duck she said, "Spoilsport. You're just jealous."

"Oh yes," Devon said, "I can only *imagine* the pleasure of having so many close friends I've never actually met before. What a rich life you must lead."

"What'd he say?" Rhonda asked.

Annie shook her head, "You don't want me to translate everything, trust me. He's a literary demon with a forked tongue."

"And a rapier wit," Devon said. "Now on to business. How are we going to get on campus and prepare the ceremony?"

"He wants to know how we're setting up the ceremony with the campus under quarantine."

Rhonda considered this, "The steam tunnels hook up to

every building on campus. We stashed some summoning supplies in the boiler room of the math building and a few other places, just in case. I'll need the spell though."

Annie nodded, "Devon and I can search for that if we can get an Internet connection. Hopefully its nothing we have to pay for."

Rhonda said, "I have a credit card if you need it."

"That's not the kind of payment I meant," she said. "Some websites are demon contracts in disguise. Beware of the 'Accept Terms' button."

Rhonda nodded in grim understanding.

"What about Fake Blake?" Devon asked, "He will have to be released, and we will need his summoning name…"

"Devon wants to know if we can spring Blake," Annie said.

"And get his summoning name," Devon repeated.

"So we might need that credit card after all…"

"Ask her for his damned SUMMONING NAME!" Devon squawked.

Annie sighed as Rhonda jumped at the fowl language. Annie translated, "Devon wants to know if you remember Fake Blake's summoning name. I gave him Devon's name so he'd tell us about you and David. Now we need his."

Devon looked eagerly at Rhonda as she tried to recall the words. The girl mouthed a few phrases to herself over and over, her hands going through the motions. Devon watched and waited. Still she pondered. Devon muttered to himself. Many moments passed.

"Perhaps she can find it on Wikipedia? *My* name was listed," he said smugly.

"Yeah, and you weren't too happy about it either,"

Annie reminded him.

"Huh?" asked Rhonda.

"I found Devon's summoning name listed on Wikipedia, and he got upset. We think demon soul brokers like Gothraxess made them available so people could use them for those entrapment spells."

"Wikipedia?" Rhonda said, surprised. "Blake said he found it in some ancient scroll. That big fake."

Annie shrugged, "Guys lie about that stuff. Makes them seem more mysterious. Any idiot can surf the web."

"Speaking of which," Devon said, "Why don't you see if they have one of those computer machines here. You can search for the proper spell."

"What time is target practice around these parts?" Annie asked Rhonda.

"Um, early usually."

"Let me know if they run out of clay pigeons," she said, as she glared at the duck on the bed, "I hear it's duck season."

"Oh, touché," said Devon wearily.

The girls stayed up into the night, surfing the web, researching dark magic spells and demon summoning names. Devon fell asleep on Annie's bed, sleeping comfortably, until she shuffled in around 3am and put him unceremoniously on the cold floor. He grumbled in protest, but his minion was snoring before he could quack a suitable reprimand. Muttering, he waddled over and settled himself on her dirty but warm laundry.

Morning came with a pale blue light, and the grinding of pickup tires on the dirt roads as the compound members came and went. Devon awoke and flapped onto Annie's bed, examining his minion. Her pillow was soaked in the usual drool, and her black hair draped her face like a thick spider web; her gentle snoring was accented with the occasional rhinoceros-like snorts.

Best to give her more time, Devon decided. *She has earned it, I suppose.* He looked to the other girl across the room, sleeping soundly on her bed, appearing innocent, dainty, and refined. *To think, had she summoned me, I might well have eaten her by now. Perhaps I did act too rashly. Oh well, live and learn.* He settled down next to Annie and fell asleep until the sun peeked in through the blinds.

"G'd morning, duck," Annie said, surprised to see him snuggled against her. Devon blinked in the slatted shadows of the blinds. Annie's hair was plastered to her face, a red mark on her forehead where she had slept on her arm.

"Ugh, good morning Annabelle Puckett. Please tend to yourself as soon as possible," Devon said, hopping off the bed and waddling towards the bathroom. He had a habit of using the tub as a toilet, for it was easy to clean and safer than perching on the narrow seat.

Annie woke up and shuffled over to the printed pages from the night's research, which were sitting on the metal dresser. She glanced over the data, hoping it was enough to save Blake's bacon and send his demon back home. They had found Fake Blake's summoning name, so Devon would be happy. She tried to pronounce the bizarre word, fumbling with her dry tongue. "Ra-fia-tha-si-mos. Funny, he doesn't look like a Rafiathasimos."

Rhonda woke to the name, her breath catching, as if she was suddenly pulled from a disturbing dream. "Oh, it's you, Annie. Good morning," she said weakly. She got herself out of bed and made for the bathroom.

Annie called, "You might want to wait a bit, Devon's doing his trick in the tub."

Quacking came from the bathroom down the hall. "I am finished with my 'trick' thank you. Be so kind as to rinse out the drain."

Breakfast was served in the community hall where they had first met, and Rhonda sat with Annie and her uncle at one of the folding tables. Devon was given a bowl of runny porridge with bread crumbs and extra butter, and everyone else enjoyed pancakes and eggs. A young man about Annie's age, who looked nervously at the newcomers, soon joined them.

"Morning, son." Jim Parker said, "This is Annie, she's a friend of Rhonda's, come to help her out."

Annie smiled and nodded at Doug Parker, feeling a bit guilty for the grief that had been laid at his feet by certain present parties. He looked like a typical football jock; big and sturdy, with a crew cut, pronounced cheekbones, and buff frame. He gave Annie a quick once-over, taking in her tattoos, black pigtails, Egyptian eyeliner and dark lipstick. He nodded silently and sat down, his brow rising by a hint. Annie's 'jerk alarm' went off like a klaxon.

"The police seem to be under the impression that Dougy here was involved in that… unfortunate incident with the Banks boy, and all that property damage," Jim said, as if Annie didn't know. "We've been hoping that someone might come forward and testify on his behalf, say, someone who was there that night?" He looked hard at Annie, making her squirm. She felt like he was asking her to enlist.

"I've told the cops all I saw, and I never saw Doug at all," Annie complained, "I don't know why they think he was involved." She really didn't want to be pressured into altering her story for the police. "I mean, I'd love to help any way I can, but I don't know what else to say."

"They think I offed Tommy and set a bunch of rabbits on fire," Doug said, "just because of who we are. They're looking for any excuse to send in the troops to take us down. Bunch of fascists." He poked at his food without interest.

"Well, that's not gonna happen, son. We'll fight 'em to the last man, and you can tell Chief Wagner that yourself," he directed the last comment at Annie, pointing like a sword thrust and making her blink.

Annie wasn't here to feed anyone's martyr complex, and she looked to Rhonda for help. But the girl had her head down over her food, avoiding anyone's gaze. Her guilt radiated like a heat haze; she couldn't just come out and admit to unleashing demons on the sleepy town, so she kept quiet and let Annie take the heat. *Bitch.*

"So did you two come up with anything to help Rhonda with her problem?" Jim asked Annie. "Anything you can share that might illuminate this situation?"

Annie gulped her mouthful, wishing she were somewhere else. "Uh, maybe…" she said meekly.

"So what's this Mystic Star and Circle?" he asked point-blank. "Some offshoot of the Free Masons or something?"

Rhonda looked at Annie pleadingly; she obviously hadn't shared her extracurricular activities with the family. "Uh, no, not really," Annie said, "It's kind of a secret campus society with some weird initiation rites."

Not too far from the truth, she decided.

"What, like having sex with animals?" Doug asked. "Sick shit. Is that what the duck is for?"

"Hmph," Jim scoffed, "Damn liberals running our schools, what do you expect?"

Devon raised his head and frowned at the pair, wanting to say something scathing, but he decided not to draw further attention. After all, they had guns. "Cretins," he muttered into his porridge.

"No, the duck is not for fucking," Annie explained, "He's an escaped sacrifice. Rhonda turned on the society and set loose the animals they were going to kill. Now they're pissed at her." The lie spilled from her mouth with surprising ease. She was really getting too good at bullshitting.

"So some college punks are threatening you? Why didn't you tell us this before, honey? We can give their names to the police, or… pay them a visit ourselves." Jim Parker seemed genuinely concerned for Rhonda, which made Annie feel worse somehow for lying.

Rhonda looked up from her food and said; "I didn't think it was that big a deal until the murders. I knew those kids who died in the dorm on Halloween. They were MSC too, and I got really scared." She looked down at Devon, who was finishing his porridge, shuttling it down his neck; she wondered briefly if he had done the same to those freshmen, picturing him covered in gore and awash in demonic power. She shivered violently and excused herself from the table.

Annie was left alone with the Parker men, wondering how the hell she got recruited to cover for this girl and her misdeeds. *Maybe it's pity*, she thought. *No, I'm doing it for Blake; I'm saving his soul from*

Rafiathasimos, or whatever he's called.

"I-I better go check on her," she said, excusing herself. "Poor kid had nightmares; something about commie vegans chasing her, trying to give her an abortion..." She took her plate and Devon's bowl to the kitchen, finding Rhonda leaning over the sink. The girl looked a bit green around the gills.

"You okay?" Annie asked.

"Not really," Rhonda said. "I just wish I could undo everything, you know? Everyone would be alive and safe, Blake would be himself, and no one would have to suffer for what I helped to do. Those poor kids wouldn't have been killed..." She looked at Devon, who had just waddled into the kitchen, and her stomach roiled again. "Ugh. I feel sick."

"You know," said Annie, "I never found out the names of those kids." It was partly curiosity, but mostly to remind Devon of the atrocity he committed, to poke at him for breaking his word and ruining his chance to go home the easy way.

Rhonda steadied herself. "Oh, their names. I'll never forget them. They were..."

"We got trouble!" came a shout from the front door of the hall. A bell could be heard ringing frantically in the distance, immediately raking Annie's nerves. Jim and Doug Parker jumped up, rushing to the door to confer with the watchman.

"Cops and Feds!" Jim called to the girls. He marched to a gun case in the next room, selected an assault rifle, and slapped in an ammo magazine. "They're coming up the road to the gate! Get ready!" He chambered a round to punctuate his order, looking for all the world like an old 80's action star. *He probably practiced that in the*

257

mirror, Annie thought grimly.

"What?" Rhonda cried, "You mean they're storming the place?"

"Not if we can help it. We have rights, damn it! And we're gonna make sure they respect that." Parker headed outside to direct the defense of the compound, calling as he went, "You girls get to the hardened shelter near the center and don't come out until we say it's safe. If they decide to open fire, I don't want you getting hurt."

Devon flapped onto the counter asking, "What's going on? What did he mean by 'open fire'?"

"The cops and the FBI are coming for Doug Parker," she explained, "with lots of guns... I think they decided he was involved..." Annie trailed off, mentally kicking herself. *Serves me right I guess. It's not like I told them otherwise when I had the chance. I let this happen. God, I'm an asshole.*

Devon groaned as she picked him up and followed Rhonda to the concrete shelter, "Oh, why am I not surprised?"

Devon, The Demon Duck From Hell

Chapter 21
The Obligatory Chase Scene

The girls walked quickly through the compound buildings to the central shelter, looking nervously at the tree line as they went. They didn't see anyone lurking out there, but that didn't mean it was safe. If the feds had the place surrounded, they'd have snipers set up by now. *How did the feds get up here so quickly?* Annie wondered. *Were they already in town?*

They heard the echoing squawk of a bullhorn as the cops called to the militiamen, the words muddled as they passed through the trees. They made out 'warrant' and 'Doug Parker', but the rest was unclear.

"Do you think they have us surrounded?" Annie asked, as they opened the heavy metal-clad door. "Maybe we can sneak out a back way?"

Rhonda bolted the door behind them, looking at the shelves full of food and water. "Can't say. Uncle told me

259

they have motion sensors and cameras around the perimeter, so they'd know if they were being approached. Right now it sounds like they're only on the main road."

"What's all this?" Annie asked, as she peeked into a side room. It had many shelves stacked with radio equipment and TV screens. Wires ran from the back and twisted on the floor like angry snakes, all leading to metal wire conduits mounted to the wall.

"It's the communication center," Rhonda said, "It's supposed to be manned during emergencies."

"Why is there no one else here?" Annie asked. "Doesn't this qualify?"

Rhonda shrugged, "I don't think they were expecting a visit from the authorities today. Most of them only come up here on the weekend for meetings."

Annie sighed, "What's the point of preparing for the end of the world if you only show up on weekends?" She poked at the controls on what looked like the master panel. "I guess it's a good thing. At least no one will feel confident enough to start trouble."

"You think uncle is just going to let them take Doug?" Rhonda smirked, "Not likely. They'd need more than just their suspicions."

The monitors came to life and Annie squinted at the images. "Oh cool. They really do have the place wired. Look, it's the cops at the gate." She pointed to one of the images; it showed a dozen vehicles, half were police cruisers and half were dark SUVs. "Those must be the FBI," she said. "A few plainclothes guys, and what looks like a SWAT team. Crap on a stick."

Devon flapped onto the desk, kicking up dust on the electronics. "Are these pictures happening now?" he asked, "or are they, what do you call them, reruns?"

"Nope, these are live." Annie said. "There's Chief Wagner with the bullhorn. Wow. All feds *do* wear sunglasses." She moved a little joystick on the control panel and the camera panned to the right, showing the road into the compound. Jim Parker walked up boldly, his rifle slung over his back, with two lieutenants in tow, weapons at the ready.

Devon said, "It appears that there will be a parlay. Perhaps this will all be over soon, and we can get to campus to prepare the ritual."

"Hope so," Annie agreed. Rhonda didn't ask what he said, but could guess. No one wanted a shootout.

Annie took a few moments to figure out the controls, and scanned the compound's perimeter. The woods looked clear so far; there was no movement, no armed task force closing in. She adjusted the camera at the gate to watch Parker chat with the chief. As the camera swung back into position, she saw something odd.

"What was that?" she said, moving the joystick and zooming in. A light shape moved from the road to the wooded area near the fence. It was carrying or dragging something behind it, keeping to the underbrush.

"What did you see?" Devon and Rhonda asked her together.

"Not sure, looked like an animal, maybe a dog." She flipped some more switches and found another camera's point of view. This one was farther up the road towards the compound; the men and vehicles at the gate seemed much farther away. Annie turned the camera towards the woods and focused on the fence.

"There!" Rhonda said, pointing.

Devon leaned nearer to the screen, but found to his

dismay that the picture looked worse up close. "Just dots," he said. "Wait… that's…"

"Oh my god, a monkey," Annie whispered. "Is that a Rhesus monkey? The one we're after is a Rhesus monkey."

Devon cracked, "What does it matter what kind of monkey it is? How many monkeys do you *think* are running around in these parts? It's him, definitely."

Rhonda agreed, "Yeah, that looks like the first one we…" her words trailed off into a guilty memory.

The monkey scaled the fence like a monkey, and leaped inside the compound, landing with a dark object in its hands. It seemed to be wearing a belt across its chest. It reminded Annie of Chewbacca from Star Wars.

"I think he's carrying something," Rhonda observed. "Is that what I think it is?"

Annie zoomed the camera in and gasped, "That's an assault weapon. God. It's a fucking assault monkey."

The creature scampered towards the camera, making an effort to remain hidden from the men at the gate. When he reached one of the perimeter foxholes, he leaped in, turned, and opened fire on the authorities that had unwittingly given him a ride.

"Holy crap!" Annie shouted, as the 'pop-pop-pop, pop-pop-pop' shattered the peaceful forest morning. The men on the video monitor dove for cover behind the vehicles, police and FBI drawing their sidearms or aiming assault rifles. Jim Parker turned and shouted in confusion and anger, waving his arms at the shooter, thinking one of his men had gotten trigger happy. His lieutenants had their weapons at the ready, facing the enemy at almost point blank range, deciding whether to go down shooting or run.

From outside the door they heard the running of feet and frantic shouting. "Incoming fire!" yelled one man, as he ran past the bunker. Annie watched in growing dread as the militiamen took up defensive positions, training their weapons on the gate. Jim Parker and his lieutenants were belly crawling away from the gate as confused officers shouted and took aim at them. More shots rang out from both sides of the fence, as militiamen tried to provide cover-fire so their leader could crawl to safety. The cops and feds were shooting at the muzzle flashes, unsure of their targets.

"This is really, really bad," Annie said, as she tried to track the monkey on the monitors.

"Really?" Devon sneered, "Do you charge money to state the obvious, or is the first one for free?"

Annie looked to Rhonda, who was hugging herself and shaking her head. "What's likely to go down here? Will they surrender?"

Rhonda shrugged, "Maybe, given enough time. The cops would be stupid to push through the gate; they're going to call in reinforcements first. Then it'll just be a matter of time."

"A siege," Annie said. "How long can they hold out?"

Devon butted in, "Not as long as you'd think. The Plague Monkey needs only to sneak in and bite someone, and before long the whole camp will be infected."

"What did he say?" Rhonda asked.

"You don't want to know," Annie replied, "but we've got to get out of here. The demon monkey is coming for you, or Devon, or both."

Rhonda asked, "Won't we be safe in here?"

Annie said gravely, "Not if he spreads a plague through the compound."

"Oh god," Rhonda whispered.

"Do you have a car or something?"

"My car is in the barn, but it's not made for forest getaways," Rhonda said.

"Well, we can't stay in here," Annie declared. "Maybe if we leave, the situation will settle down a bit." She picked up Devon and made for the door. "Where is this barn of yours?"

Rhonda led them to the barn near the hillside as bullets sang by and gunfire echoed over the rooftops. They swung the barn doors wide and ran inside, where Rhonda's little Honda and Doug's pickup truck were safe from the prying eyes of surveillance satellites and black helicopters.

Rhonda went to open her driver's door and shrieked, "Keys! My keys are back in the barracks!"

They jumped at the stuttering bark of an assault weapon; the sound of hot lead punching through metal rang beside them. The commando monkey had found them, and was firing from the roof of the central bunker. Bullets peppered the hood and windshield of the subcompact, making the girls scream, and Devon hiss in fear. Frantic, they dove between the car and truck as more bullets tore the air around them. Annie poked her head out when the noise let up.

"I think he's reloading," she said.

They both got up to look, and saw the creature fumbling with the weapon, its hands just inhuman enough to cause problems. Taking advantage of the pause, she rushed to the truck and opened the door. "Bingo!" Annie shouted.

Devon recoiled, "What? Where? We killed Bingo, surely!"

"Not the bunny, silly duck. 'Bingo' as in 'good'. There are keys in the ignition!" Annie tossed him onto the seat and jumped behind the big steering wheel as he squawked in protest.

"Is it a stick?" Devon asked grimly, looking at the strange controls.

Rhonda dove into the passenger side as Annie gunned the engine, saying, "Nope, it's an automatic transmission sent from Heaven!"

"Then let's get the Hell out of here!" Devon cried, as a new burst of gunfire slammed into the tailgate. Annie obliged him, and they kicked up a huge cloud of dust as the pickup tore from the barn.

As Annie turned to avoid hitting the other vehicles parked nearby, she asked, "Any clue where to go? Preferably away from the firefight?"

Rhonda pointed the way, "There's an access road that leads toward the firing range on the other side of the hill. We can probably reach the main road from there, if I can remember where it is."

"Oh good," Devon remarked without enthusiasm.

"Hang on!" Annie shouted.

Devon was about to ask what he was supposed to hang on to, and with what appendage, when she spun the wheel and threw the truck into a sharp sliding turn. Devon was thrown onto Rhonda's lap and the girl screamed, shielding her face as the hapless duck tried to steady himself with his wings.

"Quack wak wakwak!"

"Um, would you mind, like, holding the duck? He's cranky." Annie said, cringing.

As they sped past the buildings, the truck endured another smattering of bullet hits, whether from the monkey on the roof, or the shootout at the gate, they could not tell. The pickup roared down the access road, heading for the trees. Devon strained to see over Rhonda's shoulder as the central compound receded in the distance.

"Well. That's over with," he said with a sigh. "This little skirmish should keep the authorities occupied for the time being."

"Occupied? People could die, Devon!" Annie barked. "Innocent people; crazy and paranoid, maybe, but innocent. Chief Wagner's down there too. I hope there's a car wide enough for him to hide behind, the big lug."

"He's the one that you have to keep lying to," he reminded her. "It might make our lives easier if…"

"Shut up!" she shouted, "Haven't you learned anything yet? I don't want people to die! I don't care if it makes my life easier, I'm not going to have it on my conscience, you hear me?"

Rhonda sat uncomfortably as Annie tried to drive while shouting at Devon. Having the murderous demon on her lap was unnerving, but to hear half of the argument as a series of quacks was bordering on absurd. She wondered how this Annie girl coped with it. Maybe she had some good drugs. Maybe she would share.

"I think I see the firing range up ahead," Rhonda said, trying to change the subject. "It's just a little farther until the trees thin out and we can go off road."

Annie checked her mirrors and did a double take. "No way!" she shouted, just as the driver's side mirror exploded and bullets riddled the truck bed. The monkey was coming down the dirt road, sitting on the back of a quad-runner, one hand gunning the throttle and the other balancing the weapon on the handlebars. Annie hunched down so she was just peeking over the steering wheel, shouting to her passengers, "We got company!"

Rhonda squealed and ducked as far as she could, her movement hindered by the seatbelt. In her panic, she gripped Devon a bit too hard.

Devon squawked as her fingernails dug into his flesh. "Ow! Tell this strumpet to stop clawing me, or I shall burn her hands off!" he quacked.

"Ease up on the duck," Annie warned, as she tried to navigate the dirt road. "Okay, I see the break in the trees. Hang on!" She steered into the forest hillside, just missing a pine tree, and roughly bouncing the truck over a fallen log. Rhonda's arms were jostled about, causing Devon to be shaken like a Martini.

The gunfire ceased as the monkey put both hands and all his weight into turning the quad-runner into the underbrush. The pickup kicked a cloud of pine needles and dust as Annie swerved through the forest, narrowly missing the thick trunks, as little squirrels scampered for their lives. Looking in the center mirror, she saw the monkey losing ground as he picked his way more carefully, shifting his entire body to turn the handlebars, avoiding obstacles that the truck had just muscled over. She was about to share the news when she saw the main road ahead.

"The road! Yay!" she shouted, and promptly drove into an unseen ditch, making everyone lurch forward. Devon slid unto the floor and got kicked as Rhonda tried to steady herself.

"Daaamn," Annie groaned. The truck spewed mud and foliage as she stomped the accelerator pedal. "I think we're stuck." She gingerly felt her forehead and found blood. "Ow. I'm gonna have a goose egg for sure."

"This is no time to be thinking about food," Devon said shakily from somewhere under the glove compartment.

She grinned despite the pain, "A 'goose egg' is a big bump," she explained. "I smacked my head on the steering wheel. Thanks, I'm fine."

Rhonda took a gulp of air and coughed, turning to look behind them; the angle of the truck was blocking any view of their pursuer. "I can't see him," she said, rolling down the window. The noise of the wheels spinning in the dirt made it impossible to hear the quad-runner, so she picked up Devon and held him outside, turning him to face the forest. "See anything back there?"

The duck was not happy to be thrust out the window like a big white target; he was about to bite the girl in protest when he saw the monkey, only a stone's throw behind them, stopping his vehicle and taking aim with the weapon.

"Pull me in! Pull me in, you moron!" he quacked, as bullets whistled by him, shattering the passenger-side mirror. Rhonda shrieked, instinctively letting him go and pulling her arms inside. Devon flapped to the cold ground, ducking behind a tree to avoid the bullets and the big spinning wheels of the truck.

Stupid girl, he thought. *Pity I can't devour her soul for that.*

The monkey ceased fire, and Devon peeked around the tree. If he was right, the creature was trying to reload the gun again. *Time to act.* He leaped from cover and spread his wings, hissing fiercely, his eyes glowing red. He couldn't cast a proper spell as a duck, but he could always burst into flames and turn the monkey into roast beast.

The creature gave a primal scream, exposing its fangs.

Devon triggered his flame power, preparing to engulf the monkey in an inferno.

But nothing happened.

"Um…" he said, as he tried again.

Nothing.

"Well, shit," he muttered.

Chapter 22
Truce or Consequences

The plague monkey smiled a toothy threat and finished reloading, chambering a round. He called to Devon in a rough, high voice, "I come for the wench, and find another demon with her! Tell me before I kill you, where is their leader, the one called Blake?"

Devon's mind was racing. *My idiot minion gave Fake Blake my summoning name*, he thought bitterly, *and now he's managed to use it to suppress my powers. And I still don't know his yet, or the monkey's for that matter. I am so unprepared.*

"I can show you where to find him," Devon called, thinking fast, "but you will have to let us take you there."

Annie had stopped spinning the tires and was now peeking out the window. She threw up her hands as the monkey swung the weapon on her. "Don't shoot!" she cried. "Can't we talk about this?"

The monkey barked a laugh, but Devon said, "It's true! She can understand us! She is my minion, and bears the mark of Babel. She can speak to demons in whatever form."

The creature narrowed his eyes and lowered the weapon slightly.

"Stay in the cab," Annie said to Rhonda, who was listening to the zoo noises in fear. The girl nodded and said nothing, keeping low. Annie opened the truck door and climbed out, her hands in the air. "Hey there, mister Plague Monkey," she said, as she stepped out of the ditch. "Um, what do I call you?"

The simian replied, "Call me… Nikko."

"Hi Nikko," Annie said, eying the gun. "I'm Annie. Uh, nice to meet you."

The monkey seemed to deflate as he heard his name spoken back to him, a look of relief crossing his face. The gun lowered further. "It is true! You *can* understand!" said Nikko in awe. "Never have I been so pleased to speak to a mere mortal."

"Yeah, it never gets old for me either," said Annie. "So, why all the shooting and stuff?"

Nikko's eyes went back to the cab, "The mortal girl inside; she helped summon me. Her soul is mine by right, and I need it to gain strength."

"Yeah, about that," Annie began, "See, Devon here made the mistake of killing the ones who summoned him…"

The monkey looked impressed. "The three in the dormitory were your work? Quite gruesome."

"Thank you," Devon said, looking smugly up at Annie.

"Anyhow, it was stupid, because if you keep them alive, they can do a ceremony to free you and get out of your contract," Annie explained, "That's where we're going with Rhonda, so it might not be in your best interests to kill her. Or me." She paused, "Or Devon."

"Are you meeting with the Blake boy for this ceremony?" asked Nikko.

"Yeah, he'll be there," she said, hoping he would be there, "so you don't have to make everyone sick. You can lift the plague before its kills anyone... right?"

Nikko shook his head, "I cannot undo the spell while trapped in this body, but if I am returned to Hell, the plague goes with me."

"Awesome!" Annie said, lowering her hands a bit. "Everybody wins. Now, we need to get the truck freed, so if we can all just settle down and work together, we can be on our way."

The plague monkey looked from Devon to Annie, and after a moment's thought, slung his weapon across his back and nodded.

"Okay then," she said, "Let's see what we have here..." She gave Rhonda the 'thumbs up' sign as she walked around the truck. The vehicle was only three feet from the road, but the front bumper was hung up on a ditch, with the front wheels suspended over loose dirt.

"Hey, a hoist thingy!" she exclaimed. The truck had one of those hooks and pulling cables mounted on the front; she looked across the road and saw a likely tree to attach it to. They were as good as free!

"I got an idea," she said as Devon watched her pull on the hook, uncoiling the cable. "If I can... umph, attach this... to that tree... ow. This is hard."

"What are you doing, Annabelle Puckett?" he asked, following her.

She crossed the road with the cable and began to circle the thick pine, "If I can get this around the tree and tie it off, I can pull us out, just like in that *Jurassic Park* movie. Only it's not raining, and there won't be a spitty-saurus after me."

He gave her a sympathetic look, "You realize of course, that dinosaur bones are just a little trick God is playing on humans, right? They never really existed."

She stopped dead in her tracks. "No way! Seriously?"

"No, not really. Adam and Eve used to ride them. But they all died in the Great Flood because they were too big to fit in the ark."

Her eyes narrowed at him, "You're bullshitting me. I *know* you're bullshitting me."

"I am," he admitted with a chuckle. "Everyone knows that Noah's ark was much larger on the inside."

"Sure it was," she said, hiding a sly little grin. "But I guess you'd know, being a fallen angel and all."

Now it was Devon's turn to glare, "I told you, we are *not* fallen angels."

She shrugged, tugging more cable from the hoist, "Says so in the Bible."

"*Revelations* was an analogical criticism, written by an anti-Roman activist who was high on opium," Devon retorted. "One of my colleagues was responsible for its fame; he's one of the few literary demons to draw commission from biblical scripture, and he's quite smug about it."

Annie smirked, "Kind of annoying when someone screws with your origin story, ain't it?"

"Speaking of monkeys," Devon drawled, "Nikko seems very amicable, considering all he's been through."

"Yeah," Annie agreed. "You're lucky he didn't pop a cap in your ass."

"Lucky indeed, since I have lost my powers," he said quietly.

Devon, The Demon Duck From Hell

"What?" she gasped, "You're helpless again?"

"Shhhh!" he hissed. "It seems a certain demon who now knows my *summoning name* used that knowledge to surpress my powers. I can't even burst into flame much less channel a spell through you again."

Her shoulders sagged, "Well, shit."

"Yes, my sentiments exactly."

"So the monkey has a machine gun and a deadly plague bite, Fake Blake can cast all kinds of spells..." she trailed off.

Devon nodded, "And all I have is you, Annabelle Puckett. I hope you are up to the challenge, since this is all your fault."

Keep mouth shut, she thought. She finished pulling the cable around the tree, and securing the hook on the cable, stepped back to examine her handiwork. "Not bad. Maybe I'm a 'truck girl' after all, you know? All that horsepower, four wheeling and haulin' ass..."

The duck smirked, "Need I remind you, we are stuck because of you, Truck Girl? Trust me, you'd be better off on the back of a mule."

She glared, "Just as long as the damn thing can't speak." She stomped back across the road calling, "Let's get moving! Nikko, hop in and be nice to Rhonda."

The monkey climbed in the window, making Rhonda shrink in fear, but he ignored her and settled on the seat. Annie handed Devon across to Rhonda and looked for the hoist controls. "Okay people and demon-types, we have a truce. Rhonda, this is Nikko; Nikko, Rhonda." The monkey and girl reluctantly shook hands. "We are going to help him get back to Hell without killing anyone, so let's all play nice." She flipped the switch and the electric motor hummed to life, pulling the cable taut across the road; soon the truck began to move slowly out of the ditch.

"Yes! I am awesome!" Annie shouted. "Go baby go baby go!"

Just then, three police cars came up the road, sirens blaring and lights flashing; no doubt they were heading to the standoff at the Parker Compound.

"Hey, it's the cops!" Annie said. "Better late than never."

"Um," Devon said frantically, "Annie…"

The first cop car hit the cable, metal groaning and tires squealing as the taut steel crushed the grill. The second car tried to stop, but it slid under the back of the first car, flipping it over the cable. The third police vehicle, an SUV, managed to swerve and roll into the pileup, blocking the road completely. The pickup truck was yanked out, ripping the hoist free as it tipped sideways into the ditch. Annie's face kissed the dirt through the open driver's window. Devon and Nikko fell on top of Annie, but luckily Rhonda had her seatbelt on and only dangled helplessly above them.

"Ow," Annie groaned, spitting dirt. "I think I broke my shoulder."

"Annabelle Puckett," Devon's weak voice came from near her feet. "You are *not* a Truck Girl."

"Thanks duck. Nikko, get your monkey-ass off my face."

"Sorry," said the monkey, adjusting his weapon and bandoleer before climbing for the open window facing the sky. Rhonda stared squirming to right herself so she could unbuckle her seatbelt. The sound of warbling police sirens and idling engines filtered in, along with the smell of burnt rubber, oil and dirt.

"Someone is coming," called the monkey, who was now sitting on the passenger door. "It is another truck."

The sounds of tires on gravel stopped a few yards away and running feet approached the scene. "Hello? Anyone hear me?" called a deep, familiar voice.

"Wayne?" Annie called. "Is that you?"

"Puckett?" Wayne answered, as he ran around the front of the toppled truck. "Puckett, are you okay?" He pressed his hands to the windshield and took in the scene.

"Not really," she said, "I think my shoulder is broken or something."

Wayne looked up and froze. "Is that a monkey with a machine gun?"

"Uh, yeah," Annie called. "He's with us. And it's a submachine gun."

"I thought it was an assault rifle?" said Rhonda, as she fumbled to free herself.

"Aren't assault rifles like, bigger?" Annie asked.

"I think it depends on the kind of ammo," Rhonda said.

Wayne shook his head incredulously, and began climbing the truck to help them out. "My question was more about the monkey than the kind of gun," he said. "Is he one of your ah... demon animals?"

"Yeah, he started some shit at the Parker Compound, but now we have a truce," Annie explained as she untangled herself. "We need a ride to the campus."

"What happened to these cops?" he asked, helping Rhonda out the window and down to the ground.

Devon quacked, "That was Annie's achievement. She saw it in a dinosaur movie."

"It worked out different in the movie, duck." Actually, the guy in the movie had been eaten, but she didn't

276

mention that. "Are they okay?" This was really going to sour her reputation with local law enforcement.

"We can check in a minute. Gimme your hand," he called, reaching in for her. She passed him the duck and Wayne took him with reluctance, setting Devon next to the monkey. Annie was hard to pull out because she couldn't use her left arm.

"Ow! Owowowowow..." she whimpered. Her big black boots searched for traction on the upholstery as he drew her from the window; tears were forming in her eyes but she refused to start crying openly. Not in front of the duck.

Wayne ushered them all towards his truck as he looked over the pileup. "Get in, I'll check on the cops."

Annie scooped up Devon in one arm as she and Rhonda got in the cab. The monkey leapt into the cargo bed.

Wayne went from car to car, looking in on the injured policemen. *God, I caused this,* Annie thought grimly. *If anyone dies here, I'm going to curl up and puke myself to sleep.*

Wayne came running back as one of the policemen worked his way out of his flipped car. "I'll get help!" he called to the cop. "I've got to get around the mountain to get a signal." He jumped in the truck and made a U turn, skidding in the mud and dirt as his passengers hung on to whatever they could grab. He tore down the mountain road, passing his phone to Annie. "Tell me when I've got bars," he said.

Annie nodded as the pain in her shoulder grew. "Thanks for stopping by. What were you doing out here anyway?"

"Coming to get you," he said. "I felt kinda crap,

277

running off yesterday. When I heard the cops were heading up there with the feds... well, I know you can't keep yourself out of trouble." He smiled without humor.

Annie nodded, "You have no idea."

"Annabelle Puckett, we must talk," Devon said. "We are heading into a very dangerous situation. Do you have the summoning names of Fake Blake and the monkey?"

She fumbled in her pockets for the printed documents. "Yeah, I think it's here," she said, as she checked the cell phone. "I got bars, Wayne."

"Give it here," he said, and he dialed 911.

"Are you going to use the phone while driving?" Annie asked, "That's dangerous."

Everyone looked at her with the same accusing expression.

"I'm just saying..." she cringed.

As Wayne called in the emergency, Devon demanded to see the paperwork. "Hmmm, not bad; the ceremony seems to be simple enough," he said as he browsed the print, "It looks like all we need is... um..." He trailed off.

"What?" Annie asked, sensing a problem.

"Um, candles," Devon said. "Do we have uh... candles?"

"Yeah, Rhonda said so last night, remember?"

"Oh yes. Yes, now I remember. Good." He continued reading, glancing at the back window to see if the monkey was watching. "Fake Blake does business under the name *Leddess*... why is that familiar? Ah, here we are; his summoning name is Rafiathasimos. Excellent. Have you memorized the name?"

"Not really," Annie said, "Do I need to?"

"Only if you value your life," Devon said. "Either of us can use it to temporarily bind him, like I did with

Haggarath, the burning bunny."

"But that only lasted like, a second."

"Yes. Use that second well if it comes to that," he warned. "Besides, this is Fake Blake's *summoning* name, not the one on his business card. It will be more effective than what we did to the bunny."

"Okaaay, we are planning to *save* Blake, right?"

"If he allows us to," he said. "Neither he nor the monkey would have much reason to let me live. We will need to be careful and clever if I am to survive this."

For a brief moment, Annie considered what her life would be like if Devon became a demon snack. She wouldn't have to be his minion for seven years, she wouldn't have to challenge the supremacy of Gothraxess, the Spider Queen of All Media; she'd never have to put up with his crap, or get zapped with a killer migraine when he lost his temper.

As if he could sense her reluctance, Devon looked up at her and blinked.

Oooh, he had such a cute little bill... Why had she protected him for so long anyway?

"Annie?" he asked, uncertainly.

Could she really go back to a normal life, knowing what she knew? And what about what she didn't know? How much more was there to learn about the unseen world, the world of vampires, aliens, demons and angels, ghosts, magic, and unicorns?

"Are there unicorns?" she asked.

Devon's bill dropped open. Wayne and Rhonda looked at her quizzically.

"Uh, no." Devon said. "Does that matter?"

"Nah," she said, disappointed. "Just wondering."

Chapter 23
The Good, The Bad and The Monkey

The truck sped down the mountain roads until it reached the edge of town. Once on the streets of Bueller, Wayne took extra care not to draw attention to himself, obeying the traffic laws to the letter. His eyes darted to and fro like those of a trapped animal. Annie, muttering in pain, was trying to fashion an arm sling from some bungee cords she found under the seat; Rhonda was holding the papers for Devon to study, trying to memorize her part of the spell. Nikko was in the empty truck bed, trying to hide himself in a corner. He kept his weapon at the ready in case he needed to gun and run. Annie had told him he was a wanted monkey, although she left out the part about who had ratted him out.

"So we just have to wait until nightfall to do this spell?" Annie asked. "I thought this stuff was done at like, midnight."

Devon shook his head, "Once the sky is dark, the barriers between worlds are thin enough."

"Because of what, solar radiation, or quantum particles, or something like that?" she asked, "Or is it just magic?"

He looked at her uncertainly, "Yes?"

"Which?"

"Probably both. They say magic is just science you don't understand yet."

"Do you understand it?" she asked.

"Sort of... demons don't really study *why* magic works, we just... take it for granted."

"Maybe if you studied it, you could find better ways to do things," she offered, "like humans do with science."

"I don't believe such an endeavor would be wise," he said. "Consider what humans did with the splitting of the atom."

"Hey, it's not all nuclear weapons and flipper babies. Science does lots of good stuff too."

"Well, until science can find a way to save my soul from eternal torment, I'll stick with magic."

"Fair enough," she said. "It's your ass."

Wayne muttered, "This is so frickin' weird..."

They drove past yellow fliers on the light poles, advising people to call the police if they spotted a monkey, and not to approach it. Animal control vans were driving up and down the main streets, and some people were carrying make-shift weapons, looking in bushes, up trees, and around buildings. Annie could see no police in town, either because they were at the Parker Compound, or on their way there.

Or flipped over on the road. God, she felt awful about that.

"Where to first?" asked Wayne. He had been unusually quiet during the drive.

They had a good six hours until sunset, so there was plenty of time to plan, but hiding the monkey was going to be a problem. "Hey, what about going to the café? The monkey can wait on the roof, and we can see the main streets and the campus from the front tables."

"Okay," was all he said.

"Is everything OK, Wayne?" she asked.

"No Puckett, nothing is OK. I talked to my grandma last night; she says you're a witch and I should stay as far from you as possible. She says it doesn't matter which Way you follow, which religion, you know? Evil is evil and a witch is a witch. Just because you don't put on animal skins and change shape doesn't make it okay."

Rhonda looked over, "Animal skins? Like skin-walkers?"

Wayne looked sharply at her, "You're the worst of all, girl; calling the spirits and corrupting the animals, getting people killed so you can become powerful. I'm only helping you because you're with Puckett here, and because I know she doesn't know any better."

"Hey!" Annie frowned, but her face softened when she saw Wayne's typical smirk. *Got you again, white girl,* he was no doubt thinking.

Rhonda said nothing. She had far more guilt and self-loathing than Wayne could heap upon her with a single remark.

He pulled into the parking lot behind the Mountain Perky Bean. "I just felt like crap for running off like that, but don't think I'm going to get any deeper than this. If you and your talking animal demons want to cause more trouble, you can do it without me. I've got my own spiritual health to think about. Grandma wants me to talk to a holy man and protect myself."

He opened the driver's door and Annie thought she heard a hawk cry overhead… or maybe it was a squeaky door hinge? "Protect yourself?" she asked. "Like a ceremony with a medicine man or something?"

"Yeah," he said. "I don't want anything to happen to me or my family because of this."

"Well, we're going to prepare a ceremony to send these demons back to where they came from tonight. I'm trying to fix this, Wayne."

He nodded, looked at her shoulder, and said, "Lemme try and fix this too. Hold still." He felt her shoulder, kneading the muscles painfully but gently, assessing the damage.

"You have some medicine of your own, Wayne?" she joked, then grimaced as he found the sorest spot. "OW."

Wayne replied, "If you wanna call it that. You got a dislocated shoulder. I can fix it, but it's gonna hurt."

She laughed, "If I can take having a demon shoot magic through me, I think I can take- AAARRGH!" He had shoved her shoulder against the side of the truck, making a sick popping sound. She resisted the urge to knee him in the balls; he was trying to help after all.

"Feel better?" he asked with a big grin.

She had to admit that it did. It was still wicked sore, but she could move it now. "Where did you say you learned that?"

"Ancient Navajo tradition called Greco-Roman wrestling. I'm on the team, remember? It happens all the time." His mood sobered as he watched the monkey clamber out of the truck bed, adjusting the weapon on its back before climbing a drainpipe to the roof. He shook his head in resignation, "I wish you luck, Puckett. We all got to do what we got to do. Have Wendy look at your arm. She used to be a nurse."

"Thanks Wayne," Annie said, placing a hand on his shoulder, "You're a good guy."

He smiled one final time, "Thanks Puckett. You're not bad yourself. Take care, crazy white girl."

He got in his truck and drove away, leaving Annie, Devon and Rhonda in the cool shade of the coffee shop's back wall.

Rhonda set Devon down on the pavement and said, "He's kind of superstitious, isn't he?"

A Red-tail hawk called loudly overhead, making them all jump.

"Goddamn!" Annie exclaimed, "The thing must follow him around!"

The electronic cow announced their entrance to the café. Wendy greeted the girls, her smile turning to worry when she saw the state they were in. "Annie! What happened? You look like you were in a car wreck!"

"Uh, something like that, Wendy. I messed up my shoulder. Wayne fixed it, but it still hurts like hell." Annie limped to a table and sat heavily in the chair. There was no need to limp, but it might get her a free comfort drink.

"You should get to a hospital," Wendy fretted. "What in the world happened?"

"We were up at the Parker Compound when all hell broke loose. Someone started shooting and we had to bail."

"Shooting! What were you doing up there in the first place?"

"It's a long story Wendy… do you think you can look at my arm? Wayne said you were a nurse."

"Ten years, yup." She examined Annie's arm. "I think you bruised some tendons, but nothing feels broken. You need to get some x-rays to be sure. In the meantime, I can make you a proper sling." She helped Annie into the back room, leaving Rhonda with the duck.

Business was slow since the college quarantine and the killing spree, so they had the café mostly to themselves. Rhonda sat studying the spell instructions, taking her mind off of the horrors she had caused, and avoiding looking at Devon. The duck had nothing to say to her, even if she could have understood, so he was content to wait. Besides, he didn't think she could be coerced into buying him a biscotti; not without a great deal of pantomime on his part. It just wasn't worth it.

Annie returned a bit later with a nice sling made from an apron and gauze from the first aid kit. She looked cleaned up and less disheveled, her pigtails had been re-pigged, and her scrapes and scuffs had been cleaned. She held a bag of ice to her forehead, and when she removed it, he saw that she indeed had a 'goose egg' that had grown alarmingly in the time she had been out of sight. Devon wondered if her brain might be damaged beyond use. She was so erratic already.

"How are you feeling, Annabelle Puckett?" he asked, concerned.

"Not too bad, considering. You?"

"I am undamaged, surprisingly. I wonder if consuming souls has made this body more resilient?"

She avoided the idea, turning to Rhonda, "How about you? Holding up okay?"

Rhonda ran her fingers through her golden mane, as if

her health could be judged by her hair's volume and shine. "I'll be better when this is over," she said. "I still don't know what I'm-" Something caught her attention outside the window, and her eyes grew wide. "Oh god... Blake?"

Annie and the duck spun around, seeing the young man across the street near the campus. He hadn't changed clothes in days, and his hair was messier than usual, but he still looked darn cute, even if he probably smelled. *He's possessed*, Annie thought, *so don't drop your panties just yet.*

"How did he get out of jail?" Annie asked.

"Probably the same way he muted my powers," Devon said. "The spells I cast on him wore off, and now he is able to use magic at will, like at your father's house."

Fake Blake closed his eyes and turned his head to and fro; when he opened them again, he was looking right at them from across the street.

"Uh oh," Rhonda said. "We may be in trouble."

Annie rose and picked up the duck, "We should go out and meet him. I mean, we're trying to have a truce, right?" She moved out the door before Devon or Rhonda could protest.

Fake Blake gave her an evil grin as he saw the duck in her arms. "Why, Annie! You brought me a snack. You are too kind."

"He's not a snack, Blake! We made a deal, remember? I have Rhonda and the spell." She turned and motioned for Rhonda to come out of the cafe. The door mooed as she reluctantly went outside. "We can fix this," Annie pleaded.

Fake Blake walked across the street, his hands bursting into flames. "Very well. Then there's no reason for

Malgamadalard to trouble you any longer."

Devon whimpered as his most secret name was used so openly. "Annie..." he muttered, pathetically.

A simian shriek came from overhead. "A Demon! You did not say Blake was possessed!" The monkey's angry cries caught the attention of bystanders, who screamed and ran from the suspected plague carrier. Some who thought to capture it quickly reconsidered, probably because the beast held an assault rifle. "You lied to me, Devon!" Nikko shouted, enraged.

Fake Blake paused at the sidewalk, looking up at the barrel of the gun. The fire he held in his hands did not go out. "So, you found the coven's first mistake?" his gaze fell on Rhonda, who looked back with a combination of fear, worry, and loss. "Or did he find you?"

Annie said, "We found each other. We have a truce, *Leddess,*" Fake Blake's eyes flickered at the sound of his business name. She pleaded, "We have the spell to send you both back, all we need to do is get to the supplies on campus and do the ritual at nightfall."

"I still don't see why we need the duck," Blake said. "He owes me for my inconvenience."

Devon hissed helplessly.

"No!" Annie said. "I won't help you if you hurt him." She shielded Devon with her body. *Why am I doing this again?*

Nikko leaped over the edge of the roof onto the awning. "You did not say Blake was possessed, duck." Fake Blake's hand twitched with power as the monkey took aim at his head. "Why would *he* help me get home? Or did you intend to use me as payment?"

"It was nothing like that," Devon contested. "Annie, Rhonda and Blake can do the spell. We can send you back, then Fake Blake next. It's easy, really…"

The monkey shifted his aim between Devon and Blake, uncertain and agitated. "The two of you made a secret pact, do not lie!"

"But he wants to kill *me*!" Devon whined.

"And why not?" asked Nikko, "You are useless for the spell. You would only benefit from our deaths!"

Flashing yellow lights came down the street as an animal control truck approached, followed by white vans from the CDC.

"Guys," Annie said, "we're running out of time here. They're coming for the monkey and the cops won't be far behind for Blake. We can either stand here pointing guns and spells at each other, or we can work together."

Fake Blake lowered his hands, "Perhaps you're right," he said, relaxing. Then his wrist snapped and flame shot up at the awning as he rolled to the side. The monkey's finger jerked on the trigger as the awning beneath him burst into flames. Bullets riddled the sidewalk in front of the girls, then the monkey leaped for a table parasol, and Blake gained his feet.

"God-damned demons!" Annie yelled, as she and Rhonda bolted across the street in front of the oncoming traffic. Devon could do nothing but stay tucked under her arm like a football, as her thick, black boots beat the pavement, and tires screeched around them.

The animal control vans took up a perimeter, but the men with nets were not prepared for a monkey with a machine gun. Blake continued to cast balls of fire at the nimble simian, as he took cover behind the patio furniture in front of the café. The storefront was burning as Wendy called the fire department from behind the counter. Bullets pierced the glass after ricocheting off of

Fake Blake's protective magic shield. It was chaos.

Annie ran onto campus, darting past the quarantine notices and yellow caution tape. Wilson Hall was only a few buildings away, but that wasn't her destination; she needed to get to the math building. That's where the diabolical deeds had taken place, and that's where tonight's ceremony would be. She darted to avoid the security guards posted near the danger zone, and made her way around the dining hall towards their destination. Rhonda kept up rather well, her sneakers more suited for running than Annie's combat boots. She was in better shape too, obviously. *Bitch.*

They came to a halt in the alley behind the 24 hour T-Stop and the math building; Annie was out of breath, and Devon was rattled by all the jostling. Rhonda's hair looked windblown, and her skin was flushed and lovely. *Damn her.*

"We need... to get in... the basement," Annie said, panting. "There's a window around here... somewhere."

"It's too small for either of you," Devon said, "and there is no point sending me in alone, because I can't open doors."

Rhonda said, "If we only had a monkey..."

"Well, mister monkey is shooting up the town with Blake the Flake," Annie grumped, hearing the burst of fire in the distance. "There has to be another way in."

Rhonda shrugged, "We can go in through the front doors."

Annie's jaw dropped, "Why didn't you say so before?"

"I was following *you*."

"Ugh! Whatever. So the building is open?"

"Of course, it's a school day." Rhonda said.

Annie huffed, straightened her clothes, and marched

towards the front of the building, swearing. The halls were empty; apparently classes were in session. The trio made their way to the side stairwell and headed to the basement, where the boiler room door was located. It was unlocked, but they were not alone; one of the maintenance men was maintaining something, so they crept down the access ramp and hid behind a stack of cardboard boxes, waiting for him to leave. The man seemed to be getting the heating units ready for winter.

"Is the stuff still here?" Annie whispered.

Rhonda shrugged, "It's all in the next few rooms, closer to the steam tunnels. I hope the candles aren't melted."

"Devon said candles were important," Annie said. "Maybe one of us can make a run for some."

Devon said nothing. Eventually the man finished his work and made for the door, locking it behind him.

"Can we get out that way?" Annie asked in a panic.

"We can travel through the tunnels if we need to; there are more than a few places to get out." Rhonda said. "Besides, all the locked doors open from this side."

"Good, I guess we can start setting up," Annie said as she set down the duck. "Lead the way."

Rhonda took them through a couple of storage areas to a basement room behind a rusty door. The smell of damp concrete and mold permeated the still air. As the door creaked open, Annie half expected bats and a foul wind to come pouring out. She carried the duck into the dark room. Through one of the open, blackened windows, a glimpse of sunlight cast a beam through the dank air. Devon shuddered as he saw the dim pattern of a summoning circle on the floor, recalling the night nearly a month ago, when he first appeared in this cursed avian form. He asked her to put him down so he could get a closer look.

"This is where it happened," Devon said. "I was summoned here, and the sacrificial duck was there," he pointed with his wing towards a small, makeshift altar over which was draped a dusty tarp. He looked about the room, reliving the moment.

The entrance to the steam tunnels was against the far wall; the iron grate stood like a dungeon portal, guarding the passages that spread heating pipes and electrical conduits all over campus. Annie wondered briefly if there were orcs down there, or rapists. Or maybe orc-rapists.

"Okay," she said, "We've got a few hours to burn, so let's get started. Maybe the boys will join us if they don't kill each other first."

Chapter 24
The Cost of Doing Business

The beam of light creeping across the floor was the only indication of the passage of time. Devon supervised as the girls drew the symbols of power with chalk and charcoal, following the direction on the printed forms. He waddled about, inspecting their work and taking care not to break the lines. *This could work*, he thought, *for **them**, anyway. Maybe Annie was right, maybe I was being stupid trying to get revenge above all else.* He sighed and peered into the box of candles. They were soft and misshapen, but they would serve. The real issue would be the payment. *Best not to bring it up*, he decided. *Annie would certainly not approve.*

"Not too bad," Annie said, as she took a step back to admire her handiwork. "It looks like a real magic circle."

"Have you ever *seen* a real magic circle?" Devon asked.

"Not outside of a video game or the Internet," she said, "or the movies. But it looks good enough to be in a movie."

Rhonda looked up, "Maybe a crap, low budget cable movie."

"That's still a movie," Annie said defensively. "It's a little slice of cinematic immortality."

"Hmm," Rhonda said, "It's sad when you think about it; a crap little movie or book might be someone's legacy to the ages, their main contribution to the universe."

"Better than nothing," she said, "love you or hate you, at least *someone* has an opinion."

Something clicked in Devon's mind, something that had been bothering him ever since reading Fake Blake's business name. "Leddess!" he exclaimed. "Now I remember."

But Rhonda only heard quacking. She said wistfully, "I wonder if that's the point of life; to give future generations something to argue about."

Devon piped up, "Actually, the point of life is to maximize the p-"

He was interrupted by the crash of a body against the iron grate to the steam tunnels. They spun at the noise, and in the dimming light, they saw a dark shape hunched near the lower half of the door. It was about monkey-sized.

"Let me in," Nikko said from the shadows. "He is not far behind me."

Annie rushed to the gate and fumbled with the latch, admitting the bedraggled simian into the room. He no longer wore his bandoleer, but his weapon was still slung across his back; his fur was scorched and patches were missing.

"I was running out of ammunition," Nikko explained, "and the animal catchers were closing in. I had to make a run for it to evade them both." He glared at Devon.

The duck raised his wings in a plea, "It was not my intent to deceive you... well, it *was* actually, but not for the reasons you think. We hoped that Leddess would see the wisdom of the situation, and agree to help for his own sake. It seems he was a bit more upset with me than I surmised."

Nikko made his way across the room, looking for a place to hide. "I do not want to argue about it now, I just want to get home and out of this useless body." He looked at Devon again, "But I guess I should be grateful; some had it worse." He gave the duck a toothy grin before closing himself in a metal cabinet.

Annie looked back down the tunnel into the receding darkness, broken only by regular patches of orange electric lights. She thought she saw something moving in the distance, and she slowly closed the grate, latching it with a metallic clang. "I think he's coming," she said quietly.

The dark form in the tunnel seemed to absorb the light as it came on, drawing the darkness about itself like a cloak, its steps echoing through the passage like the beating of a stony heart. Sparks burst from the fixtures as it passed under the orange lights, yet a hellish glow seemed to illuminate the figure from behind, despite the darkness it left in its wake. Annie thought for a moment that she glimpsed the glowing of eyes like coals, and a devilish countenance, with horns, wings, and a tail swishing dangerously. She shivered and backed further into the room, away from the portal. The smell of sulfur and burnt popcorn permeated the air, rising like a foul wind from the bowels of some movie theater from Hell.

But when the figure reached the grating, it was only Fake Blake, looking rakishly disheveled and dirty, a few splatters of blood covering his shirt and neck. His pale skin seemed to radiate a sickly light, as if a fire was consuming him from within.

"The gang's all here," the demon said in the young, masculine voice of his host. "And you've been busy too. I'm impressed." He reached through the grating and opened the latch with ease. "Hello, Malgamadalard," he crooned.

Devon shrank back behind Annie.

"Not so mouthy now, are you?" said Blake, "Perhaps you'd like to say goodbye to your dear, faithful minion, before I return to Hell in possession of your soul?"

Annie folded her arms, "Damn it, Fake Blake! We're trying to help you! You have a free ticket home, so don't waste it on revenge."

Fake Blake smiled, "Are you saying you *won't* help me if I kill the ducky? You'd *refuse* to save dear Blake, who has endured so very much because of your weakness?" His face looked pained and desperate.

"*My* weakness?" she spat, "You're the one who possessed him!"

"But you gave me the way, Annie dear. So trusting and easy to manipulate; it's no wonder Devon values you so. Pity about his summoning name though." He scratched his chin and grinned wolfishly at the duck.

Devon spoke from behind Annie's boots, "I remember him now! He will one day become more dangerous than we can imagine! Leddess is *Stephanie Meyer's literary demon!*"

Annie blinked and said, "Wait. What?"

Leddess drew a cold smile, "Yesss, I'm so pleased you know of me, he said to the duck. "I've always admired *your* work, if not your choices. So few of the old-timers ever considered extended marketing licenses. At the end of her short, mortal life, I will draw commission from the vast cache of adoration from her *entire* franchise; books, films, clothing, posters, lunch boxes, *everything*. Then *I* will have a mansion in the Karrkan Pits! I've already picked out the plot."

"Oh my god…" Rhonda muttered, putting the pieces together, "When she dies, he'll be able to buy his way out of his contract with Oprah!"

Realization struck Annie like a hammer, and she cried, "*He's* the reason that sparkle-vamps and stupid, angst-ridden, teen heroines are so popular?" She turned to Leddess, her voice cold, "You bastard son of a bitch."

He let out a laugh of pure evil.

Devon pleaded, "But you are still bound to Gothraxess *now*, and if that body dies *before* you become rich, you will be hers to feed upon for eternity! I am trapped, but you need not be! Would you risk your one chance at freedom for vengeance? I made a mistake…"

"I silence you Malgamadalard," Fake Blake said, and Devon's throat closed up, choking him off mid-sentence.

Annie picked Devon up, holding him protectively, "Stop it! He's powerless, isn't that enough? You don't have to bully him."

Fake Blake started to laugh again, but his mirth was cut short by the bang of a metal cabinet opening.

Nikko stepped out with weapon raised. "I can hardly miss you from here, Leddess. I have only a few bullets left, but they will serve to send you into the spider queen's belly!"

Devon, The Demon Duck From Hell

Fake Blake turned slowly, a dark expression clouding his features. "There you are, I thought you might still be in the room. Do you think you can take me with that mortal weapon?"

Nikko said, "You are not immortal. I sense your powers are waning, and I have the gun." Seeing Blake's smirk, he added, "Besides, I think if we fight in this small space, we might kill the humans. Without them, we are both trapped here."

Annie looked at Rhonda, "Not good."

Rhonda agreed.

Devon just coughed.

Fake Blake folded his arms. "Very well," he said, "But what do you care about the duck? You could just as easily kill him yourself."

"Not if it jeopardizes my way home," Nikko said. "Release him."

Fake Blake thought a moment and sighed, "Oh very well. Malgamadalard, I release you. Happy?"

Devon coughed and sputtered. His eyes widened, and he whispering something in Annie's ear before addressing the demons. "If I may, ehem, I have a suggestion on how to proceed. I've had some time to think about this…"

"Ugh," Fake Blake groaned, "He loves the sound of his own voice."

"Hrmm," Devon glared, "I was thinking that Nikko should go first, as it will take three human voices to invoke the spell."

"This was supposed to be about me," Blake said angrily. "Not the monkey. What am I supposed to use for payment after he's gone?"

"Um," Devon lowered his voice, "I think Nikko has his

own arrangements. It need not interfere with the second ritual."

Nikko nodded, "Yes, I have one of my own. There is no conflict."

Annie gave Devon a little shake and said, "Hey, what's this about payment?"

"It's a demon thing; bookkeeping, really. Nothing you need be concerned about," he said reassuringly.

"Bullshit," Annie said. "You guys deal in souls and stuff. What kind of payment are you talking about?" Rhonda took a step back and Fake Blake shuffled his feet. Nikko cleared his throat.

Devon sighed, "Payment for the ritual is a soul, the life of one of the original conjurers."

"What did he say? What's going on?" Rhonda blurted. She had been trying to follow the conversation, part of which sounded like 'quack wack' and 'Oooo ooo ook'. She knew something critical had just been said.

Annie translated. Rhonda gasped and whimpered. Fake Blake and Nikko tensed up.

"They can't!" the girl cried. "They just can't!"

"No…" Annie shook her head, setting down the duck. "No, I won't do it."

"Annie," Devon said desperately, "It cannot be helped. These two demons have the right to slay those who summoned them, just as I did. There are rules and consequences. Once they summoned us unbound, they forfeited their lives."

"NO!" she screamed. "No, I won't do it! I don't care about your rules, no one else was supposed to die!" She backed against the wall, "We were going to fix this, we were going to stop it…"

"It *will* stop, Annie. It will stop once the contracts are

finalized. The damage is already done; it is just a matter of collection." The duck shuffled nervously. *This was not the time for second thoughts.*

Nikko spoke, "My payment will be the boy in the hospital: the one I bit to carry my plague. Once he is dead and I am gone, the plague will end. Is that not fair?"

"David," Rhonda moaned. Her friends were being dragged into Hell all around her and it was all her fault.

"So what, that leaves Rhonda as payment for Blake?" Annie cried. "No way!"

Rhonda stiffened, "I'll do it," she said quietly. "I'll be the sacrifice for Blake."

"It's settled then!" Devon said brightly.

"No!" Annie yelled, "You can't do that! Rhonda, you can't!"

Rhonda turned to Annie, tears in her eyes. "It's okay, Annie. It's okay. I want to do this. You have no idea what it's like… this is all my fault and I don't want anyone else to suffer for my sins." She took up her position at one end of the magic circle and began lighting candles. The evening approached, its fading indigo light giving way to the flickering of burning wicks.

"No…" Annie said, as Fake Blake took up his position and Nikko carefully entered the middle of the circle. He kept his weapon at the ready, but his face held anticipation and relief.

"Annie, you must." Devon said quietly, "Do your part and many lives will be saved."

She shivered and shook her head, her Egyptian eyeliner running with her tears.

"He will die anyway," Nikko said. "I cannot stop the plague without returning to Hell, and I cannot return to Hell without his death as payment."

Annie's head was spinning, and she felt like puking all over the duck. Not only was she supposed to help with a black magic ritual that needed a human sacrifice, but she had to do it twice in one night? This was insane. She was going insane. Maybe it ran in the family after all.

Darkness fell and Nikko said, "It is time. Please."

Annie shuffled forward to her place on the edge of the magic circle, feeling numb as she lit the candles. The words were in her hands, but she could scarcely read them through her tears; the salty drops were making the ink run as well. Fake Blake began the chanting, followed by Rhonda, and then reluctantly by Annie, whose voice squeaked around the lump in her throat. *I'm never going to Heaven now*, she thought. *This is dooming me for sure. I might as well renew my Time Vampires subscription and take the name of Chuck Norris in vain until I die.*

The ritual concluded as Rhonda spoke the summoning name of Nikko the monkey, raising her hands as if in prayer as the candles blew themselves out. "I free thee, Bathekashass. Return to Hell!"

The monkey smiled as his body went limp, the weapon clattering to the concrete floor. His fur began to smolder, and within moments, his entire body was reduced to ash, much like that of the snake originally inhabited by Blake's demon.

Fake Blake picked up the weapon before anyone could move for it, and he popped out the magazine, ejected the round in the chamber, and pushed the remaining bullets out of the cartridge with his thumb, one by one. "There, that nasty thing is no longer a problem." His eyes fell on Devon, "So dear Annie, your association with Malgamadalard has already led you to kill a boy in the hospital. How many more deaths will he require before he's done with you?"

Annie just stood numbly and looked at the charred remains of the monkey. Devon inched behind her.

"It's such a little thing, his death. If you like, I can take him into the other room so you don't have to watch." He dropped the useless weapon to the floor and walked slowly around the circle. "Once I am gone, you will be free. No more demon duck to worry about. You can even get your tattoo removed, so you don't have to be dragged into this again."

"Annie?" Devon whimpered, "Don't let him kill me, please?"

Fake Blake smiled and raised his hands, "I don't even have to use magic. I'll just get a hold of his scrawny neck and twiiiissst." He wrung his hands to demonstrate. "No harm… no fowl."

"Oh, please, *please*," Devon said, with a hint of courage, "Don't let me die with that amateur tripe ringing in my ears."

"Cheeky to the last," Fake Blake said, "This will be sooo satisfying."

"Annabelle Puckett," Devon said, as he darted out of Blake's reach, "Now would be a good time."

Fake Blake raised an eyebrow, "Annie to the rescue? I don't think so. She's in no position to help *you*, and in no position to deny *me*. She wouldn't want me on the loose just because she didn't go through with the ritual, now would she?" He leered at her. "She'll be a good little minion and do as I tell her."

Annie looked up through her tears, her lip quivering. No one was going to order her around anymore, at least not if she could help it. "Scientia potestas est;

Rafiathasimos, I take your power." She braced herself, jerked, and doubled over, landing on her hands and knees.

Fake Blake scoffed, looking at the girl quivering at his feet. "Nicely played, dear. But Devon has no power to give you. I suppressed it."

Devon stepped forward, "You released me. At the monkey's request, you released me without being specific. I have my full power again, and you…" Devon burst into flames as Annie got shakily to her feet. "You are nothing but a scrawny boy that needs a bath."

Fake Blake's eyes grew wide as he tried to call up a spell, but found himself powerless. "Damn you!" he cried, reaching for Annie's throat, but Annie broke his grip, pushed him back and kicked him squarely in his mortal nuts. Fake Blake sank to the floor, gasping in pain and rolling onto his back.

Annie glared, "You have five minutes to get yourself together, demon. Then it's your turn to get the Hell out."

Devon sat smugly as the second ritual began. Fake Blake chanted his part in a strained voice, and the girls took up their lines, rising as a chorus in the small, candlelit room. The duck had triumphed, finally triumphed. Of course, it would have been better had Annie let him devour the soul of Rafiathasimos, but then her precious Blake would perish too, and he'd have to listen to her bleat about it for the next seven years. Still, it was a victory and he intended to savor it.

The ritual came to a conclusion as Rhonda, tears welling in her eyes, raised her hands and offered her life for her friend. "I free thee Rafiathasimos. Return to Hell," she said solemnly. *And take me with you*, she thought. *I deserve it.*

The demon stepped into the circle, and with an eager smile on his face, held out his hand to Rhonda. She took it with a sad expression of finality.

Annie stifled a whimper and shook her head, unable to bear it. *Forgive me, Rhonda. Forgive me, Blake. God, forgive me.*

Rafiathasimos spoke, "I take as payment... Blake Kingsley." His body fell to the floor in the magic circle as the demon left him; his face going slack, his hand slipping from Rhonda's. The girls just stared at the body for a moment, not comprehending. Then the reality struck them both like a thunderbolt.

"No... no!" Rhonda cried, falling to her knees, weeping. "Take me... take me..."

Annie sobbed helplessly, and sank to the floor beside her. *The bastard lied to the very end. He wanted to hurt us no matter what.* She looked at Devon, who waddled over and put his wing around her.

"It was probably for the best, you know." Devon said, "All the magic he used was fueled by Blake's spirit; I doubt there was much left of him to save." It was a practical fact, but he knew better than to be flippant about it. Empathy was not totally alien to him after all. "You did all you could, Annabelle Puckett. I am honored to know you."

Annie could only sit and mourn, as Rhonda wept over Blake's lifeless body.

The campus was swarming with police as the girls emerged with the duck from the math building, eyes and noses red from crying. *It was going to be a hell of a night at the police station*, Annie thought. *Luckily we got our stories straight*. Rhonda might not be much of a liar, but the alternative was to admit to using black magic to summon demons. No one would believe it, even with the evidence all around them. Rafiathasimos had flung fireballs at the monkey for hours as they chased about town, and the Bueller Fire Department had to call in help from Flagstaff to manage all the burning buildings.

Blake would take the blame for everything; it would be his final sacrifice for the evil he had brought on this town. Hopefully his story would spread through the Infernal Web, warning others of the dangers of dealing with demons. Annie herself intended to put the truth out there for other believers to find. Someone had to take her seriously. After all, the Internet was a haven for those who would believe anything. But it was going to be okay. It was all over and she was going to be okay.

"You have done well, Annabelle Puckett. In all my years I have never known a mortal quite like you," Devon quacked from her arms.

"Thanks," she said, "You aren't so bad yourself, demon duck."

Her cell phone rang out *Crazy* by Patsy Cline, and she fumbled to answer it.

"Hello? Mom? Yeah, I'm okay. It's been a hell of a month, but it's over. What? Mom what's wrong?" Annie looked worried, and Devon leaned closer to hear the little voice on the phone.

"Um, honey? Um you know that um, Chihuahua you brought from daddy's house? Um, yeah, honey, is there something... special about him I should know?"

"Oh..." Annie sighed. "Shit."

CPSIA information can be obtained
at www.ICGtesting.com
Printed in the USA
JSHW020943130323
38858JS00002B/5